# Tears
# of a
# Phoenix

# Tears
# of a
# Phoenix

## Helen Noble

Winchester, UK
Washington, USA

First published by Soul Rocks Books, 2012
Soul Rocks Books is an imprint of John Hunt Publishing Ltd., Laurel House, Station Approach,
Alresford, Hants, SO24 9JH, UK
office1@o-books.net
www.o-books.com

For distributor details and how to order please visit the 'Ordering' section on our website.

Text copyright: Helen Noble 2011

ISBN: 978 1 84694 988 3

A CIP catalogue record for this book is available from the British Library.

Design: Stuart Davies

Printed and bound by CPI Group (UK) Ltd, Croydon, CR0 4YY
Printed in the USA by Edwards Brothers Malloy

We operate a distinctive and ethical publishing philosophy in all
areas of our business, from our global network of authors to
production and worldwide distribution.

# Acknowledgements

Heartfelt thanks and warmest gratitude go out to:
Emma, Imelda and Eileen for their unwavering support
and guidance
Roger, Stephen and Rick for their invaluable writer's advice
and assistance
Jordan for her unique artwork
Don, Emma, Doug, Jane and Marta for sharing some
inspirational experiences
Johnny and Kate for their kind and patient proof-reading
And Alice for her brave belief in Jed's Tale

# Chapter 1

# NSOROMMA: Child of the Heavens

The thrust of the knife and the sickening crack of my fractured rib is the last thing I feel, as our entangled limbs collapse into a communal pool of blood. Around us there is screaming, shouting, noises, people rushing. I am being dragged along the gravel path with a sense of panic. Amidst an overwhelming stench of hot, fresh blood and human fear, I cannot utter a sound or even open my eyes to let people know I am still alive. Drifting in and out of consciousness, I am confused and weak; I am utterly helpless. 'This one's still alive,' I hear. 'Get him in the ambulance.' Seconds later the furious pounding of my heart stops and there is silence. Floating on the edge of the scene, I see horror on the faces of onlookers. My body is on a stretcher, being lifted into the ambulance. Danny is splayed unconscious on the ground. The paramedic at his side stands up and takes a deep breath. His eyes glaze over, listening to the voice in his head telling him to just follow procedure; whilst his heart echoes with the pain of another senseless loss.

Lost in a fog, the faces of my loved ones loom towards me. With her gentle smile and outstretched arms, Ma is beckoning to me; and Alisha's tears of grief are drawing me back into her arms. I am torn between the two. Smiling at both, I reach out to hold each of their precious faces in my hands; but they cannot see me or sense my touch, and my leaden soul sinks into the mist.

When I emerge once more, it is into some ancient, stone place. A distant, cold and empty memory; a long-lost home. The once-thatched roof is now open to the clear, midnight skies, and the only signs of human existence are the faded Adinkra symbols, the ram's horns, adorning the square arch to the shrine. The long-abandoned talking drums sitting beside in silence. In the inky stillness, I am so cold that I feel that I am turning into stone. My senses tell me that soon I will be dust, lying in-between the flagstones of the temple floor. Staring motionless at the sparse, stone shrine, I accept that I am nothingness. My body is dead and I am here to pass over into the spirit world.

In preparation, I let go of the people in my mind's eye, the places in my memory and the pain of my body. I am nothing; I am free. I am nowhere; yet I am everywhere.

I am empty, yet full of everything. There is a sensation of being pulled apart, there are now vast spaces where parts of me used to be; and yet, curiously, I have never felt so connected.

I am expanding further in all directions, yet also spiralling, and turning inwards, into an unfamiliar space. This is a dance between utter darkness and pure light, and I am the partner blindly stumbling along, trying to follow the unknown steps; until I notice a pattern emerging beneath my feet. It is an elaborate trail of white grains, strewn across the flagstone floor. I trace the intertwining lines and curves, to find nearly all of them ending in a star-shaped emblem, all except for two curved lines, which end with what appear to be the forked tongues of snakes. Where they meet, the bare feet of a figure wrapped in a white cloth emerges from the darkness. A female with glossy, black skin, powdered white. She is holding an elephant's tusk in one hand, a coconut in the other, and dancing with her eyes closed. From her mouth I hear whistling and a hiss; and when she opens her eyes to look at me, I feel an urgent rush of energy surge through me. Fixated by her ghostly stare, I am helpless in the face of her all-pervading power. She has total possession of me, her energy charging every fibre of my body. The heat fires through me, rewiring every synapse and reinstating the natural function of every organ. When the ricochet of shock subsides, I become aware of a faint pulse, a gentle stirring deep inside of me. It is the incubation of a weak, yet familiar rhythm. Instinct tells me I have been here before. With each pulse, beating stronger than the last, I warm to the realization that I am alive.

Gently energized, I brave a breath, and then another. The air is fresh, clean and pure. Silky and cool, I feel it travelling through me, permeating the network of my arteries and revitalizing my organs. I feel it massaging the muscles in my arms and legs; and the fresh tingling in my fingers and toes, tells me I am connected, I am whole, I am reborn.

Inspired by my breath, echoes of ntumpane drums are gathering; increasing in pace and volume as they are drawn towards me; their rhythm spiralling in celebration of my return. I catch the intermittent chime of a gankogui gong. And as if to destroy any doubt that I am alive, my whole body reverberates with the hypnotic rattle of axatse beads.

The Ancestors are surrounding me, chanting for the ntoro, the spirit to re-enter my being, and the blood to pump once more through my Oyoko veins. Gone is the white powdered face of the priestess, it is now the gold gleam of headdresses and black robes of the ancients I can see; and a silver staff is thrust in front of my face. I look intently at its intricate carvings and as I focus to see the three faces etched at the top, an image of Danny flashes at the sacrificial shrine before me. Smiling, his shirt is ripped, and saturated with the crimson blood pumping from his neck. I look for the gold dust in his eyes; for the sparkle of the crystalline bones of the shaman. I see none, only a soul that is passing. I am staying in this world, for a little while longer.

Each time I relive that experience the details become more vivid in my mind's eye. The thrust of the stab and the slump to the ground echo through my body, and I can taste the hot, fresh spill of blood from Danny's throat. My heartbeat and the rhythm of the drums merge to the point where I feel that my being and the instruments are one; that the universal life force is being channelled through my body by the Ashanti ancestral spirits. My wide eyes are leaking silent tears, yet I am unable to move or to cry out at the pain and the horror. The drums and the voices subside, yet the indelible images are tattooed in my memory. Am I a new soul in an old body? Is this how we get second chances at life?

When the hot-poker-like pain rips through into my consciousness, I find myself lying in a hospital bed, gasping for air and tensing all over; as if holding my breath will stop the pain. I am awash with the feelings of sadness at the death of my closest friend, yet at the same time in shock at the sheer madness of it all.

I know Danny didn't want to kill me. The thing is I believed that he, like me, had changed, and wanted to leave that life behind. We had a history and I trusted him, but I guess part of his soul was still back there, trapped in that old lifestyle. I will never know the truth.

That day he had talked about being cursed, who knows what was really going on in his mind and his life. We are all fighting our demons; and some of us are just stronger than others.

Occasionally the fury feels like it's about to flame right out from my chest and scorch these hospital sheets. But it never does. I manage to temper it, persuading myself that it wasn't his fault. Sometimes I shake from head to foot, uncontrollably and inexplicably. One moment I am just lying here quietly in this hospital bed and then it as if the fear decides to work its way out of my body, in its own time. When I first became aware of it taking over my body I tried to fight the corrugated wave of energy; to stifle it, stop its violent riptide through my body; but gradually I've learned just to let it happen. It always passes, eventually, leaking out through the ends of my fingers and toes, leaving me feeling exhausted but still and calm.

And it's the same with the crying. It's as if there is a wave inside of me, intent on working its way out. I have no control over the tears. Water always finds a way to flow. Sometimes they simply pour out without any warning, leaving tear- tained stripes on my face. However, I've learned that any resistance to the crying is pointless. It too is working its way through me, for some reason, or so it seems. The doctors refer to it as 'shock' – I don't know if that's a recognized medical condition, or a word for stuff they just don't understand. They can't give me any medication for it and its one of many things about me that they are monitoring. All I know is that I have to trust. It has taken me so long to build up that trust, in myself, and others. I know that life can be different. I've felt the changes shifting from within me and I don't want to lose that momentum now. I was meant to be here and to do something with my life. I have a reason to stay around a bit longer and finish what I've started.

'Same dream Jed?' asks the serious-faced nursing sister who is charged with keeping a close eye on me.

'Yeah, same dream,' I let her think it. It's far too complicated to explain it any other way. If I say that it's real, that it actually happened, then I will be subjected to yet another psychiatric assessment. Better that they think it's a bad dream, a symptom of post-traumatic stress – then they can box it off, all neatly diagnosed, treated and folded away.

'You know there are people you can talk to about that, don't you?' She asks, preparing the medication to kill my pain.

'Yeah, I know. I just find it easier to write about stuff than to talk to people,' I explain to her, not for the first time. She tries to not make a big deal about logging the incident on my chart, but I'm really not that bothered about it. I'm used to every aspect of my life being documented.

The police were hanging around, waiting for me to answer some questions when I regained consciousness in the high dependency unit. There weren't many details I could give them, and the nurses made sure they didn't hassle me. All I knew was that Danny was dead and I was lucky to be alive. They must have had some eye-witness accounts which put me in the clear; and as I had no weapon they can't say I provoked the situation. However I know I was lucky not to get my life licence revoked and to be recalled to prison. This was my chance, my second chance at building a decent life for me and my son. A momentary lapse of judgement had led to the death of Danny, who I had once thought of as a friend; and left my own life hanging in the balance for a while.

I really cannot afford to fuck up again.

Some people think we need to travel the world to appreciate the many different ways in which to see, hear, smell, touch and taste life. Although I think we can learn much from the experiences of others, ultimately all the answers are inside us. That's what I realized after spending seven years in a prison cell. As I navigated my way through the criminal justice system, I learned what was real, who was just playing mind games, and how I was the only one with the power to turn my life around. I realized that we all tell ourselves stories about our own lives, and of the lives of others. These stories are but a fraction of the truth about our existence. All of our lives are a consequence of the actions of those who came before us and of the intentions of those who walk alongside us. The courses of our lives are influenced in ways of which most of us are barely aware.

Ultimately, I've realized that it's our choices in life which determine the way things work out for us. It was a bit hard to swallow this at first, having blamed everyone and anyone else for everything bad that had ever happened in my life. It was even more painful to acknowledge the ways in which I had caused hurt to others – especially my own family. These were the hot coals I had to conquer as I trod my path to freedom from jail. I'm not proud of who I was back then, or how I behaved. It was only by being honest with myself that I could start to be on the level with others, and hope to make the changes that I wanted so desperately in my life. When you believe that just that one thing will transform your life, you expect that on achieving it, every-thing else will fall into place. However, each step closer comes with extra choices and greater responsibilities. My journey towards freedom took me into the dark and desperate places of my past, where the dredging up of toxic memories made me physically sick. However, in doing so I found myself on unexpected horizons, where my greatest fear was no longer of someone taking their revenge by sticking a knife in my back. I panicked at the thought being rejected by the important people in my life. No longer dodging the violent intentions of street rivals; I was now acutely fearful of incurring the revulsion of those I now respected. After all, the sordid details of my life were being laid bare for all to see.

However, once I had acknowledged where I had come from there was no turning back. Those first terrifying steps into the unknown are the only way to change the course of the future It's much easier to slide back into a place with which you are familiar, however bad the reality of the situation. The first time you turn around and realize that familiarity or comfort no longer exists, then you are faced with a choice. You can just waste the opportunity and carry on creating the same old hurtful life; or you can start out on something new.

After a few wobbles I decided there was never any going back and I started heading in a new direction. I was both lucky that there were some people who wanted it to work out for me; and unfortunate that I sometimes placed my trust in the wrong people. When you find yourself in a dark alley with a dangerous man you have to hope and pray that you have enough time to back away unseen, or that you are agile enough to turn and run. Failing that, you have to put your faith in the hands of others and believe that someone somewhere will always have your back. It helps to be aware that the good guys are not always the ones wearing the uniforms. Yet it is only when you face your immortality and fully accept your inexorable death, that you become free to start living again.

The only fighting I get involved with these days is for the chance to play a positive role in the life of my son. The facts of the past may be detailed in court transcripts; prison reports and private love letters; however the future is unwritten. The more you learn about the world and yourself, the wider the selection of words that become available for you to construct your future. Yes, there are people who believe they can predict my next move; and those just waiting for me to fulfil the destiny that their twisted judgement has prescribed for me.

However, they cannot control my actions; speak their words through my mouth, or force my hand to write about their dreams and desires. I script my own destiny.

I'm well aware that I will be judged on my actions and I have to comply with the terms of my life licence. One false move and I will be banged up again, making a mockery of all of the progress I have made and showing a blatant disregard for all of the help I have received. Nothing could be further from my intention. I've served my time and tried to make amends as best I can. Now it's time to move on and make something of my life, for me and for the benefit of my son. I can't relive my life through my son, but I can help make him aware of his choices as he creates his future. We are all, to a degree, the product of the people around us and of the places where we grow up. Our family and friends try to tell us who we are and what we can expect to achieve in life. Yet we can take responsibility for our own education, live by our own principles and become who we want to be. We can influence the way we appear to other people; but only when we can clearly see ourselves. I discovered mirrors in some unexpected places and learned to deal with the shame of my past. It wasn't easy to acknowledge all of the pain and suffering I had caused. However, only once I had accepted all of myself and my actions, could I take responsibility for the changes I was able to make.

People are very cynical about convicts who 'find God' in prison. Some will use anything to manipulate others into believing they have changed and can safely be released back into the community; but that's not how it was with me. My spiritual initiation, or cultural awakening, however you come to see it, was a challenge that I tried to dodge many times before finally rising to meet it head on. On occasions the process was very uncomfortable and disorienting, often I wanted to bury my head and not face the realizations unfolding in front of me. However, once there was a shift in my inner landscape, there was no escaping the reality of life around me. Once I started to see myself differently, this also affected the attitudes of the people around me, in many different and often surprising ways. As an outsider looking in at my life you might think I didn't deserve any help or second chances. As an outsider looking at the lives of others, I would probably have made the same judgement call. It's when you start looking at your own life from the inside out, that the nature of your relationship with others changes too. For so many years I was sure that I knew who and what I was, and this was reinforced on a daily basis by people who had no desire to watch me grow or change. However, when I learned more about my family and heritage, my self-image shifted to the point where others started to take notice and eventually to accept that there was more to me than anyone, including myself, had ever thought possible.

Sometimes we need to look back to get some sense of where we came from, yet we cannot allow whatever it is that we find to hold us back. The knowledge may set us on a different path. For me, finding out about my heritage shocked me into realizing that essentially, I was who I chose to be; how I chose to relate to others was reflected in how they saw me. Ultimately, we have no real control over others, just ourselves, our own feelings, thoughts and actions. We can't change the past, but we can learn from it and choose the future. I know that some people don't need to serve a life sentence in prison to learn that lesson. I also know some for whom a life sentence made absolutely no difference, riding the downwards spiral of crime and punishment, until they disappeared off the face of the planet.

I am one man who chose to look back, to learn, to accept the mistakes of my uncensored past, and to take full responsibility for my future.

This is my story.

# Chapter 2

# EPA: Handcuffs

'You alive in there, Jed?' That sarcastic shout, followed by the heavy thud of the door jarring the foot of the bed, had been my daily rude awakening for the best part of seven years. I experienced the regular intrusion of many different prison officers over the years, none of whom thought I deserved any human privacy, as I found myself bouncing in and out of prison on short sentences for drugs and violent offences. *Fuck off!* I would think to myself, much preferring to be woken by the voice or touch of a woman. It was a challenge, trying to remember the warmth and softness of a woman's skin after just a few months in jail.

'Yeah, cheers' I would grunt, as soon as I could manage to cover my arousal, knowing that the dull voice would then move on to the next door, leaving me alone with my daily prison-issue breakfast pack. I had served enough time before I eventually got the life sentence, to get used to the drill. Some preferred being unlocked for breakfast; they charged out of the cells like they had somewhere to be…me, I liked the time to come round in the morning – to get myself together before I had to face the crowds and the conflict. It suited me better that way. That's what it was all about in there, so I figured out after a couple of years, looking after number one, the best you can. I went my own way, as far as the system would allow. I took more care who I was hanging out with from the start. It was better to avoid the jokers, than having to drop them out when they let you down.

I had always had this sixth sense of both people and places – a sort of knowing or feeling that someone was bad news or that something was going to go down around me, it just took me a long time to pay attention to my feelings; listen to my own thoughts, and trust my own judgement. No lifer can afford any of the shit sticking to him, its hard work getting out of prisons these days. It's no longer a case of lock you up and throw away the key. Back in the day, you'd do the time then carry on regardless. Now things have changed. Someone plans your sentence out for you, tells you what education and skills you need and how you can address your 'offending behaviour'. Sounds like bullshit, I know, but these people have the power to tell the parole board whether or not you are 'ready' to be released. Playing the game and jumping through hoops is how I saw it at the beginning on my life sentence, give them what they want and they give me my freedom, but I have changed. I'm not the jumped up jerk I was when I went in on that last stretch. It's a result of the events and experiences of the last seven years of my life. Some people might think that seven years in jail is a waste of a life. I think that my life before I went in was a waste. I was always running, looking over my shoulder. Paranoid, seeing guns pulled behind the windows of passing cars and hearing threats whispered by strangers with knives on the streets; always thinking something was about to go down, and take me with it. At the time I told myself it was life in the fast lane, cool, exciting. I did whatever I wanted, regardless of anything or anyone else. Life was a game, and I was a fucking main player. But I remember it all ground to a halt for me at the start of the life sentence when I met Tiny. Someone who had been in jail most of his adult life, Tiny was so fat that there was no room in his cell for a mate, and if any newcomers to the induction wing were tempted to try and get close to him, the rank smell seeping out from his cell kept them away. Even the screws shouted to him from halfway up the landing, knowing that he always left his door wide open during unlock, listening to what was going down on the wing around him. Tiny was regarded as part of the prison furniture. He rarely left his cell, so if you braved the stench to get to Tiny's corner of the landing you would hear him talking to himself, usually about the weather; like it mattered when you're banged up in jail for twenty-three hours a day! 'Rain coming in from the West, and North Easterly winds, cold and fucking wet again,' he would announce to the caged bird he kept for company, in his cell. Perhaps it helped him predict the seasons or something. No-one else ever talked to him – screws or inmates – and I never heard him talk about anyone on the out either.

He was the butt of many cruel jokes and actions by bullying inmates, who had a keen sense for the most vulnerable individuals. He was regularly rooted out by those who wanted to vent their frustrations on an easy target, until they got moved off the wing.

Then one day, late December, when I was looking at the first of many Christmases in jail, they cut him down from the bars of his cell window, where he had been found hanging, and took him to the morgue. Although the rest of us were all banged up in our cells, those with windows overlooking the compound could see the two paramedics and six officers it took to carry his dead-weight body out of the wing and across the concrete yard, to the ambulance parked just outside the perimeter fence; closely followed by the dead bird, its squashed head and broken neck swinging loosely from the hand of one of the senior officers.

I guess he simply had nothing left to live for, poor old bastard.

That was the first time in my life I realized that I could die, lonely and mad, like that poor old fucker. No woman to hold; or kid's hair to ruffle and no-one to care whether you rotted away in your own stench. At twenty-eight years of age, I had finally woken up. I was not prepared to die slowly in jail, eating slop from some plastic tray and watching life pass me by through some cheap TV screen in a prison cell.

Those first few weeks in a maximum-security jail at the start of the life sentence were sketchy. Lying on the bed in a dimly lit cell, I could just catch a glimpse of the sky between the bars on the window frame and the top of the prison wall encasing the Victorian monstrosity of a building. I got passed some smack by some "well-meaning" inmates, who said it was the only way to get through the first couple of weeks, to numb yourself. More like it was a way for you to find yourself in debt to the main man on the wing and then having to pay it all back when the favour was called in. I knew how these things worked. I'd used the stuff myself in the past to block out the sounds of the guy in the next cell paying for his drug debts with his arse. I passed it on, so now it was someone else's problem, and I took extra care to watch my back. I remember the scrape of the coarse blanket through the thin, stained sheets on my back; and the burns on my numb toes from the ancient heating pipes running along the wall next to the bed. This wasn't my first time inside, but things had changed now, this was for real – this was my life now, for as far into the future as I could see. I didn't want it to end with me being cut down and carted over the compound by strangers who couldn't care less. When I woke at night, the air in the cell was chilling; and the strange voices and noises of the weird, wailing fuckers around me on the induction wing made me shudder. I was in with all the other new 'residents' of the prison and the most vulnerable – the ones who constantly rattled the pipes and cried out the names of their mothers and girlfriends...all night, until, like Tiny they could call out no longer.

I didn't want to see or talk to anyone else. I disconnected myself from everyone in there. I didn't belong there and I couldn't, I wouldn't relate to anyone. In jail, you are surrounded by strangers, who view every intimate detail of your life. The staff have access to the 'official version' of your life – police printouts of your convictions, transcripts of juries' findings and judges' comments at trials; copies of probation officers' reports all forming part of your prison "dossier". The other prisoners know you by prison reputation and who you align yourself with on the wing. I had been there, done all that and knew I could trust none of the fuckers. I was going solo.

Until, *she* walked in and threw me a lifeline. That's not how I saw it at first, though. It took me a while to realize that I was being offered a chance to change things. I was unlocked and told I was being taken to the interview room on the wing to see 'some bird from psychology'.

Although my body was present, my mind was somewhere else during that first ever interview. I was desperate to be somewhere else, anywhere but there. Slumped in the chair, I was facing her, but not looking or listening. She was telling me that the officers on the wing were concerned about my behaviour. I was marked up as a suicide risk and the staff had requested a psychiatric assessment for me. The doctor had prescribed pills for my depression; and now she had received a referral for psychology to assess me to see if I was suitable for some course or programme to help me think straight. But it was as if she was talking about someone else's life, I felt that none of it had anything to do with me, we were in different worlds and she had no idea of how things were for me. However, the one thing I did know was how to handle women. Looking closely at her, I found myself wanting to feel her long, shiny, brown hair in-between my fingers and wondering what her face would look like without the black-rimmed glasses. I shot her a charming smile, just to let her know exactly who she was dealing with.

At that very moment, as if she could read my mind, she looked me straight in the eyes and said, 'you are appearing cold and remorseless, and if you don't start to make progress, by talking to the staff, you will be left alone on this induction wing whilst everyone around you moves on.'

*Move on? Where the fuck did I have to go?* My life had ended the moment I got a life sentence. This bitch had stepped into the lion's mouth; got herself into a situation she knew nothing about. No woman had ever told me what to do. I felt angry and confused. I wanted to react, to set her straight and take control of the situation, and yet I was feeling paralyzed, powerless. She had floored me; unearthed a vulnerable part of me and spoken straight to my soul. Feeling rattled, I defensively told her some bullshit story about how I didn't need any shrink poking around in my business, unless it was a part of my sentence plan. If it was on the page then I would have to do it as part of my "rehabilitation". But if she was expecting me to pour out my heart, divulging my darkest, deepest secrets in the hope of making me into a respectable citizen, she could fuck right off.

There was something in her look, though, something that told me I wasn't off the hook. And there was a part of me that didn't want to be, and she sensed it. This was a new experience for me. She wasn't my mother and she probably wasn't looking to fuck me, so why the interest?

She had with her a tape recorder, some forms and a pen. 'I need you to sign here to say you consent to the sessions being taped, Jed' she said. 'You have to realize that whatever you tell me will stay between you, me, and the psychology department for as long as we are working together, unless you tell me anything that I have a duty to report. If you say something that makes me think that you or someone else is at risk, I will have to pass it on to prison security and perhaps the police'. *Yeah, right!* As if I would be telling her anything to incriminate myself. 'And of course it means that you will move off this induction wing and onto the lifer wing, one step closer to getting enhanced status.' That was the juiciest carrot to dangle – images of TV in my cell, use of the gym, the chance to buy and cook my own food. Enhanced prisoner status had to be earned, so if this was a short cut I was taking it! That's how I thought back then, so I signed, with a smug smile to myself, and started planning to move home.

We sat in the interview room opposite the office, with the lazy bastards in uniform leering at her through the glass panel in the door. I laid it on the line at the start, as soon as the tape recorder clicked on. 'I'm not talking about the death of my mother.'

'That's okay, this isn't bereavement counselling, unless you want me to refer you to see a counsellor?' She must have interpreted my silence as a "no" and so just carried on. 'Let's make a start with the assessments. Take a look at these patterns and try to figure out the next shape in the sequence.' Although these assessments were totally new to me, being back in "class" again soon brought back the old, familiar feelings of frustration and fear. Labelled a "bad influence" on the other kids in my class, I was never really in school long enough to achieve anything. I would get bored really quickly and look to see who I could wind up, which usually ended up with me being sent out of the class. The time I spent in exclusion fuelled my imagination, working out ways to provoke a response from people. I enjoyed watching people lose their cool. Although my "formal" education was non-existent, I taught myself to become a keen observer of human behaviour, trying to predict the next move. It was the most valuable form of education for anyone living on their wits and at the mercy of the streets. I started to feel the frustration rising and, as when under any stress, I was struggling to breathe properly. In the past my strategy for getting out of such a situation had been to stand up and throw over the desk; or threaten the teacher with the chair, just to get away, just to find some space so I could breathe again. I hadn't signed up just to relive this childhood nightmare. As I stood up to call the officer to come and unlock the door so I could leave, she stopped me, with a look. A look that said she expected me to do it, that she expected nothing more and nothing less. It wasn't one of those "you are a waste of time and space" looks, just one look from those intense green eyes that said she believed I was going to do it.

Although I hadn't said a word to her, with open palms, she gestured to me saying, 'it's your call, Jed'. Just one look and a few words and she had (as I now realize) planted the ball firmly in my court. Life took a double take for me at that point, there is no other explanation. It seemed as if someone, somewhere flicked a switch and I took a trip along an alternative reality. One where I was playing a different role, and finding it surprisingly easy. I went from wanting to escape, to sitting relaxed, breathing freely and able to simply follow the instructions being given to me. I felt calm and completed the first task, feeling a little surge of excitement and a sense of curiosity as to what was going to happen next. I'd never finished anything in my life. Something had changed. She was right, the ball was in my court and it was up to me to do what I wanted with it.

As I walked back along the wing I remember feeling light with a silly, smug smile of disbelief creeping across my face. I didn't try to stifle it.

However, it took me a while to trust her. Quite often I would panic in my head asking myself, *why should I be telling a stranger all about my past? What the fuck did it have to do with her? What was she going to do with all that information? Probably use it to stitch me up for some of the other stuff I'd done in the past.* And so I kept reminding myself to be careful to keep up my guard with her. Meanwhile, I kept my head down on the wing.

'I've got some interesting news for you', she announced smiling, some three days later, as she unlocked the gate and stepped onto the wing for our next appointment. I showed no interest until we were both in the interview room with the door closed. There was always someone hanging around the wing, lurking in the shower recess or licking some arse in the office, waiting to pick up a titbit of information they could use against you. I relaxed in the interview room, reading the prison anti-bullying strategy poster that had been sellotaped to the brick walls. Once a cell, the bare bricks of the wall had been painted over with some masonry paint that was now peeling and flaking on to the desk between us. Being around her was starting to feel familiar and more comfortable. 'You have a high IQ score' she announced. 'Do you know what that means?'

I remember switching on my disarming smile. 'Why don't you tell me?'

She continued, unperturbed, 'You have the potential to reach a high level of academic achievement.'

'And...?'

'And you haven't.'

'So, what's interesting about that?'

'It suggests the interplay of other psychological factors, developmental, educational, emotional, personality, cognitive style, behavioural factors.' She rattled them off before I had decided whether or not to show any interest in what she was saying. The truth was none of it really meant anything to me.

'All of them?' I asked.

'Probably a combination', she replied thoughtfully.

'So how do you know which ones?'

'I don't, yet. There are more assessments we can do to find out, if you're interested'.

'What sort of assessments?'

'OK, we call them semi-structured interviews to assess your cognitive skills. Then there are psychometric questionnaires to get a feel for your attitudes and beliefs; then we can move onto personality assessments...' It was all going over my head; all this jargon meant nothing to me and my concern was with what it could reveal about me. I mean, it's not like anyone can read your mind, unless you want them to. I knew I would still be in control of what I said. I'd been through too many police interviews to be fooled into saying anything that wasn't good for me.

'How long will it take?' I asked.

'The more you engage with the assessments, the greater the details you can recall, the more meaningful the whole process will be,' was the answer.

I had never sat down with someone, as an adult, and had a conversation, not one that I can remember, anyway. I had been lectured by teachers, and interrogated dozens of times by the police. Other than that no-one, except for Ma, had ever shown so much interest in me, or just listened to me without calling me a lazy, good-for-nothing thug who would only end up in prison, if I didn't get whacked first. As I said, there was something different going on here. I was now playing a game with different rules. Our fingers touched as she handed me the pen to sign up and I felt a shock shoot right through from the ends of my fingers to the core of my being. The look on her face told me she felt something too.

# Chapter 3

# SANKOFA: The Importance of Learning from the Past

I spent the first six months or so of my life sentence talking to her and writing about my past. She was helping me to create a picture with words of where I had come from, a jigsaw puzzle where she was asking me to fill in the gaps with my early memories. It was as if I was in some alternative reality, somewhere vaguely familiar, somewhere long forgotten. I wasn't doing any drugs, as a positive MDT test would have resulted in me going down the block, and then I wouldn't have been able to participate in the psychology programme. However, there were days where I felt as if I was in a trance, walking around in one place, with my mind full of the events of another time. Some scenes from the past were easier to stomach than others; and the ones that proved the biggest challenge for me often became the subject of journal assignments, I reluctantly agreed to write. By the end of the assessment process, I was well and truly hooked on journaling. I had established a new habit, it became compulsive; some of it I showed to her, other bits I kept to myself. I will always remember the first journal assignment. We were talking about the power of personal memories, how they can influence us without us being fully aware of their affects. She asked me to write about one of my earliest memories. It was tough for someone like me, who tried never to look back at stuff, but she was certain that this was the way forward and so at lock up that night, when I couldn't sleep due to stubborn thoughts of her filling my mind, I wrote my first journal:

## Our Father

*Our father taught my older brothers, Jon and Tommy, how to throw punches. He made them practice on each other, usually when he came home from the pub. It was like a game to him, and there always had to be a winner. I remember my father getting really agitated when one of them forgot and used their left hand to defend their selves, or started to back down. His face would go red and he would drag them both into the middle of the room, demanding that they finished what had been started. 'Call yourselves warriors? You are a disgrace to the Ashanti ancestors, to the Oyoko tribe,' he would rant. Sometimes he would fold back his sleeve and make us all look at the black tattoo on his right forearm, shouting, 'strength, bravery and power!' These words meant nothing to any of us, as kids. I guess as the youngest I was too young for the training, but I was always watching and learning from the sidelines. The loser would always get a swipe from our father; and how much it hurt would depend on how drunk and incapable he was. Some days he would just sit in the chair all day and drink. On these occasions, he would wear his brightly coloured tunic of red, gold, green and black stripes, and raise glass after glass of whiskey, in toast to his dead relatives. He would warble on about life in Ghana, which meant nothing to any of us kids, and there was nearly always a fight between him and Ma. She would accuse him of being lazy; and he would slur something about paying his respects to the ancestors and that she should do the same. Ma's response was usually something insulting to him. Her hazel eyes would flash in anger and she would say things like, 'What world are you living in? You useless piece of shit! No wonder your family all disowned you.' I usually closed my eyes when she snatched the whisky bottle from him as he lay slumped in the chair, fearful of what might happen next. Once I watched wide- eyed as she smashed his whole stash of spirit bottles in the kitchen sink, but had to close my eyes to escape the sight of her smearing angry tears across her face with blood-stained hands. It didn't work, that angry, deep, red flash is carved into the flesh of my memory. I crept behind the sofa and sat hugging my knees for hours.*

*One day our father just didn't come home. He had a heart attack in the pub and was dead before the ambulance arrived, according to the policemen who came to the door to deliver the news. I remember Ma collapsing on the doorstep of the flat and the uniformed guy helping her back inside. He didn't hang around for long, though, leaving us all alone in a state of shock, with no-one to help. The week or so leading up to the funeral was deadly dark and quiet. Jon and Tommy got sent off to school in the days as if nothing had happened. Jodie and I were allowed to stay home with Ma, who hardly spoke a word, except when talking on the phone to make the funeral arrangements. I heard the words 'family', 'Ghana' and 'shame' and watched as the tears poured down her face. Our father's belongings, which were still scattered around the flat, seemed to take on an uncomfortable presence. The sight of his tunic discarded on the chair gave me a pain in my chest and an ache in my belly, so I shoved it into the bottom of a drawer, out of my sight. I looked for the African drum with the broken skin, the one that Jon and Tommy had damaged during a fight. We had tried to hide it away, fearful of the inevitable beating someone would get when our father found out about it. I put it away with the cloth tunic. There was also a small ornament, some cheap trinket in the shape of a golden stool, that our father kept by his bed. I don't know why, but I nervously took it when no-one else was around and kept it hidden in my in my pocket. I still shiver when I think of that big, cold stone church and the horde of downcast strangers standing around on the day of his funeral. I didn't know any of them. From the back of the church I was straining my neck to find my mother. I'd been told to stay out of the way, with my brothers, Jon and Tommy; whilst Jodie our sister got to be with Ma at the front. I was jealous of Jodie, angry and scared all at the same time. When I started to cry I got a sharp elbow in the ribs from Jon. 'Shut it, don't start,' he warned me. As the eldest, he was always the first to discipline us younger kids, especially when we complained or got upset. When I couldn't stifle my sobs any longer, Tommy, always more aggressive than Jon, landed a heavy boot heel blow to my shin, and I howled. Then, amongst some side shoving and slapping, the three of us were dragged from the pew by two black-suited, muttering men and pushed outside of the church. 'Fucking yobs!' they called us, with disgusted looks on their faces. With the slamming of the old oak door, my stomach felt like it had hit the floor, and I cried silent, hopeless tears. Meanwhile the scuffle between my brothers escalated into a full- scale fight; with Tommy rolling around in the gravel, and Jon furiously kicking his arse. He only stopped when Tommy eventually curled up, snivelling amongst the stone chippings. 'Leave it out Jon, leave it out,' I begged. Jon brushed himself down and marched off to watch the coffin slide into the furnace. Tommy and I could only sit in the dust, waiting for the sickly smoulder of our father to fade from our lives. Those were the last tears I ever cried.*

*Jed Johnson JD9063*

I remember feeling very nervous when I handed my work to her, I didn't know what to expect, and was wondering what I'd started…She was wearing her hair loose over the same long black jacket, buttoned to cover her curves, and a skirt that fell loosely almost to the floor so it was hard to make out the size and shape of her arse, although it didn't stop most of the men on the wing screws and inmates alike all looking in that direction the minute she walked through the gate. She read through my work and then asked me questions about my brothers and sister. Where were they now? Were we in contact? That sort of thing. But she didn't offer any criticism, or judgements on what I had written. I replied that Jon was now living alone at the family's flat; Tommy was in jail, doing time for drugs and violent crimes; and Jodie was training to be a nurse, like Ma. She took off her glasses and placed them in the space between us, on the interview desk. Smiling at me and for the first time, I noticed the crinkly lines at the edges of her eyes. She seemed older than I had first thought, there was a knowingness about her expression. I felt that perhaps she might appreciate where I was coming from. Then she asked, 'so how were things after your father's death? Could you write about that? I don't know what it was, her smile, the warm feeling I got when she was around or the leery looks from the screws and cons as we went into the interview room and closed the door; but I knew that I wanted to keep this thing up for a while.

'Yeah, no sweat,' I replied, and when I got back to my cell I wrote the second journal entry.

## The Brotherhood

*My brothers ruled my childhood. When our father died, Jon and Tommy stepped in to pick up from where he left off. As kids, we never talked about him. Only later on did we mull over stuff from the past. I remember Jon saying he felt really pissed off when the old guy died. I guess as the eldest, he thought that the responsibility for the family lay squarely on his shoulders. He looked angry a lot of the time. As kids we knew nothing more than what was being played out in front of us. For all we knew, this is how things were in everyone's house. When Ma wasn't around, Jon and Tommy continued to practise the fighting that our father had taught them. Tommy always came off worse in the fights as he was much smaller and weaker than Jon, who would taunt him, calling him a "pussy" when he cried.*

*However, Tommy would wreak his revenge by giving me a few sly slaps when no-one else was around. He knew that if he was caught hitting me, he would get a beating from Jon, so we both came to recognize the "safe" times when no-one else was around, me with panic* and fear; and Tommy with sadistic glee. However, as kids do, I soon learned how to hurt the bastard back. Tommy had got burned on his neck and shoulders when he was a baby. I never knew how it had happened, or who was to blame. What I did know was that Tommy was sensitive to any mention of his scars. Sometimes when he had hurt me, and sometimes when he hadn't, I'd taunt him with names like "fritter" and he'd freak out. It was a weird sensation; exciting and frightening, not knowing how far he was going to go…but I would be entranced by the crazy bastard and repeatedly risked getting another black eye or bruised balls. Kids just don't understand loss of control, and my curiosity often led to more pain for both of us.

I lost my fear of Tommy when he got into drugs. He was too mellow to bother me anymore. I guess he was getting his kicks in other ways. Although Jon stepped into the old man's shoes, he took control in a different way. Whereas our father had been too fond of the whisky bottle, John was anti-drinking and started working out, big time, at the local gym. His sense of power and control seeming to increase in relation to the weight he'd brag about bench-pressing that day. I thought I respected Jon, although it was probably more out of fear that I did whatever he told me to. Jon hated the drugs scene. Because he was into bodybuilding, he found the junkie scene too pathetic for his taste. The joke is he was heavily into steroids. Jon would challenge Tommy, winding him up by insisting on arm wrestling. Tommy's refusal was usually met with anger from Jon, and on one occasion his frustration got the better of him. Jon pinned Tommy down on the floor by the shoulders and mouthed the word 'pussy' in his face. He finally let up and laughed when Tommy spat his contempt in his face. He had got what he wanted. However, late one Saturday afternoon he got more than he bargained for. As he leaned over Tommy, who was lying trashed in his bed, with the intention of riling up a reaction from him, Tommy pulled a shiny six-inch blade from under his pillow. 'Yeah?' Tommy goaded Jon. Jon backed off immediately and I froze, holding my breath as Tommy had him pinned up against the wall, the tip of the blade pointed precisely at his throat. Meanwhile, Ma was in the lounge *ironing her new nurses' uniform ready for her first night- shift as an auxiliary at the local hospital, whilst watching the All New Generation Game on TV.*

'Good work, Jed', she commented. 'I like the way you're starting to write down your reflections and ponder your own past choices. There is also some important insight in there, for example when you theorize as to how Tommy might have felt when your father died, leaving him as "head" of the house. I also liked the bit where you say that you listened to Tommy because you felt scared of him, and not because you necessarily agreed with what he said, or did'.

'That's just how it was,' I shrugged.

I was just writing about what we did and what I thought about it. But it did start to make me feel uncomfortable about my past. What did it say about me? I didn't want her to think my childhood was all shit; that my whole life was a mess, and so I also wrote about some of the good stuff I could remember, to show her another side of myself.

## Good Times

*There were some good times ...*

*Although Tommy had been a mean bastard to me, I did sort of miss him when he was sent to a secure unit for the first time. I felt a pang of guilt as Ma cried when trying to explain to me that Tommy would be away for a while. He had been thrown out of the local youth club for fighting and he had got his revenge by setting fire to the community centre. He denied it, but the truth was that he'd been so off his head on glue he didn't really know whether he'd done it or not. So our house became more quiet and peaceful for a while, especially during the evenings. Jon was seeing this girl, so when my sister Jodie and I were sent to bed, I would wait for her to fall asleep and creep back out into the lounge. Ma and I would curl up on the sofa and watch TV, or a video film. I remember the warmth of her faded pink sweater, where I always hid my face in any scary scenes in her favourite film "Ghost". I didn't like the part where the shadows came to take away the "bad" souls, but I always laughed at the scene where the ghost, Patrick Swayze, was ripping the piss out of the bad guy. I also remember the creeping fear which gripped me at the point in the film where Ma always cried. I could never understand why she was so sad about the scene where the woman was alone at the pottery wheel. But I never asked her and she never said. Ma spoke and I listened. That's just how it was.*

*It's funny, the way you think when you're a kid. I often wondered whether our father was watching over us, like the character in the film. One evening, Ma made me promise that when she died we would not have her cremated, so she could come back and keep watch over us.*

*'I'll be watching over you Jed always, wherever you are.' Ma also told me that I was a good boy. She said I was different from Tommy, and that I wouldn't go the same way as him; that I took after my father's younger brother, Cliff, who had gone back to Ghana before I was born. I remember her pulling out a photo from her purse, one of my father and Cliff from their younger days. 'You've got the good genes, Jed. You'll make the right choices.'*

*I didn't know what she meant but I liked hearing her talking this way. Ma always had this calming effect on me.*

*When Tommy was away and Jon hit sixteen, he got a job at a local garage for a couple of months. One Saturday morning he came home on an old bike, a purple Kawasaki 750, with a spare helmet he'd also "borrowed" from the workshop and said he'd come to take me out for a spin. We had a right old laugh bombing around the estate; weaving in and out of the concrete pillars, car wrecks, and piles of burnt rubbish before we headed out on to the main road. I gripped tightly around his middle; with my face buried in his back as we sped passed the queues of traffic and towards the Royal Gardens Park, North-West of the City. I remember the excitement of the wind rush on my face as we circled the ponds, statues and flowerbeds; wheel wobbling our way around unsuspecting dog walkers and bemused tourists. I was breathless with the excitement by the time we got back to the estate and it took three puffs of my inhaler before I could breathe easily again.*

*'What on earth have you been doing? Jon, what's happened? You two look as if...as if...'*

*'We've just been having a laugh, Ma.' A smile smoothed out her frown-wrinkled forehead, and there was a sparkle in Ma's pretty hazel eyes. She couldn't be annoyed with me for long.*

*Jon lost his job a few weeks later. The reason given was something about him being "underage" and "unreliable". I didn't really under-stand at the time, but I did know that Jon was a moody bastard. There were times when he was up for a laugh, and times when he'd just lie on his bed for hours, not talking, not doing anything. And when he was dumped by his girlfriend, he went car crazy for a while; out all hours of the day and night, driving any car or bike he could lay his hands on. Ma didn't say anything about it all. She just looked tired all the time.*

As I walked out of the interview room, feeling lighter and happy to leave that journal piece with her, I was summoned into the office by the fat, bastard screw lying back in his chair with a knowing grin on his face. 'Hey! Johnson. Enjoying the lady? I can see why! Don't know what she sees in you though.'

I stopped and stared directly at him. This guy was tricky, all proper in front of the other officers, sly and spiteful when he got you on your own. On the outside I would have laid into the guy just for talking to me. Here I had to be on the lookout, 24/7. As much as I would have loved to pin him back by his flabby neck in that chair, I had to be sure that no-one was around to see it. I was fighting back the urge to throttle the smug bastard, when the click of the door handle turning behind me brought me to my senses. The fat bastard looked over my shoulder to smile at her as she came out of the interview room. 'Is everything alright? Johnson not giving you any trouble is he?'

'Everything's fine thanks, Jed is no problem,' she replied stiffly. She had his number; she was much smarter than him.

'Good to hear it. Any problems, you just let me know,' he

winked at her. She left without acknowledging him, and as I started to walk away he took great pleasure in saying, 'I'm watching you, Johnson. You might pull the wool over the eyes of the pretty girlies from psychology but you don't fool me. Leopards don't change their spots and you're nothing but a piece of scum.'

I don't know if it because of this comment or was all the thinking and writing about the past but I suddenly realized I had told someone about some of my most private stuff; things I had never told anyone, and I started to panic. *What did she want to know any of this shit for anyway? What was she going to do with it?* I could feel the old paranoia creeping back. *What did she really care? What was she really asking me all his stuff for? Was she compiling a profile of me? Gathering evidence to pin other stuff on me?* She had me fooled. I had let down my guard and forgotten that I could trust no-one. I stopped writing for her, and after a couple of days she came up on to the wing to see me. I was ready to tell her it was all a load of crap and that I wasn't going to be writing for her any longer. 'Find someone else to tell you bedtime stories', I goaded her, hoping she would get angry and call an officer to take me back to my cell.

Cutting straight through all of my crap she asked, 'Jed, are you feeling uncomfortable with the history you've unearthed? I understand that this may be painful for you but that isn't the intention. The purpose of this is to see where you've come from, how you got to be where you are at today. There's no-one judging you Jed, you can't change the past and you're not responsible for the actions of others; but you can choose to create how you want things to be in the future'. Then she continued, 'let me introduce you to some of the "tools" we use in the programme. Perhaps one that you could start applying right now is "old/new me".'

'Old me versus new me?' I asked, hooked in.

'They're not necessarily mutually exclusive,' she explained. 'There may be parts of the "old me" that you feel it would be best to keep, and "new me" helps you to develop new parts of yourself ...just like you do when you're learning a new skill, take on a new job, that sort of thing. But it is useful for looking at parts of your behaviour that you would like to change.' She had planted the seed. She just did that – when I tried to shut it all down she somehow opened it all up again and I just couldn't ignore it. She was interested in learning where I had come from, what had happened to me, and so was I.

I was back on side with her again. Perhaps there was a point to all of this? I got my enthusiasm back, and that's how it was for a while. Every week I took a trip into this bubble world – an alternative reality where I could talk about stuff that had happened to me and start to think about it in different ways. I talked and wrote; she listened and read, and gave me ideas in return. She never judged what I said or wrote as "right" or "wrong", although she was quick to challenge me if she thought I wasn't being completely honest about anything. Talking was easier as I could sometimes get off track for a while with a smile and a joke, when things got a bit heavy. Those crinkly green eyes of hers would sparkle, and a knowing smile creep across her face, just before she was about to interrupt me and try to get our conversation back on track.

The journal assignments were still the hardest. When I wrote about certain things from my past they became real again. I walked around with a heavy feeling in my stomach for a few days; started having bad dreams and was constantly thinking that this was just too hard for me. How could this be good for me when it made me feel so bad? It was hard to look the truth in the face, yet it was impossible to write anything other than how it really was.

## Sex, drugs and shoplifting

*The first time that Ma caught me smoking puff, she screamed at me that I was going the same way as Tommy. 'You're not making the right*

*choices, Jed' she yelled, 'this is wrong, this isn't the way it's meant to
be, this isn't the way for you'. Well, I couldn't see any other way. I was
looking for my own path, but only in the places I already knew. I guess
I was like most other kids from around my way – didn't have much but
felt I deserved it all. And it was easy to make money. Shoplifting was a
bit of a buzz at the time and an easy way to make money for blow. I had
to hide lots of stuff from Ma, and became very helpful to her when I was
feeling particularly guilty about something I'd stolen. However,
thieving was just a game of outwit to me and I was a smug little
bastard. Someone once told me that my innocent smile would get me out
of trouble; and it did help me get whatever I wanted most from life at
that time. Although I had heard about fucking girls, listening to the
alleged exploits of Jon and Tommy, the first time I experienced it first
hand, so to speak, was rather unexpected. Following a "delivery" of
stolen goods to a mate's house, his sister took me into her room and
locked the door behind her.*

*'I want to make a payment on the next order. I've seen a new pair of
Levis that I want, and I always get what I want,' she said, unzipping
my jeans and pushing me back onto the bed. I remember looking around
at the posters of a young Madonna plastered around the walls, and
thinking that this girl looked a bit like her, with her red lipstick and
rattling bracelets. It wasn't until my cock was in her mouth that I
realized where we were at; and she too was shocked when I came really
quickly. As I stood up to make my exit, she pulled me back on to the bed,
insisting that I stay around a bit longer. So the rest of that afternoon's
deliveries were on hold, whilst I touched and tasted the bits of a girl's
body I'd heard my brothers talking about; and all to the soundtrack of
Madonna's "Like a virgin". Even now, hearing those old 80s tracks
brings a smile to my face.*

*My career prospects, as I saw them at that time, increased consid-
erably when Tommy came out of the secure unit. Inside he'd made some
interesting contacts and developed some more expensive habits. He
came on like some big-time dealer, but he was only really interested in
putting the stuff in his own veins, so I became a trusted runner for him.*

*This was a step up from petty shop thieving to serious business for me, with an increase in rewards and risk factors. I managed to pocket "official" payment from Tommy, and unknown to him, some "extras". I was confident that Tommy wasn't really interested in the finer details of the business, and so without my help he would have lost his grip on it all sooner rather than later. He always owed some guy or other for supplies, so I was under increasing pressure to deliver more and collect sooner. I guess it made me feel important, dealing with kids older than me. It's when I learned to stick up for myself, when I learned how to get what I wanted by using violence. It was nothing for me to threaten some kid shitless with his face rammed up against an alley wall, my knife at his throat, before I relieved him of his watch or mobile phone if he couldn't pay his debt there and then.*

*One time when I wasn't looking out for him, something came on top for Tommy, and he got cut all down the left side of his face. And the loser got two years in a Young Offenders' Institute, convicted of affray and ABH.*

*That's when I really started to make a name for myself. At thirteen, I was a full-time, self-employed wheeler/dealer (as I saw it at the time), with a reputation amongst the older guys for taking no shit. Suddenly it felt like I had arrived. I was in my rightful place in the world. I had respect. From then on everything I did was connected to the building up and maintenance of my reputation. There was always the next challenge, the bigger risk to take to bolster up my reputation. I had to live up to my reputation, my reputation was me.*

'That's how I saw things then,' I was keen to let her know, as she turned the last page and placed the assignment into her folder.

'Seems like something of a turning point for you, Jed' she suggested. 'How do you think that writing these journal entries has changed things for you? Have they given you some sense of perspective on your past?' I had never experienced someone looking so deeply into my eyes, and seeing into my soul. For a moment I felt naked in front of her. She wasn't expecting me to answer there and then. It was a question designed to make me think a bit further about things. She knew that she would read my answer in the next assignment. Neither of us felt the need to break the almost tangible silence between us.

We were creating something in that space. I didn't know what it was, at that time. I remember feeling excited and a little confused. I had never experienced this intensity of feeling with a woman, or a man. This was something more than just the sexual tension between two people attracted to each other, or the passion of lovers locked into a power struggle. It is only on reflection that I realize something was happening on another level, outside of us two individuals sitting in that cell; in an area that wasn't confined within the perimeter wall of the prison. Would I have fucked her at the time, if I had the chance? Of course, given the constraints of the physical situation, it would have been a great challenge. I can't say I would have passed up the opportunity if it had been presented to me. However, it was never on offer and I can now see that might have led us both down a very different path. We were breaking new ground and this experience was unique.

## Turning Points

*One of these was definitely the time Ma got a letter from the authorities telling her that I was going to be expelled from school. I remember being dragged into the headmaster's office and having to sit there and listen whilst the big fat bastard poured out a load of lies (and some true stuff) in front of Ma. Mr Rogers was a big man, with a big mouth to match. He didn't know all the details, but he didn't have to. He had the additional weight of authority behind him. All the kids feared him, he had a booming voice and a vicelike grip, which meant that no-one really protested too strongly against his harsh rules. And he never gave second chances. Although he didn't really know anything about me, in his mind, my family's name and history was enough justification for his actions. There was all this talk about me being a truant and a bully and*

34

*Ma being told that she had failed to respond to previous letters home about my conduct. They were the letters that I had routinely intercepted so she would not find out about my extra-curricular activities.*

*I remember the devastated look on her face as the sneering Headmaster told her that there was no way I could be allowed back to school. 'We will not tolerate such behaviour. Your son is a bully and a thug.' Ma started to cry at this point and asked him to reconsider. 'Just one more chance', she begged. "He needs to be given another chance. I'll help him make the right choices this time...I'll help...'*

*'He'll get no more chances here, we have to consider the decent kids, the ones who want to learn', he announced with a sense of satisfied smugness. As we were ushered out of the office door in disgrace, the school secretaries looked at each other knowingly, and Ma dropped her head in shame.*

*I turned to Mr Rogers, telling him that he would live to regret his actions and to watch his back. I don't know what I meant at that time, but Ma was hurting and I felt like shit, so I wanted him to hurt too. Looking back, being expelled was a major turning point for me. If anything, it reassured me there was only one way to go, for definite, and that was my way. I had no choice but to carry on the only "work" I knew.'*

'This is very interesting, Jed. So you see this as a major turning point?' I closed my eyes and took in a deep breath of her now familiar scent, a light, citrus sensation which often breezed along behind her as she walked along the wing. It was a sharp contrast to the acrid smell of my own prison-issue clothing which had become infused with the smell of the wing – of the of two hundred men having to eat, sleep and shit daily in a confined space with small windows, which never opened. Regardless of how many showers you took, or what detergent you washed your clothes in, you couldn't shake off the insidious odour. I opened my eyes and tried to push the thought of the prison stench out of my mind, hoping she would realize the smell was not me.

'Yeah, it's like, if I could go back to this point, if I didn't get expelled, things might have turned out differently for me.'

'Different in what way?' she had that curious expression on her face, a sort of half-frown where she pressed her lips together and a dimple appeared on her left cheek – which always made me smile, secretly, to myself.

'It set me off on a path that I couldn't get off' I was thinking aloud. 'Looking back, if I'd stayed in school, I might have made Ma more proud of me, I think she gave up on me that day, and the only thing I could do was pretend like I didn't care. I just thought that was how it was meant to be.'

'So what your mother thought of you was very important to you?' She asked.

'It was the only important thing to me, back then,' I answered, knowing that what *she* now thought of me was of ever-increasing importance to me.

## Chapter 4

## TAMFO BEBRE: Jealousy

**Ma**

*There I was, enjoying the game, cruising my neighbourhood, spending
cash like there was no tomorrow on girls and blow and fun, when my
life was suddenly turned upside down. Ma was seeing a man. I don't
know how long it had been going on, because I was only ever at the flat
to stash some stuff or lay low for a night. I knew of the bastard, through
other people, and was gutted to think of him with MY mother. I made a
point of hanging around the flat for a week, just to give the guy the
message that he wasn't welcome. One afternoon I caught him coming
out of Ma's room, smug smile on his face and smelling of sex and sweat.
I stared him straight in the face until he looked away, then I blanked
him when he tried to make conversation. But he was cool, took it all,
and didn't give any back. So, I thought we had it sorted. Then Ma said
she was going away for the weekend with him.*

*I plotted my revenge. I couldn't hurt Ma, but I knew she would be
better off without the joker hanging around, so while they were away I
put out some feelers for help from the guys on my manor. I would show
him not to mess with me and mine.*

*We were waiting from him when he left work one winter's evening.
As he walked into the otherwise-deserted car park, we flicked the
headlights on full and headed straight towards him. Following the first*

*impact and as he lay collapsed in front of the bonnet of the car, semi-conscious with both legs broken, we dragged him around to the back of the car and bundled him into the boot. To teach him a lesson he wouldn't forget, we needed to be somewhere more private than a public car park. We heard that he turned up a couple of days later on the side of a country lane. He was found lying in a filthy and barely conscious state by a passer- by who called for an ambulance, but didn't hang around to wait for it to arrive.*

*The guy spent 3 days in intensive care. His smashed-up face never looked quite the same again. Although they pinned his cheekbones back together and put some metal plate over his right eye brow, he never regained his sight in that eye and would always look as if his face was part-way through re-constructive surgery .*

For some reason, this piece of writing really caught her attention. It was one that she would not let pass without performing a full autopsy of the event and of my thoughts and feelings about it. 'It's funny how you can sometimes start to feel the same way that you felt at the time, when you're thinking back to a situation. Have you ever had that experience, Jed?'

It was as if she could sense my hackles rising. There was no point in denying it. 'The thought of that man still makes me feel agitated'.

'Is that how you felt at the time?'

'No I felt totally justified in my actions at the time. Why is it so important anyway? It's just one of many acts of violence, I've told you about loads of others already'

'Yes it wasn't the first time you used violence to get what you wanted. But I think there is something different about this'

'What are you on about?'

'What's different about this Jed?' This felt like she was trying to pull something out of me, something that just did not want to see the light of day. Although I had written about it as if I wasn't involved, perhaps to distance myself from the whole incident, she knew I had been right there, playing a part. How could I answer her?

After a few agonizing seconds of silence she asked, 'Was it the first time you lost control, Jed?'

'I just wanted him out of the way'.

'Out of the way of who or what?'

'Out of Ma's way, he wasn't good for her'.

'Is that the way your 'Ma' saw it?'

I couldn't say "yes".

'It was for her own good'.

'Did she say that?'

'He was taking her away from us'.

'Who's "us" Jed?'

'Me, Jon and Tommy and Jodie. We'd lost our father, he was dead, and we weren't looking for another one.'

'And what do you think about that situation now?'

'Back then I told myself that violence solved problems, so I had to feel good about it,' I reasoned.

'Perhaps you weren't being honest about your true feelings? Perhaps this incident was about you making yourself feel better and not in the best interests of your mother? You might want to rethink the title,' she suggested. I couldn't ignore the sudden rush of shame, and then that familiar low feeling. She clocked it and suggested that we had done enough work for the session. 'Perhaps you can continue with this in your next assignment?'

I charged straight back to my cell, telling the screws I had no appetite for their fucking lunchtime slop, and the words came pouring out:

## Care

*Even when I found myself locked up in a secure unit for my part in that assault on Ma's man I was still telling myself that using violence was the only way. She had sided with him over me. I was the only one looking out for me now. At first I kept my head down, just sussing out those around me. It didn't take long, I soon had everyone pigeonholed; those I could take on, and those I could wind up. Those were my only interests, and I had only one intention, to cause as much turmoil as possible. If I was suffering, so would everyone else. There was one creep who I noted straight off. I worked out his shift pattern and then watched him carefully. He was nasty, but boy was he slick. No-one saw anything he didn't want them to, except me. I didn't give him too much trouble at first, so he didn't really pay me much attention. He knew which boys he could bully; I think he had picked out his favourites before I arrived. I was watching and judging the bastard, waiting for the right moment to do whatever I wanted to. I told myself I was righting what was wrong about the situation.*

*"Those that make the rules shouldn't be breaking the rules" was one of my favourite sayings back then. If we weren't allowed to fight, then the staff members weren't allowed to use violence against us either. That's how I saw things back then, "them" and "us". Either you were on my "side" or you were a straight-goer, an authority figure. And it followed that if you weren't on "my side" you weren't allowed to use my tactics. This was all the justification I needed. I got in the know of who could get stuff into the unit and I managed to get a blade in through a brown-nosing friend-of-a-friend and plotted to put the frighteners on Mr Slick. I told myself that the weapon was for self-protection and I let it be known to everyone that they couldn't afford to get in my way. I had contacts. I had family. My brothers would be there for me if I needed them too, so whoever took me on, took them on too. At night I felt a surge of power as I smugly slid the knife under my pillow. I was back in control.*

*When I realized that I was not going to be home for Christmas that year, I started to plan my actions. I had decided that Christmas was going to be crap for everyone. It started off with kid's stuff, smashing furniture through windows; throwing pool balls at the TV; wildly flinging punches while the staff tried to restrain me. It felt like I was on the outside looking in at myself laughing at the supervisor as I threw paint all over him. Then it went up a gear. Mr Slick appeared on the scene with my knife in his hands. Some two-faced slime bag must have split on me. I thought I had been careful in my choice of confidantes. Now I was humiliated in front of everyone. Once again I felt small and powerless.*

*Mr Slick Bastard later denied threatening me with my own knife. He wrote in the incident report that he was merely showing me the knife to verify my ownership of it. No-one dared speak out and tell me like it really was, that he held it to my ribs and begged me to give him a reason to stick it in and twist. Locked away in isolated misery, I plotted how to hurt those I held responsible for my unhappiness. And I began to get a real kick out of rehearsing my future plans for inflicting pain. When I left the unit at the end of that six-month sentence I had a carefully complied list in my head, consisting of the names of everyone I felt had ever done me any wrong'.*

I wasn't writing about stuff that no-one knew about anymore. All this was on record – the public record of my life; my life as seen through the eyes of the criminal justice system. It was about time that I started to have a say, in how it really was.

'I've written two journals – one about the past, about my time in care, and another one to let you know how I am now,' I said, handing her both pieces, the following Monday morning, which I insisted she read there and then. My racing thoughts and feelings spilled over into restlessness and fidgeting as I could do nothing except sit and wait in painful silence for her to read about my first time inside. I wanted only for her to skip through that account and be impressed with who I had become, and not judge me on where I came from.

**Time**

*It's funny how the nature of time seems to change as you grow older. Everything seemed to last for ages when I was a kid. School days were long and boring; the wait for Ma to come home from work always dragged; as did the days I faked sickness so Ma wouldn't send me to* school. I had learned how to wheeze really effectively, even on days when the asthma wasn't really a problem. When I was home alone I would make up stories about other people and places and about myself. As I couldn't read, or write, I had to use my imagination to make up stories. In my head I was someone, a leader, someone who told other people what to do.

Then as my brothers grew up and I followed in their footsteps, it was as if this was how I was meant to live, just doing exactly what I wanted; until I took it too far and lost my grip on things. When you're not looking it can just come on top for you – you've got to be in control, as there's always some sly fucker watching and waiting to steal your glory. I learned that lesson good and proper, the first time I got a custodial sentence and was sent to a Young Offenders' jail.

That's when time became heavily segmented. My first time in prison I remember in slots, shared with others as we were squashed in and shuffled around by the system; and silent night-time sessions of darkness, and sometimes despair. Breakfast at 7:45; shower at 8; 8:15 exercise time in the compound; with official movement to work or classes at 8:45. It was back to the wing at 11:30; lunch at 11:45; then bang up at 12:30 so the screws could (officially) skive for an hour, lazy bastards, most of them.

Then it was the same sort of routine in the afternoon too with the addition of wing association time at 6:30, if you found yourself on an enhanced regime with privileges. I stopped playing pool at association time. It was just too risky, too easy to lose your head over pool; and clock some twat with the end of a cue. And when the pool balls went missing, you could find yourself in the crap, until they were eventually found during a laborious cell search, awaiting the opportunity to be used as a weapon. The screws knew only too well the pain of a crack on the back of the head from pool balls concealed within a sock, so they never gave up on a search. Bang up from 8 o'clock in the evening could make for a very long night in there, especially in summer when it was light until after 10. If there was nothing decent on TV, you were quite often left alone with just your music, your thoughts, and your memories. Imagine *all that frustration and tension just building up amongst all of us young males. Lots of weird stuff went on in shared cells, so I always made sure no-one wanted to stay long in my cell. I preferred my own space and let everyone know it.*

*I used to read books – gangster tales, true-life crime and stuff like that. In fact, I learned how to read in young offenders' prison. For a while it opened up a new world for me, and I got lots of kicks out of learning what had happened to people like me, but now I find that it sets me off thinking about my own life and stuff I would rather forget. I realize that I used to try and get rid of the bad memories and feelings by taking it out on others. If I felt hurt about something, I'd go out to make someone else feel the hurt. Then I'd justify it by blaming them and saying that they had done something to deserve it.*

*Recently I've begun to look at things differently. I used to tell myself it was the victim's fault for being in the wrong place at the wrong time; now I find myself thinking about his family, his mother or his kids. I used to tell myself 'forget about it, there's nothing you can do now to change it' and try to put the pictures out my head. The thing is, you never really forget. The foul memories are just festering away and seep out to disturb you when you're least expecting them. Now I am trying out different ways of dealing with the hurt. When I start to think about hurting others; I know it's time to move away from the situation, if I can't deal with it any other way I just have to get out of there. It sounds easy, but it's tough when you're used to hitting first and not even asking questions later.*

It was important that she knew who I was now. She knew all about my family and childhood misdeeds. I felt naked and powerless in front of her.

'So where do we go from here Jed?' She asked when she had finished reading both pieces.

Looking back, I can see that she was the first person, the only person, apart from Ma, who has shown me any warmth, accepted me for all that I was and all that I had done. Since Ma had sided with *him* against me, it was the first time I had thought there was someone who was on my side. However, I wasn't sure how long that would last. How much more bad stuff could she hear about me, uncensored, from my own mouth? Was I just burying myself so deep that if the prison authorities got to know about this stuff, they would never let me out of jail again? What if I was just shipped out of the jail in the middle of the night, to some psychiatric hospital jail, the ones where you had to prove you were sane or you stayed there indefinitely? I knew these places existed. What if I never saw *her* again? It was at that point that I realized I knew nothing about her, other than the details of her that I could see, smell and longed to touch.

'Are you ready to move onto the next level, Jed or are there still some past experiences or situations you want to explore?' She interrupted my desperate panic of thoughts. As I was trying to concentrate more and more on how I was thinking and feeling now, it seemed like she was pushing for more of the stuff I didn't want talk to her about.

Trying to cover myself, I played it cool, saying that I thought we had covered most of my violence, except of course for my index offence, the stuff for which I was serving a life sentence. But somehow she knew there was more to be told and I found myself caught up in a loop of wanting to offload it, yet not wanting her to hear it and think badly of me. She sensed my reluctance and was not letting me off the hook.

'We can refer to your list of pre-convictions here on your file if that will help you to remember...' she offered, opening the file that profiled and detailed me right down to the offensive racist categorization of "B.O." meaning "black, other". *What the fuck did that mean?* Out of the limited choice of 'Caucasian, Asian, Black Caribbean and Black Other', I guess that was the easiest fit. Yes, that prison profile detailed parts of me, including the positioning of unique birthmarks and tattoos on my black ass, but still only provided a two-dimensional image that was in no way representative of the whole of me.

I looked straight into her knowing eyes and said I needed some more time and space to think straight.

There was one past incident that was really bothering me, so I when I was alone in my cell, late that night, I wrote about it:

## Women

*After the time spent in the secure unit I was holed up in my room at home, inhabiting my own imaginary world. Ma was tiptoeing around me and HE made himself scarce. I was rehearsing revenge. Revenge on everyone who had ever done me any wrong. When Ma told me she was going to marry that guy, I knew I had to get myself out of there, for his health and my sanity. The easiest move for me was out of that flat and in with Denise. That was my first "relationship". Denise already had a kid by some other guy and her own place in the block, which was convenient for me. She was having trouble with him calling around uninvited at all hours of the day and night and getting abusive when he didn't get what he came for. I stepped in to play the big protector. That role made me feel good for a while. I was the only man in my life. I was in control. No father figures or older brothers telling me what to do. I was calling the shots in every aspect of my life. Denise didn't have much but she knew exactly what she wanted, and how to get it. It was hot between us at first, she was hungry for me, physically, and was happy to give as passionately as she took. Having sex with such a fiery woman, I learned about my own power and passion. For a while being with her was all I could think about; we had such a strong pull towards each other, that the sexual energy we generated engulfed us both for a while. This was a whole new dimension of experience for me and for a while I just couldn't get enough of it. However, we also fought with as much passion as we fucked. I hung around with Denise long enough to see my daughter Shauna, my first kid born. Then things changed between us. Denise got all demanding on me, wanting me home at night, and stuff like that. When I refused to play it her way, she told me to leave. The power struggle between us overtook the passion. I told her that she was an ungrateful bitch and told her that there were many others willing to let me move in with them. There were always a couple of willing young molls hanging around, looking to hook up with a local "gangsta" with cash to flash, or that's how I thought about it at the time.*

*Looking back, all my relationships with women have ended because they wanted to keep me close; stop me going out and doing stuff. As soon as I got that "trapped" feeling I was out of there looking for someone who would let me do what I pleased and would be happy to see me whenever I turned up. I called round one day to see Shauna only to be told by Denise that she was pregnant by some snide bastard who I had thought of as a mate. Denise is the first and last woman I have ever hurt in my life. I just lost it with all her mouthing at me, telling me it was my fault for not being there for her and that she had found a real man to look after her and my kid. I remember this great feeling of pressure in my chest and my mind going really vague. Before I was aware of what was happening, she was dripping blood from her busted nose and her bruised, swelling eyes were pleading with me to loosen my grip from around her throat.*

*The next thing I remember was sitting on a train heading out of the city to God knows where.*

*After that day Denise refused to acknowledge me and I was too ashamed to try and contact my daughter. Perhaps Denise was right, that the man in her life would be a better father than me. Shauna would nearly be a teenager now; with younger half-brothers and sisters. I remember her as a quiet little blonde kid who always wrapped around her mother's legs, peering up at me with the biggest blue eyes, whenever I was round at their flat.*

*She wouldn't know me as her father now, though. She got adopted by Denise's man and changed her name. I figured there were more than enough other women around for me and so I put them both out of my mind. There were lots of different women for a while. I just didn't give anyone the chance to get close to me and I wasn't really interested in getting too deep into anyone else's life. Alisha was the little sister of a mate. He wasn't too happy about it, when he knew she was messing about with me. I got with her when I got tired of roaming from bed to bed and wanted somewhere to lay low for a while. Alisha was cool. She was easy to be around – just a kid when we met, but she grew up quickly when our son JJ was on the way.*

Thinking I was ready, I decided to hit it head on. After breakfast with this "confession" shaking in my hands I tried to focus all the way from the second landing down to the ground floor interview room. This was going to be a major turning point for me, talking about something so personal and admitting to something so shameful. This was something I had never talked to anyone about, not even Ma. I needed to acknowledge it so it would lose its power over me; and somehow by telling *her* about it made me feel stronger. Yes it was a huge risk, she might hate me for it, I guess that was my biggest fear. I was rattled, but something inside me said she wouldn't abandon me over that one incident and so I calmed down. I reasoned that she would help me understand it and close the door on that chapter of my life, the one that I was most fearful of opening up for all to see and judge. And if she didn't understand and help then I would just forget the whole thing. I it would be over. I could accept that this is who I am that this was how my life was supposed to be. It was now or never. I didn't know if I would be able to summon up the courage to do this again. She wasn't there. The door was locked and the room was empty.

As I was desperately turning the handle on the interview-room door, in the hope it would suddenly open and she would be sitting there, a sarcastic voice spoke over my shoulder. 'Problem, Johnston? Been stood up?' Fat Bastard was on duty in the wing office, and had been sat at the desk feeding his face with a bacon sandwich from the mess and watching me with interest. With his gut bulging through the buttons of his white, uniform shirt and a smug grin on his fat face he said, 'your lady phoned and said she wouldn't be making it today, something about an audit in the department...aw she hasn't got time to waste on you anymore'.

I felt panic rising – I wasn't prepared for this. I saw myself shoving that sandwich down his throat until he choked. The picture filled me with an almost uncontrollable energy. I wanted to feel him struggle, hear him splutter, gasping for air and pleading with his eyes for me to stop. I could feel myself getting sucked in to the picture until the clanking of the gates and sound of hurried female footsteps broke the bubble. 'Sorry I'm late,' she said, cheeks flushed and slightly out of breath. 'Shall we make a start?'

*Who did she think she was? Cheeky fucking bitch, thinking she can pick me up and drop me just as she likes,* I thought, my head still pounding with anger and thoughts of violence.

It must have showed, as she stopped and looked straight into my eyes. 'Has something happened Jed?'

'I thought you weren't coming,' was all I could manage between clenched teeth and deep breaths.

'Oh, mixed messages?' she asked looking at Fat Bastard, who was grinning from ear to ear. 'Not a misunderstanding, more a case of *miss-information*', I emphasized, aware that I had to slow my breathing and calm myself down.

'I see. Are you up for this session now or shall we arrange it for another time?'

Breathing steadily now, I couldn't risk getting wound up again. I needed to get away from him and her. I asked for her to postpone the session and headed back up the landing to my cell, face to the ground, to avoid any dickhead stupid enough to take a pot at me when I was in that mood. After a smoke and a brew I got out the piece of work I had just nearly handed to her and re-read it. I realized I was still angry with Denise, and now I was angry with *her*. I was being straight with her and she could so easily be pissing me around. Trust is such a fragile thing. I knew it probably wasn't *her* messing with me but I just couldn't be sure

– I had never really trusted anyone and now, I just couldn't risk trusting *her* again.

A week passed; and neither of us made contact with the other. I thought that we were both playing the waiting game. The "old me" came to the surface and I started to doubt that I had done the right thing by opening up to the stuff of my past. Nothing had changed – no-one could be trusted and I was so fucking stupid to have been sucked into thinking any differently by some posh bird. I picked up my game with the other inmates on the wing, letting them know I was not to be messed with. I was seeing more opportunities for the other "names" on the wing to challenge my reputation and taking precautions against it, and I went back into my previous ways, strategically placing tools adapted for use as weapons around the wing. If anything was going down, I was going to be ready for it. I was back in control.

Then the rumours started. I caught snatches of conversation between the officers supervising the evening recreational hour. 'She's in a bit of a state by all accounts' one muttered as they stood in the doorway watching the cons in the games room. I got up from the scrabble table and headed towards the door, as slowly as I could, to try and hear a bit more of their conversation.

'They've been trying to keep it quiet, but you know what the jungle drums are like in this place.'

'Prison ain't no place for women, I don't know why they do it!' said the other as he turned to head back down the corridor.

Somehow, I just knew this was something to do with *her*. My thoughts had raced and my heart had pounded when I thought she had been hurt. I knew they wouldn't tell me. I'd have to wait until Fat Bastard was on shift. I was sure he wouldn't be able to contain himself. I didn't have to wait long. He was on early shift the next morning. That always put him in a bad mood. I waited until after morning movement and made my way down to the office. I could smell the bacon from his breakfast sandwich wafting up the wing. 'What are you doing unlocked?' he barked, a small piece of rind falling out of mouth and onto the paper he was reading.

'Psychology appointment', I answered.

'Oh no you haven't!' He said with a grin. 'That little lady's out of action for a while.'

'What do you mean?' I asked, feigning surprise.

'Had a bit of a hiding by all accounts' he spoke in between loud chews and in a manner which suggested it was only to be expected.

Desperate to not seem too interested I thought I could try one question, 'What, from her old man?' I had looked at her ring finger enough times to know there was no gold wedding band on it. He stooped chewing and stared at me with his mouth open. 'Some piece of scum in the segregation unit, but he's had what he deserved. He's gone on Rule 43 now, so nothing no-one else can do about it. If you're on the wing all morning make yourself scarce, I don't want to see or hear you'.

My head was buzzing. I was livid. I didn't know why. I was confused. With increasing breathlessness I climbed the stairs to the second floor landing and headed towards my cell. I remember thinking that men shouldn't hit women, not women like her. Men who hurt women and kids got what they deserved. That was the rule in this place. Ma had always told me not to hit girls. But I had hurt Denise. Why was I having so much trouble with the fact that this woman had been hurt?

I was a fucking hypocrite. What could I do? I knew what I couldn't do. I could never show her that journal entry. Perhaps I would never get to show her any of my work again. The idea of not ever seeing her again left me feeling cold and empty inside. I reminded myself that people come into your life and people leave, no sweat. Yet I couldn't seem to shake off my constant thoughts and stubborn feelings for her.

# Chapter 5

# ANANSE NTONTAN: Spider's web

It was at this time that I started talking to Danny. He was a young guy with the respected position of "Listener" on the lifer wing. He was allowed in to other peoples' cells overnight, if they asked the screws for someone to talk too. The screws liked him – he gave them no shit and he got their trust. The first time I met Danny was when Principal Officer King, as I later got to know him, opened the hatch to my cell in the early hours of one morning and asked if I wanted a "listener". I didn't reply; I didn't care. I didn't even know who I was anymore. I had been living for the weekly sessions with the psychologist in the hope I might get some clarity, insight and warmth. Now she was out of my life, the road ahead looked bleak and unforgiving. I can't remember what Danny said. I could see his mouth moving, but I wasn't tuning into his frequency. I must have fallen asleep at one point, because I remember waking with a start to find his big, dark eyes peering into my face. I froze in fear, despite the voice in my head telling me to get the fuck out of there before this weird bastard did something evil to me. Then there was another voice, reassuring me it was ok, I was safe, and Danny turned away from me and banged on the door for the screw to unlock the door for him to leave.

We walked past each other on the wing with our heads down for a week or so, until in the feeding queue at midday one Wednesday, Danny leaned forward, close enough to speak to me without being heard by anyone else.

'You ok,' he muttered in a muted tone of voice.

I don't know whether it was a question or a statement, but I remember a sense of calm wash over me. 'I'm ok,' I heard myself say.

'Well you know where I am.' He ended the conversation and we continued the wait for our daily slop in silence.

However, that was the start of a long conversation between us, as I found myself listening to and learning from Danny. He didn't look like anything, a thin guy with sallow skin and a sulky expression. His face always downcast, with brooding eyes set deep beneath a heavy brow. But there was something about the way being around Danny made you feel. When he fixed his gaze on you, you became the most important person in the world; and when he froze you out you started to question your reason for existing. This guy, who always provoked an initial sense of uncertainty in me, also had a way of steadying me, of smoothing out my nerves. I was intrigued by him, and sometimes in awe of his knowledge.

He seemed to know the system really well. Looking back, I guess it's because he had been in at "Her Majesty's Pleasure" from a very young age. Rumour had it that he had killed both of his parents when he was about 14 years old, choked them in their sleep, sliced off the old guy's balls and the old girl's tits, then doused the house with petrol, lit the flame and watched it burn. When the fire and ambulance arrived, it was said that Danny was found in the garden shed, listening to Nirvana through headphones whilst flicking through some hard-core porn mag. That was the story that echoed round the wing, but was never confirmed or denied by Danny. He never discussed sentences or tariff dates, and it just wasn't done to ask Danny direct questions. He would never answer any sort of question about himself, but he would talk for hours when you got him on a subject he was interested in.

When you listened to Danny it sounded like he'd been all over the world, some places I hadn't even heard of. He knew loads about all sorts of stuff, but I never saw him reading any books. Danny liked to draw. His cell was decorated from floor to ceiling with ornate, mystical pencil sketches, and despite the lack of colour the power of the hawks' heads and the detail of the dragon wings was pretty impressive. When I closed in on one reptile-like creature I could see that the whole thing was made up of hundreds of small, scrap pieces of paper so carefully placed together that it was hard to see the joins. Danny called them his "journeying maps". He said that he had never learned to read or write properly, something to do with him being dyslexic, but he had spent time talking to all sorts of people in and out of the system. The screws seemed to let Danny have more "favours" than most of the other lifers. From what I could see, he didn't give them any shit and so they left him alone. I think it was because of the time he'd been in the system. Everyone else around seemed to accept it; although some guy put it around once that Danny was a screw-loving grass. Later he was found in the laundry room with steam burns all over his face and shoulders. The screws didn't seem to make much of an effort to find out who was behind the attack and the culprit never stuck his charred neck out again.

Danny's cell was somewhere I could go, where it was easier for me to forget where I really was, and a whole new world was starting to open up for me. He asked me if I ever played the drums. I thought of the one that belonged to our father, the one that he kept at the back of his wardrobe, away from us kids. I remembered the time that my brothers got into a fight over who could play with the drum, whilst our father was out at the pub, and accidentally broke the skin stretched over its carved, wooden base. As feared, our father had erupted when he found it and Jon, as the eldest took the beating. I could only watch as he cowered, trying to cover his bruised and bleeding face from the blows of our father's furious fists.

Trying to clear that image out of my mind I focused on the drum and described it to Danny.

'Ah the talking drum.' He knew what I was talking about. 'Do you have it in here with you?'

'No it was broken. I left it at the flat. I have some of my old man's other things though.' I don't know why I volunteered that. Perhaps I thought Danny might know something about the golden stool and the tunic – the stuff that I had taken after he died.

He asked me to bring the items to him. 'Kente cloth' he stated as I unrolled the tunic I kept in my box of personal stuff in my cell.

'You know about this?'

'Yeah, traditional African cloth – your old man from Ghana?' Danny asked.

'Yes, came to London in the fifties by all accounts, married Ma and stayed. We've still got family members over there.'

Danny rolled up his prison-issue, sweatshirt sleeve to reveal a black tattoo on his right forearm, looked like the blades of a windmill with a hole in the middle. 'Ananse,' he announced, 'the spider.' I was none the wiser. 'It's a symbol from Ghanaian culture,' he informed me. 'I lived in Ghana for a couple of years, when I was just a kid. I can remember some stuff, mainly from the traditional storytelling sessions. This Kente cloth was supposed to have been inspired by the weaving of this web by the spider. If you check out the loom they sometimes use to make this stuff, you'll see it's different from other looms in that the man, the weaver, actually positions himself within the loom itself, like a spider in its web.'

'A man, weaving?' I asked, thinking Danny had made a mistake.

'Yes, most traditional crafts, such as pottery and weaving were the work of men, not women in Ghanaian culture.' Danny continued, 'in Akan culture, Ananse is the messenger of the Supreme Being, God, Yahweh, Allah, Jehovah, John Smith or whatever you want to call him. He is the keeper of all of the superior one's stories, and the communicator between him and us. He weaves a web of energy, which spans the whole of existence, from the outer reaches of the universe to the individual cells of our bodies. And then like just as you see a spider venture out from one briar in a garden bush, weaving himself all along the hedgerow, he can then travel to and from any point in the spirit-world to the physical world along the many skeins of this web, carrying messages between the supreme and the people'.

Inspired by Danny's apparent knowledge of Ghana and its culture, I grabbed one of the pencils lying around and sketched an image from memory. 'My old man had a tattoo on his right forearm, sort of like this…'

Danny looked at it and said 'Okodee Mnowere – the Eagle's talons. This is the Adinkra symbol of strength, bravery, power. The eagle is the king of the sky and its strength is concentrated in its talons. Your old man, was he part of the Oyoko clan? He must have been, to have this tattoo done, back in the day. Anyone can have one of these now, but if he had it when he was young, then he must have been Oyoko, one of the ancient nine Akan clans, who used this symbol as their emblem.' This was all news to me. Danny switched his attention to the tunic, 'so this is authentic Kente cloth then, not some imitation.' He looked more closely at the cloth, running his fingers firstly along the black and white vertical stripes; and then across the interwoven red, green and gold stripes arranged in alternating blocks. 'Kyerekwie', he announced, 'cloth of the lion catcher. See these black warps? These represent the black markings of the animal's fur.'

'What does that mean?' I asked.

'Mate, it means that your old man was descended from the clan of lion catchers. The colours and the patterns in the cloth tell the story. This is your heritage, too'. Danny looked excited at his discovery. He became very animated, very keen to learn more about me.

'Sorry to disappoint you – I ain't been near any lion's mate. None in my concrete jungle' I laughed trying to shrug it off. It meant nothing to me. It wasn't my family history. Not the one I had lived out, so far.

Danny pulled out a small, smooth-skinned, hollow, drum-like wooden instrument. It had some circular interwoven design covering the stretched top. Danny explained it was a gift from Ireland, a Bodhran with a Celtic design. It was a present from a relative, given to him as a young kid before he was old enough to remember, and every time he was transferred to a new jail, it was confiscated by the staff who were overly suspicious of anything out of the ordinary in prisoners' cells. It had been subject to regular security checks, but somehow he'd managed to hold onto it.

Danny started to tap the drum rhythmically; gently and quietly, while I listened. After a while he told me to close my eyes and he started to tell me some weird tale.

'So you're walking along this path, right? You've turned off the road and you're cutting along some scrubland, heading towards the woods. The sound of the traffic on the road behind you is fading into the distance and the twigs that snap underfoot are the loudest sound you can hear now. You're sweating now as it's a hot summer's day; the sun is beating down on the back of your head and as you approach the entrance to the woods, a stillness descends around you and you feel welcomed by the cool shade.'

By now I'm staring at Danny, who's still tapping on his drum, eyes closed.

'Stay with me on this one Jed', he said in this firm tone, without opening his eyes. I was becoming used to Danny talking for long periods of time, and so I listened to what he was saying. I remember him telling me to find a hole in the ground somewhere. 'Use your imagination,' he said, still drumming, eyes closed; and I noticed a bead of sweat forming in the crease of his frown.

'What do you mean?' I felt uncomfortable.

'Think of the last time you were in the woods.'

'What woods? I ain't been in any woods.'

'Never, not even as a kid?'

'Hey man, I was a city kid...born and bred in brick. The only green stuff I ever saw was the snot from my sister's nose, and I don't know what sort of game you're playing, some weird fucking thing if you ask me.'

Danny looked up from beneath his frown with a curious expression, shrugged and proceeded to explain, 'This is MY talking drum. In Ghana, Jed, there is a storytelling art called 'Anansesem' by Akan speaking people. Storytelling sessions always open with some music or some rhythm, played by the storyteller. It is also the way that other people can join in with the story. In Ghanaian tradition it's also widely believed that the spirits of the ancestors are always around and that they sometimes make their presence felt during story telling.'

'So this is some religious shit? Listen, I'm not interested...' I said.

'Not religious Jed, spiritual. This stuff isn't about God or Jehovah or whoever, it's about connecting with the earth, the place where we're all from and where we all end up.'

'What's this got to do with me?' I asked, half-interestedly.

'It's your heritage, man. Your ancestors, my ancestors, they all worshipped the universal Goddess Ma'at, before they were scattered all over the globe. Before the continents split and the different religions developed, our ancestors all worshipped the same Goddess who set the order of the Universe from its chaotic state at the moment of creation. They believed that she regulated the orbit of the planets; controlled the seasons on the Earth; the actions of the Gods in the heavens and the mortals on the Earth. Ma'at bound all things together in an indestructible unity: the universe, the natural world, the state, and the individual were all seen as parts of the whole order.'

When Danny was on a roll, it was pointless trying to interrupt him and this stuff was capturing my imagination, I had never heard anything like it.

'Have you heard about the "Book of the Dead?"' he asked. I shook my head. 'The ancient Egyptians recorded all this stuff about Ma'at in there. They believed that cosmic harmony was affected by the actions of men on Earth. In the Duat, the under-world, on the Night of Weighing Words, Ma'at weighed every soul's heart on a feather scale. To balance on the scale, the heart had to be pure and free from sin. Only if this was the case, could the soul reach the paradise of the afterlife. If not they had to stay in the underworld. Heaven or hell, this was the decision, a concept that was copied by all the religions of the world; and the scales became a symbol of social justice throughout all the nations of the world.'

'So all other religions and civilizations stem from ancient Egypt and the Goddess Ma'at?' I asked.

'Yep,' Danny confirmed with confidence.

'How can stuff that people believed centuries ago still be true today?' I was starting to question Danny's judgment.

'Man, it's all in the pyramids, its science, not myth. Scientists have confirmed that the electromagnetic waves produced by the pyramids connect with the creator. The pyramids are the gates to eternal life for those who succeeded in passing from the material world into the transcendental parts of nature; they were built to help us connect with the creator. Their foundations are built on the laws of nature projecting the resurrection of spirit from matter. The four base points of the pyramids represent fire, air, water, and earth, while the top represents the fifth element, the Supreme Being. The ancient Egyptians knew all this stuff way back then'.

Danny spoke with such conviction that I couldn't challenge his beliefs. He knew far more about these things than me. I was intrigued. He continued, 'Going back to our roots is the only option, Jed. If we want to save our planet and our race from destruction, we have to return to the traditional African values. Look back through history, Jed, and see what's happened since the power has shifted from the African continent. The Greeks took over leadership of the ancient world in 332 BC, bringing us the city state and 'civilization' as they thought it should be. They taught us lots of useful stuff, but not useful enough to allow them to keep control. They lost their power to the Romans in 49 BC, who ruled for 1,500 years. The Europeans gave it a good go in the last couple of centuries, with the British trying to empire-build, and the Dutch were a main player in the African Slave trade. Of course, the USA has been in control in the last fifty years, largely down to their nuclear-weapons-building policy and interplay with the oil-rich states of the Middle East. Now China and India and Russia are the emerging economic powers, picking up where the West is leaving off, polluting and poisoning the planet. Africa must cut short China's reign if we are to repair, restore and renew our troubled earth, making it more sustainable for all who inhabit her, it's our only hope.'

I couldn't say if Danny had all his facts and figures correct, or whether he was making it all up. But he spoke with such emotion he managed to invoke a sense of ignorance, fear, pride and power in me all at the same time. I was feeling alive and inspired to learn more about my ancestors and what was happening in the world outside of the prison walls. I found it hard to settle down to sleep that night in the quiet of my cell with all that noise going on in my head.

# Chapter 6

# MPATAPO: Reconciliation, Peacemaking and Pacification

Her eyes flashed a welcoming smile at the door, their green sparkle suggesting that this was going to be something special. 'Make yourself at home,' she murmured, turning to walk towards the sprawling leather sofa behind us.

Oh I intended to...My eyes followed the length of her silky curls to the curve of her waist and I watched the rhythmic rise and fall of each firm buttock, just knowing that they were naked below that skimpy slip. As we sat alongside each other a loose strap sleeked off her smooth shoulder and I felt the promise of her warmth rising from between her breasts. I gently licked my lips in anticipation of her sweet moisture and let out a low moan, feeling a strong increase in the ache of my desire.

Then she turned to face me and I saw Denise looking at me through bloodshot, blackened eyes, fresh blood trickling from her busted nose. I closed my eyes, trying to lose the image, and opened them again only to see the face of *her*, the psychologist, trying to smile at me despite her bruised and battered lips.

I woke from the dream in a panic, feeling sick and confused. *What the fuck was going on?*

Unusually, I was dressed and waiting impatiently for the

morning unlock. The officer responsible raised his eyebrows when he pushed the door to find me fully dressed and standing in the middle of the cell. 'Got somewhere to be, Johnson?' he asked, standing back from the doorway in surprise.

'Yeah, things on my mind', I muttered as I shouldered past him and headed off to find Danny. I didn't want to confide in Danny, but I did want his help. I mentioned something about women trouble, about not knowing what was going on in my head. 'What can I do man? I'm so confused.'

Danny thought for a moment and then replied knowingly, 'Yeah, women, complex creatures, often the cause of great confusion. Look, when I've got some tricky shit on my mind I take a shamanic journey'

'What's that?' I asked.

'It's a journey people take when they want to know the answer to a question.' I had a hundred questions and no idea of what Danny was going to do next.

'In West Africa, the way is to ingest the powdered root-bark of the Iboga plant, Jed. This is how the Shamans help people to find the answers to their questions. Some believe that the plants themselves are spiritual guides and others say that the natural plant chemicals induce you into a trance state which allows the soul to leave your body and enter the cosmos where you can watch your fate unfolding before your very eyes.'

Was he going to offer me some acid shit? I had been clean for a good few months now and I was anxious not to fuck that up, but not sure how strong I would be in the face of temptation.

'But you can also do it with drumming,' he said reaching for his drum, and explaining. 'We'll pick up from where we left off, last time. You're in the woods and looking for a spot to rest.'

Danny picked up the beat on the drum and started his rhythmic hypnosis. He "guided" me towards an old tree stump in the midst of a clearing. I was told to look into it. I could see only black, empty space. 'If you look carefully, you'll see grooves dug into the sides. Climb down using your hands and feet, as if you're on a ladder,' he instructed me.

I closed my eyes and imagined myself reaching for the grooves. I had expected them to feel muddy, as if made of soil, but it felt more as if I was climbing down on the struts of a wooden ladder.

'Keep climbing,' Danny reminded me as if he sensed my attention wavering, 'you're getting there.' All this time I was conscious of the gentle drum beat in the background. Curiosity was keeping me going. 'Ok, stop!' Danny banged the drum once and announced, 'You've reached a place, where are you?'

I was in a barn, having just climbed down from a hayloft.

'What can you see? Look around you,' Danny urged.

I could see hay, wooden stalls, and the smell...

'Are there any animals around?'

I could see something moving behind one of the stalls. It was a horse, stamping one hoof and snorting.

'Go over to it and ask it a question'.

I found myself looking into the face of the horse, wondering, *why all this stuff about women?*

It was like I was tripping. I knew it wasn't real but it was happening. I opened the door to the stall and let the horse out into the barn. It was a magnificent creature, strong and serene. As I stroked its chestnut mane, it stood tall and elegant and started to walk towards an opening at the furthest end of the barn. As the heavy barn door was pushed open, I was momentarily blinded by the strength of the sunlight. Then I was astride the creature, eyes closed and head down, as she trotted ahead steadily. As the drum beat picked up and the horse broke into a canter, I leaned into the rhythmic lull with my fingers firmly entwined in the horse's mane.

When she slowed I opened my eyes to see a steep grassy incline ahead. I could feel her struggle to carry my weight to the top of the rise, and gripped tightly when she lost her footing on a few occasions, slipping on the smooth grass under hoof.

At the summit, I saw we were perched on a dusty ridge, like the spine of the earth, stretching behind and out in front of us as far as the eye could see. To the side was a steep, rocky descent into a fast-flowing river below. For me the way forward was obvious, however the horse was pacing restlessly, as if undecided on which direction to take.

I knew I had no control over this creature; I just had to trust it with my fate.

Then the fearful pounding of my heart was drowning out the sound of the drum, as I realized we were heading down amongst the loose-lying rocks to the river below. I felt angry and frightened of being dragged down this way, however, those feelings were drowned out by the thunder of the hooves and I could only succumb to the relentless pounding and dodging of the missiles the horse was kicking up around us. As we neared the bottom and she started to slow up I felt a sense of relief at the realization that I had survived.

Then the sound of scraping hooves, slipping on wet rocks. We were splashing in the shallow water, heading downstream where the river opened out as an estuary into the sea. I slopped about on the back of the horse, as all my constricted muscles relaxed and my body leaned over the horse's head, breathing deeply and slowly.

As the waterway widened in front of us, so the horse faltered, fearfully. I shakily dismounted and bent over to look into the deepening water beneath. I could see Alisha's face. It was smeared with dirt and tears, her soulful brown eyes now black and sunken. She looked so small and helpless; no longer the strong, feisty woman in a face-off with me that day in court. Then I was wading in, the water rising around me, lapping at my chest and closing in around my neck. I closed my eyes in an attempt to escape Alisha's image and walked, immersing myself in the water. I felt a hypnotic pull, far too strong to resist, into a sunken landscape. Until, with a sudden gasp, I became aware of the need to breathe. I could hear Danny's strained voice urging me to 'come back' and I coughed and spluttered. Then, feeling that I couldn't get the water out, I panicked. The next thing I knew there were two officers attempting first aid on me.

'What brought this on?' I heard one ask in a worried tone. 'I thought he was on asthma medication.'

'I bet he's been dealing it,' snorted the other. 'Look, he's drenched in sweat; do you think we should call the doctor?'

'Yeah, put a call out over the net'.

The screws made sure my throat was clear and placed me in the recovery position. I felt for my inhaler in the pocket of my jogging trousers and gestured to one of them to reach it for me. A few minutes later I was sitting up and sucking in Salbutamol. The screw cancelled the net call for the doctor and asked, 'What's been going on here, Danny?'

'Asthma attack, obviously,' Danny replied, shrugging his shoulders, 'I didn't know he got it so bad'.

The screws were suspicious. 'You're both on observation. Watch yourselves.'

I was escorted back to my cell, where I crashed out in exhaustion for the rest of the day.

When I woke it was past midnight. I was awash with old feelings and thoughts, which emerged loud and clear in the silence of the dark. I had asked to know what was going on with the psychologist, yet I had been given an image of Alisha. I needed to get some stuff clear in my head and so I wrote about Alisha. Even if no-one was ever going to read it, I had to get it down on paper so I could get it all straight – well as straight as you could make that fucking twisted path that was my life, which had led me to where I am, right here and now.

## Alisha

*It was the drugs that got in the way of me and Alisha, not the dealing, the doing. She seemed to be able to handle my line of business, so long as I kept it away from the house. That was easy as I wasn't home often. And she was all wrapped in the baby, anyway.*

*I got a short sentence for dealing and common assault when I was about 21. It didn't really bother me at the time, it was a local, low security jail. I was still on a learning curve and doing time was par for the course. I was young and thought I was untouchable. I got into the business of bringing stuff into prison, as it was the only business I knew. I wasn't up for some crappy plastering course that the prison was offering. Avoiding the security cameras and the keen, beady eyes of the screws, made for some excitement; as did watching my latest girl Friday make it past the sniffer dogs and embracing her to relieve her of the package she had concealed somewhere on her person. A lingering kiss could cover the passing of a small package from her mouth to mine; whereas a cough into the hand was a bit harder to conceal. So, I received all my deliveries with a passionate kiss, much to the amusement of the other blokes on visits and the frustration of the screws who could never quite get to me before I swallowed the shit. And they just couldn't get enough on me to insist on closed visits in one of those side booths — where they could watch you more closely. I gained some kudos from the other cons for hash, speed or any low-grade dope I could source. As with any business, though, the stakes were soon upped when some geezer got in some crack. Feeling confident I sourced a ready supply of brown, and was keen to move it quickly. I couldn't afford to be caught holding, so I chose my customers carefully and had a pretty smooth operation going for a while. Until, someone got a little jealous. At unlock one morning my door was overlooked, or so I thought as I hammered and kicked, hurling abuse at the staff for leaving me trapped. Suddenly, I was pushed backwards as the door flung open and the dogs were all over my cell. They didn't find anything, but it made people really nervous and nothing got moved for a couple of days. I was under suspicion so I couldn't afford to make any false moves. That's when I had my first taste of heroin — it was the safest way to get rid of the stuff.*

*I had tasted and handled all sorts of stuff, but had never really seen myself as a brown-head. However, on that sentence my self-image changed. When I was stoned the warm, cocooned feeling was sweet. I was light and free floating, nothing could weigh me down. It kept me safe from the reality of what was happening around me. Smack blocked out lots of unwanted sights and sounds. But I was losing my grip. I was waking up with a feeling of desperation in the pit of my stomach and acting all paranoid with those around me. When I got out from that sentence, Alisha told me I was different. She didn't like my new habits or my new friends and so we started drifting apart.*

*I was on new territory now playing in a different league and the paranoia was taking over. The stakes were higher and I needed more protection, so I got myself a shooter. Then I put the word out, as a warning to people. If they were going to mess with me now they knew what to expect. So I was feeling a little smug for a while, comforted by the contents of my inner pocket. It was easy to smile at the drivers of passing police cars, knowing the stash that they were missing out on as they pursued some petty traffic offence. The local police had learned from numerous fruitless searches that I was way too smart to be caught carrying, so with that in mind and my newfound confidence, in the shape of a 9mm barrel, I upped the stakes and soon there were shooters and crack flying all over the place. I was back in control again. It was so good to see the smile wiped clean off the face of some sly fucker pulling a knife on me, when he was faced with my weapon. And I couldn't help but laugh when the knife was blown out of his hands and he slumped to the ground in defeat.*

*This was something of a new addiction for me, until early on a dark winter's morning when I was roughly awoken by guys with flashlights, sporting body armour.*

*I vaguely remember hearing my name being shouted; and then Alisha getting out of the bed, from beside me.*

*From a drug-induced haze it seemed to take forever for me to figure out what was going down. When some bastard breaks into your room in the dark, it's usually because they're desperate for your stuff and are prepared to do you serious harm to get it. As I reached out for my* weapon, some bastard trod on my arm and blasted me blind with a flashlight. The truth is I wasn't up to too much resistance; I was far too wasted to put up any sort of fight. The next thing I knew I was on my feet, my arms outstretched being dragged out of the bed and flung to the floor. As my face hit the boards, I was cuffed with both hands behind my back. This wasn't the work of dealers; my arrest was carried out with military precision, six officers, a van and an armed response vehicle. I had gone up in the world!

I've got a patchy memory of being questioned. One guy got really agitated because of the delay between his questions and my response, but I was really struggling to think straight let alone talk and make any sense.

In frustration they locked me in a police cell to sleep it off for a couple of hours. When I came round I was cold and cranky. The video recording shows me wrapped in a blanket with both hands shaking, spilling the coffee from the hot plastic cup.

'When was the last time you saw Ms Henderson? What time did you leave her? How did you leave her? What state was she in, Jed?'

What the fuck were they going on about?

'Her father's not going to let go of this one, Jed. It ain't going away. Tania was from a good family, not like the usual low-life you hang around with. She overdosed on smack and was left for dead, she didn't stand a chance.'

They shoved some close-up pictures of the hollow-eyed face of a young girl with dried blood smeared around her dark, discoloured lips. Then a shot of her half-naked body lying slumped on a filthy bean-bag. Her ribs were protruding from beneath two tiny tits and her hip bones were both visible as her stringed panties were halfway down her thighs. A final photo told the tale – a sharp still stuck in her left arm as it lay, hanging off the bean bag, her knuckles resting on the cold and dusty concrete floor.

Then it hit me.

This was one of the girls I had been using to sell stuff for me in return for a personal supply of heroin. I didn't know her as Tania, and

*I certainly wasn't responsible for leaving her to die in that state. However, my name was in the frame, even though there was no way they could have any forensic evidence on me. Either they were just trying their luck or someone had deliberately fed them my name.*

*I coughed my way through three cigarettes, trying desperately to avoid these photos of her dead body they kept shoving in front of my face. I told the police I hadn't seen her for ages – not since I'd been out of jail. Said the last time I'd seen her was when she visited me inside and that they could see her on the CCTV footage of the prison visitors' room. I also told them that I wasn't her pimp. They asked me where I had been on the night Tania died. I wasn't sure, but I gave them Alisha's number and said I was with her. As one of the cops left to make the call, panic spread through my body like a red-hot rash and my pulsating head felt ready to explode. I was sweating and shivering at the same time, and could only mutter the words 'I want my brief'.*

*As I waited, I drank coffee and smoked endless roll-ups to help me get myself straight.*

*When he eventually arrived, the harassed-looking lawyer handed me yet another smoke and tiredly asked if I intended to confess. There was no other evidence against me, except the words of the bastard who had informed on me, and it looked as if he wasn't a reliable witness himself. They were waiting on results of tests from the scene – fingerprints on the syringe and sperm samples taken from her body for DNA testing.*

*My brief requested police bail for me, and as they had others to question and were short of interview space I was let loose. Alisha had given me an alibi, said I was with her on that night. It wasn't rock solid and the police said that if forensic turned anything up they would have my arse.*

*As I left the station I knew that this might be my one and only chance to sort this whole business out – my way. I knew where I could find the grass and there was only one thing on my mind …*

## Revenge

*I went straight round to a mate's house, one who owed me, and* demanded a piece. I was going to pay my prime suspect a visit. Tony Delannoy, who came from the same sprawling estate as my brothers and me, had made it good and bought some posh fucking pad out of his fruitful dealings in drugs, girls and debt collection. Although he threw garden parties for the local kids home; and barbecues for his snooty neighbours, anyone who knew him from before could tell you what a nasty, pimping bastard he really was. I guess I had given him a bit of competition lately and his standard of living was suffering because of it. But that was no reason to grass and put me in the frame for Tania's death, especially if it was to cover for his misdeeds. Tony liked to have complete control over his girls, so he liked to know them all intimately. I had reasoned that it was probably him that left her in that state. Pacing down the tree-lined avenue, deserted except for one sad looking kid in a hoodie, holding a skateboard, I could feel the heat rising. Heart pounding and thoughts racing, I strode up the driveway to his house hollering his name. The only response was a furtive shadow movement from behind the curtain. In a rage of frustration I reached for the wheel brace conveniently lying next to the shiny new BMW M3 on the driveway, and added a freestyle stripe along the bonnet. Then, fired up, I kicked down the gate to the rear of the property and marched around to the back door. I caught sight of a wide-eyed glance from behind the glass doors and the next thing I knew there were glass sharps and splinters flying everywhere. Once I started I couldn't stop shooting until I thought my weapon was empty.

This was all in slow motion, like time had stopped and nothing else was happening in the world. Then, there was silence.

Checking the gun, I noticed a single slug left, so walking around to the front of the house I fired a parting shot through the letterbox in the front door, before leaving the scene.

The kid in the street stood holding his skateboard in stunned silence as he watched me walk off up the road. My head was numb. I couldn't think. Adrenalin was ricocheting around my body. I couldn't see much happening around me; it was like I was switched into tunnel mode. The thing is, I just couldn't see the end of the damn tunnel. I just kept *going; dodging in and out of buildings; avoiding any main streets; but going nowhere. I felt lost and confused in a place I thought I knew well. I needed somewhere I could get my head down for a few days, just until I could get myself sorted.*

*In desperation I buzzed Alisha from outside her block. I waited nervously for the door to unlock, glancing to the side as a vehicle pulled around into the bay behind me. It was just some kids with the bass blaring; no threat to me. With relief, I eased myself inside the block and climbed the grimy, piss-stained stairwell to the eighth floor. Alisha looked me up and down as she let me into her flat. There was an air of nervousness about her. I knew I shouldn't be here, that she would be asking me questions about my arrest and having to give me an alibi, but there was nowhere else to go. She showed me into the kitchen and left me searching through the cupboards for something to eat whilst she went to check on JJ in the bedroom. I was waiting for the questions to start and picturing her accusing stare when I told her I had nothing to do with the girl's death. It really wasn't looking good for me, I knew, but I was going to have to pull it back somehow. At least she had given me that alibi and let me in the flat, so there was some hope. And then as I reached into the freezer for the box of chicken burgers, the only item in there, I heard Alisha's voice telling JJ to stay in the bedroom as she brushed past me towards the door.*

*It was on. No early morning swoop; no crashing down the door. Just swift and almost silent – by the time I heard the heavy footsteps in the hallway outside the door there was no time for me to go anywhere, or to hide the piece I had hidden inside my jacket. Fuck! Why didn't I hand it back for cleaning and safe-keeping before I came here? I wasn't thinking straight, had lost my grip and I had been fucked right over.*

*As I found out later, Alisha had been called by the police when the shooting was reported. She wouldn't give me another alibi and was told by them to call if I showed up.*

*She had gone into the bedroom to make that call and the next thing she was letting in three officers through the front door. No sirens, no screaming cars, and to top it all I had left the outside door to the block open, so there had been no need for them to buzz for entry. I might as well have just walked into the fucking station to hand myself in.*

*Apparently the skateboard kid had given them a pretty good description of me, and within minutes of walking into the flat they had the weapon. Alisha demanded to know the grounds for my arrest and the look on her face when one smarmy bastard announced 'attempted murder' was one of utter disgust.*

*She told the officer, 'just get him out of here', before she turned her back on me and went back into the bedroom, slamming the door behind her. At that point I felt I had nothing left to lose and blamed the police for everything.*

*Resisting arrest was subsequently added to my rap sheet. I gave those bastards every excuse they were looking for to throw the book at me. I wasn't a murderer. I was just trying to protect myself. I could think of a thousand and one things to justify everything I had ever done. My mind was racing and my fists and feet were flying everywhere.*

## The School of Hard Knocks

*That's where I learned about life...and death.*

*The skateboard kid from across the road provided a positive identification of me from behind a glass panel, and with the fingerprints from the gun and statements from Tony and his family, the police had enough to charge me with attempted murder.*

*My brief advised me to go guilty, said I would get a better hearing when it came to sentencing. But I wasn't guilty of attempted murder. I was only trying to frighten them.*

*I wasn't going down for life. Life sentences were for murderers and paedophiles. No-one had died and I was no fucking nonce. The thing is no-one had told me about the two strikes rule.*

*So there I was on remand in the familiar territory of the local jail, playing word games with my brief and power struggles (in my head) with the criminal justice system, when out of the blue I got a letter from Jon.*

*He said he wanted to see how I was doing and that he had some news for me that he wanted to tell me face to face. I was nervous about seeing him. I hadn't spoken to anyone in my family, even Ma, since I came in on remand. I just had too much shit on my mind with the trial and stuff, to worry about what was going on with them.*

*I waited anxiously in my high visibility vest, just one among many in the echoing visits room, all fearing the humiliation of the no-show visitor. I was telling myself that Jon had some good news for me although I didn't believe it. I felt relieved but started shaking as I saw him across the room. I was feeling very small and lost in the chaotic hum of the visits room. Jon sat down, looking awkward and distracted by the noise surrounding us.*

*I broke the initial silence with a stiff 'good to see you' and he responded with a tense 'so how are you doing? Are you keeping alright?'*

*Then I started with 'I'm sorry Jon, I meant to get in touch...' when he interrupted saying: 'Ma's ill, Jed, really ill.'*

*'What do you mean?'*

*'They've found more growths.'*

*'What do you mean more growths?'*

*'She's been having radiotherapy for a couple of months now...'*

*'Yeah, I know,' I lied.*

*'These are secondary tumours'*

*'So what does that mean – more treatment, chemo or something? What?'*

*I felt panic rising in my chest.*

*Jon looked at the floor as he quietly told me that the hospital had said there was nothing else they could do for Ma.*

*'What do you mean?' I demanded. 'What about an operation...there must be something?'*

*'There are secondary tumours on her liver, Jed, there's nothing anyone can do'.*

*Jon raised his sleeve to wipe his eyes, his head still bowed. I felt like I was being choked, as if something was trying to burst up out through my throat, but was being held back by some invisible force. There was a battle going on in my chest, and all I could do was cough and splutter uncontrollably. Jon looked at me in wet-eyed alarm. He'd witnessed my asthma attacks as a kid but nothing like this for years. As I bent over, desperate to gain control of my airways, Jon called for assistance from the screws. Two of the four officers standing at the lookout post approached us suspiciously, no doubt wondering whether this was just some stunt to distract them from their security surveillance.*

*Luckily there was a prison doctor on shift that Saturday morning, and as the prison had no hospital wing, I got shipped out to the local A&E. It proved to be just an overnight stay as I was a high-risk remand prisoner and a bed- watch shift was an expense the prison service couldn't really stomach.*

## The Trial

*Then the trial became central to my existence. I was living it, breathing it. I was filling my skull with torturous thoughts and tensing my chest against the fear and hurt I could see so clearly coming my way. Some days dragged painfully, like a rotting limb, whereas others raced roughshod over me, leaving me reeling in the wake of the unknown. There was no beginning or ending there was just this never-ending trail of dread and despair.*

*It was one week out of my life – seven days of sheer face clinging, or so it seemed at the time. Now it's something of a blur, like a bad trip. Some days it seemed like I was caught up in some strange stage play where all the other characters were reading from a different script than the one that had been given to me. On occasions the performance in courtroom no. 4 of the Old Bailey suggested that we were all players in a right fucking farce.*

*My memories are the words that people spoke and the expressions on their faces, like the look of despair on Alisha's face as the prosecutors depicted me as a mindless thug, with no concern for the lives of others, even kids. What could I say? I couldn't deny what I had done. As his damning commentary faded all I could hear was my own voice condemning me for letting her down. Tony's family and cronies were filling the public gallery behind me, trying to look like "normal" people in their knock-off designer clothes; Tony's missus with her fake, tanned tits out on show at every opportunity. I could feel the contempt creeping silently round the courtroom and I'm sure everyone else could feel it too.*

*The prosecutor also made a meal of that, telling the jury I could have made things easier for everyone by pleading guilty. Whereas I had chosen to make the victims suffer more by having to come to court to give evidence against me. Tony's missus was claiming they had done nothing to deserve the attack and saying how scared she felt that her and her eldest son, Jake, were going to die in their own house, besieged by a mad gunman.*

*Although Jake was in court a few times he was not called to the stand to give evidence. He didn't have to. He managed to portray himself as a pathetic victim just sitting there all nervous and pale. There was no talk about permanent damage to his leg due to the gunshot wound, but the brief said something about him suffering psychological damage, being afraid to go out of the house and stuff like that. No-one mentioned that Tony himself was up on remand for manslaughter charges over the death of that girl, Tania. Nothing was said about him supplying class As and pimping. But as my brief kept reminding me – he wasn't the one on trial here. The antagonistic prosecutor summed up the situation as one where I was terrorizing an innocent family up and said that I had demonstrated a 'scant regard for human life'. Those words are etched in my mind. I see them written in between the lines in books and newspapers; I hear them spoken from the mouths of people around me and shouted out by characters on the TV.*

*I only had Jon to speak up for me. As he stood there the jury must have seen a hard faced, pumped up, aggressive-looking guy, his thinning hair making him seem a good ten years older than his real age. But despite that front, Jon's only words were his thoughts that if I went to jail for life then an innocent woman, our Ma, would die without her children by her side to comfort her. On hearing that, devastation engulfed me. I saw Ma, wasting away in some hospital bed a million miles away from me and it felt as if I had all my guts ripped out and my life force was hanging in shreds alongside them.*

*So when I heard the question 'on the charge of attempted murder how do you find the defendant?' I was in a haze of weak confusion. 'Not guilty' was the reply.*

*'On the charge of grievous bodily harm, with intent, how do you find the defendant?'*

*'Guilty,' came the response from the grim-faced speaker for the Jury. I saw his small, mean mouth move and felt his words ricocheting around inside my head. There was some muttering and shuffling of papers*

*When it came to sentencing, the 'two strikes' rule was applied to me, and I got a discretionary life sentence. I think mine was a case where the authority had decided to "set an example".*

*Whereas a guilty on attempted murder would have got me a mandatory life sentence, due to some political hard line on violent crime, GBH plus two previous convictions for violence, got me a discretionary life sentence. Nowadays I would be looking at an indeterminate sentence, which would be even worse, but I wasn't thinking straight. My head felt like it was going to explode; there was all this pressure building up inside me and there was no-where for it to go.*

*'I'll remember all your fucking faces' I hollered at the jury, as I was up, out of the dock and headed for the doors. I don't know where I thought I was going, I just knew I had to get away.*

*However, my face hit the floor with a thud before I was even halfway across the courtroom. As I lay restrained, face down with some mean bastard crushing my chest into the floor; I could feel the chaos erupting around me; shocked officials barking orders at scared jurors.*

*'I want a fucking appeal,' is what I remember shouting as I was dragged out of the courtroom and banged up in a stark cell in the basement of the building.*

## A Promise to Ma

*I was grounded by the death of my mother. No amount of heroin could kill that pain.*

*I withdrew from everyone and everything. I had thought that things could get no worse for me; that my arse was already scraping the bed of the sewer, when this inconceivable trench engulfed me. Sometimes I wonder what would have happened if I'd stayed there.*

*I think the real pain started when I tried to climb out. Through the blackness I was struggling to secure a foothold, grasping for the imaginary line to haul me out.*

*Ma's funeral happened one week later. Cause of death was undisputed; arrangements were made by the next of kin, Jon and Tommy. I had to first overcome the hurdle of being allowed out to attend the funeral. You'd be right in thinking it was a human right to attend the funeral of your own mother wouldn't you? Wrong! I came up against all sorts of bollocks, like I was a serious flight risk and as a Category "A" prisoner, too big a threat to the public to be released under guard to a church for a couple of hours. Then I was told it was for my own good; that I would be putting my own safety at risk. At risk of what? Tony and his brothers, for fuck's sake, what could they to me now? Kill me? That would probably be a relief.*

*However, I think the Governor had to listen to the recommendations of the prison psychiatrist. No doubt some bullshit about me having to be able to say goodbye and let go, before I could move on, in the spirit of rehabilitation.*

*Standing in the church-like hall, waiting for the coffin to disappear behind the curtain, and oblivious to everything else, I made a promise to Ma. I knew what she would want for me and how she would like me to live my life. I pledged that I would do everything I could to make her feel proud of me. I would never let her down again.*

*The photograph of Tommy, Jon, Jodie and me at Ma's funeral was the only picture I have of us the four together. The only blot was the smirking face of the screw I was cuffed to.*

*I blacked his face out with the ash from a fag in my cell one night.*

*I was angry all of the time. I think it was my anger that got me through. I shifted the guilt I felt for not being there when she died with the anger I felt towards everyone for having Ma cremated when she wanted to be buried.*

*Then I withdrew again, giving away the anti-depressants the prison doctor prescribed to some guy looking for smack, in the early days. He said he owed me one. I told him to forget it. The wing records describe me as acting "out of character" as I kept away from the crowd; avoiding any possible conflict that would inevitably arise in the pressured environment at some point. I was on the "suicide risk" list for months, though I was never transferred to a special observation cell. I suppose they thought I was stable on prescribed drugs. I stopped giving out my supply and just flushed the pills down the toilet after a few months. I stopped running with the crowd. I stopped running, full stop.*

*At the time, I don't think I was aware of what I was doing or where I thought I was going. Looking back, I was just creating a new space for myself, before I could figure out which way to go.*

*Until **she** threw me that lifeline.*

'Where have you been, mate?' Danny asked when I surfaced, a few days later, in the lunchtime queue.

'Just getting some stuff straight in my head,' I said and nodded to the server holding up a ladle full of something – not sure what. He was getting lots of grief from the others for the quality of the offering that day and I couldn't be bothered to join in. It was a shit job, serving the food to your fellow inmates; you got grief from all angles. Every mealtime was a potential flash-point. Most people complained about the food on a daily basis; some made a habit of threatening the server for extra portions, and you could see who was a victim of bullying when they insisted that the server gave their meal to someone else.

Occasionally plates went flying in frustration and sometimes a fight broke out in the queue between people who had a problem waiting. At that point the officers would intervene, remove the inmates concerned and then everyone else was subjected to early lock down. Whenever that happened, you could feel the tension in the queue at the next mealtime and be sure that if someone had earlier gone without food; their hunger now was for revenge on whomever they decided was to blame.

With my slop tray I headed up the stairs with Danny, onto the second landing, as it would be quiet in his cell. We both sat, eating in silence, until Danny put down his plastic fork and asked me, 'So what have you worked out?'

'How I got here,' I answered.

Danny laughed, 'OK, well as long as all that's sorted out now!'

'I mean how all the stuff that was happening in my life sort of led me here and not just the facts presented to the jury in my case,' I explained. I could see that Danny wasn't the slightest bit interested in my past.

'It's just your destiny, man, you can't change it'.

'I know I can't change the past', I said, 'but I can choose the future'.

'You think?' he asked, knowingly. Before I could answer he sighed and said, 'It's all determined for us. The master plan is set. We are just pawns in the universal game.'

'Game of what?' I asked. This wasn't feeling much like my idea of fun anymore. Something had shifted inside of me. I was starting to see my life in a different light, to feel very uncomfortable about some of the things I had done. I had started to care about things, to care about people and what they thought of me.

'You're just a small cog in a large manmade wheel, on a big crazy spinning planet in a universe full of big crazy spinning planets. There's nothing you can do to change the order of things, just kick back and let it happen.'

Sometimes Danny's take on things confused me. I wanted to be in control. I needed to be in control. I'd learned that things always came on top when I wasn't alert and vigilant. I couldn't just loosen the reins; I needed to know I was going somewhere.

I decided to try and straighten things out with Alisha, by

sending her a visiting order. If we could meet face to face, I could explain to her what I had learned about myself and perhaps she would understand and help me make sense of it all. I figured that if she showed, we could go from there, and if she didn't then I knew I had to forget about her and JJ. Two weeks' notice was enough time for her to make arrangements and I was still quite local, so it wasn't far for them to travel.

On the day I awoke with nothing but the thought of the visit on my mind, and felt edgy and excited. As I sat in the waiting room at 2:30 pm regularly checking for sweat in my armpits, I chewed over the possibilities as to what Alisha might say or do. Soon the thoughts were racing around in my head and I fidgeted around on the bench between two other nervous guys, all three of us avoiding eye contact, just facing straight ahead as was the general practice in the jail's showers and urinals.

It seemed that with each uneasy shift of my arse, it became harder to breathe. In vain I tried to resist the tightening sensation creeping steadily around my throat.

Conditioned to the familiar clank of keys, we all turned to face the officer coming through the door. 'James, 406' he barked and the guy on my right rose awkwardly to his feet.

As the door was locked behind them, the flutter of panic spread across my chest, as it registered that there was no way to back out of this.

'Johnson, 063'

I was up on my feet before the words were out of his mouth, my head buzzing.

'Seat number 44' he instructed as I walked past him into the visits room.

Manically, I scanned the room, catching unknown faces, until my eyes rested in the kiddies' corner. One tiny blonde girl was sitting alone, clutching a doll. For a moment I thought of my kid Shauna, then I saw her. A small, brown, strained face staring up at me, it was her, Alisha, and she was alone. I jacked myself into a red plastic bucket-shaped chair, with "44" written in bold on the back and placed my clasped hands on the empty grey table top between us. 'Where's JJ?' I asked quietly.

Alisha looked at the table top, 'Look Jed, I...'

'Where is he?' I demanded, trying to keep a grip on it.

'I didn't think it would be good for...'

'For you, you selfish bitch'.

Too late, I'd lost it. I smouldered as I desperately tried to stop the insulting accusations from flying out of my mouth at her.

Alisha stood up, with her head still bowed, 'I'm not here to take any shit from you, I didn't have to come, Jed...looks like it was a big mistake.'

Panic set in. 'No, no...I'm sorry, I didn't mean...I was just disappointed that's all...please don't...go.' She was looking me straight in the eye now and I could feel the sweat dripping down the back of my neck.

'Look Jed, you're not the only one having a hard time, ok?' Then I noticed the dark circles under her defeated eyes.

I asked her to sit down, and wearily she slumped back into the seat. She must have sensed my desperation, perhaps it seemed greater than hers, or maybe she just had no fight left in her. 'What do you want from me Jed, I'm not sure there's anything I can do now...'

I didn't know what to say, I didn't know why I'd sent her a VO, seemed like the right thing to do at the time. For a second I thought about the image of her in the water, but I didn't know what to tell her. 'How's JJ? Is he ok?' was all I could manage to say.

'He's a bit confused, he's had some of the neighbours say some nasty things to him and he just doesn't understand, Jed.' I thought she was trying to make me feel guilty, so on the defensive I took in a deep breath in readiness to retaliate. But before I could say anything she told me something that sank like a stone in my stomach.

'So we're moving away, Jed. Me and JJ, out of the area, somewhere for a new start.'

It was like the last good thing in my life had just been washed away. The heaviness was rising into my chest and my breathing was becoming laboured. I tried desperately to tell her how I felt. Feebly, I managed to ask, 'Where will you go?' Meanwhile I was thinking a million thoughts.

*Will I ever see you again? What will happen to you? What will happen to us? Will you forget me? Will JJ forget me? Where will you be? Will I ever be able to find you again? Why? Why are you doing this? I need you. I need to know where you are....*

Panic set in, as I thought of all the places in the world that she could go. Alisha, who had never been off the estate, as far as I knew, was going away, out of my world. I felt totally powerless. There was nothing I could do to stop it.

'I'll write to you, when we've settled in,' is all she would say and then she left.

I started to cough and so reached in my pocket for my inhaler. The screws seemed to know that something had gone down, and just watched me uneasily for a few minutes. As I breathed in the steroids, something weird happened, it was like I was sucking my whole body into some great cloudy expanse and I was unaware of what was happening around me. One of the screws came over and asked me if I was alright to return to the wing. Apparently I just looked straight past him and continued to stare at something that wasn't there. That's the comment he wrote on the wing file that led me to an MDT the following morning. The only thing I remember was a feeling of being glued to the ground by my feet, as something rushed up through my body and into my head. I felt an overpowering urge to jump up to follow the feeling. Then a feeling of weightlessness took over my body and I sat within a cloak of calm. What felt like ages later, I struggled to stand on shaky legs, the screw called for some assistance to get me back to the wing. I limped back across the concrete compound like a frail old man, supported by two rather awkward looking uniforms.

I remember hearing but not responding to the screws as they led me back to my cell, just feeling peaceful and quiet. I remained awake for most of the night and the wing SO insisted that I saw the doctor the next morning, refusing to unlock me for work. I didn't know what to say to the doc's questions, I couldn't explain what had happened. He could only conclude that I'd had a bit of a shock reaction to my inhaler and changed the prescription. I was told only to use my old one in a real emergency, until the new one came through.

When I think back to that episode now, it was like a great change washed over me. I had no control over it, I just felt that I was at the mercy of something greater than me. I had no idea what happened to me, whether it was a reaction to the drugs or not, but I felt a sense of calm that I had never experienced before. Everyone around me took it that I'd overdosed on some wicked pills, smuggled in by my visitor that afternoon. I caught a few sly glances when the drug test results came back in the negative. But what did I care?

There were a more changes happening to me around this time. I was becoming less preoccupied with the details of what was happening around me and more content to be, wherever I was. I wasn't rising to the bait or watching for the players to make their moves. I could see everything going on but nothing was riling me, and it seemed that in return I was getting less crap from the screws and the other cons. I was no longer trying to avoid the tide of shit that inevitably flows your way at some point when you share a wing with some two hundred other guys, it just seemed like it was not coming my way.

Something had changed and I needed to speak to someone about it. I decided to put in a request, through the wing office, to see someone, anyone from psychology, and continue with the work I had started.

It was a week or so later when Fat Bastard called out to me from the office as I walked past on my way to the lunchtime slop queue.

'Oi, Johnson, got a note here from your lady friend. It says she wants to book an appointment with you, for later on in the week. Are you free?' His tone was mocking and sarcastic and I could feel the hairs on the back of my neck standing up. I stopped just outside the doorway to the office but kept looking straight ahead.

'She's back?' I could never be sure he was telling me truth, and no-one else had said anything to me.

'Yep, she's back. God knows why. Some people just never learn.'

'What day?" I asked through gritted teeth, trying to clamp my mind shut to stop the violent images that were creeping in.

Taking what seemed like far too long just to look at the interview-room diary, he finally looked up at me and spoke to the side of my face. 'Thursday, 10 o'clock suit you?' He knew that was the lifer wing's scheduled session in the gym. That's why there was always interview space. The bastard was just trying to make things awkward for me, knowing that I always went to the gym on a Thursday morning. But I would get to see *her* again. I was careful not to show him my frustration at missing out on a session of circuits; or any excitement at the prospect of seeing the psychologist in who I had already entrusted the details my past. There were only three days to wait, to get everything straight in my head. 'Yeah, Thursday's cool' I said, still staring straight ahead and started to walk off.

'Oi! Insolent bastard!' He shouted, agitated at my refusal to look him in the face, 'I didn't hear a "thank you", you ungrateful...' I just kept on walking.

Chapter 7

# SESA WO SUBAN: Change or transform your character

After broken sleep, I woke that Thursday morning feeling spaced. It was like there were gaps in my head and I couldn't hold any thoughts together for long and that was making me feel even more anxious. Pacing up and down in my cell before unlock, I tried to plan what I was going to say to her. Thinking back the last time we had met, I had been furious and couldn't calm myself enough to be able to speak to her. That had been about three months ago and lots of things had happened since then.

When I heard the familiar sound of officers' footsteps on the metal stairs and then on the landing, I listened for the clanking keys and started to count the number of doors being opened. There were nearly always two of them on unlock and they always started from the same point on each side of the landing. It was possible to work out how long it would take them to reach my cell – unless they had to deal with something unexpected along the way. It's amazing how acutely your sense of hearing develops when you can't see what's happening around you.

'Breakfast pack,' some faceless officer announced as he

opened my door. I stared aggressively at him, and then checked myself, thinking that I wanted this morning to go well.

'Thanks,' I said, and took it from him without any more attitude. I didn't have any truck with this guy – other than his uniform.

As much as I wanted to eat, I found myself distracted by fearful thoughts, causing momentary panics. What if I went down to the interview room again and she wasn't there?

How would I control my temper if Fat Bastard was too quick to take the piss again? What if this was all just a set up by him? *Don't be so fucking paranoid,* I told myself and started to get my journal entries together. *Don't let that fat bastard, or anyone else in this place, do your head in – take control.* From my cell I listened to the morning hum of the wing as two hundred prisoners and a handful of officers carried out the rigid, daily routine. The noise got louder as the time for morning movement approached; peaking when everyone who was going to work, education or attending rehabilitation programmes stood queuing for security checks at the gate, before they left the wing.

On Thursday mornings the noise in the queue was louder than usual as most of the guys on the wing were hyped-up for their weekly gym session. This was a privilege that you lost if you were on report for anything, or you failed an MDT. Some took the chance to get some real exercise, other than just jogging around the compound and doing sits-ups and press-ups in their cell. Others couldn't resist the temptation to get a bit too physical in the five-a-side games despite risking being banned from the gym for violent behaviour. The gym staff were always alert, especially with large groups as all it took was one man to lose it and smash a dumb-bell into another's face. Although the guys who opted for weights were often doing courses for certificates and knew better than to fuck around. I was thinking of signing up for that BAWLA course, perhaps next week.

For the next hour I rehearsed in my head, over and over, how

I wanted the meeting with her to go. She would be in the room waiting, so I wouldn't have to hang around the wing office and get wound up by the comments of any stupid fuckers. She would look up and smile as I walked into the room and it would be as it had been before her absence. She would know exactly where I was at and where to go from this point onwards. I would watch her concentration-frown deepen as she was listening to me and wait for the point at which she would tilt her head slightly forwards. That usually signalled she was about to interrupt me with a question. I would listen to her take a deep breath as she was about to sum up what I was trying to say; and rattle her pen on her front teeth just before challenging what I was saying, as she always did.

I was deep in thought as to how the conversation would go when Officer King walked by and poked his head in through my open cell-door. From what I'd seen of him so far he seemed ok – on the level, so to speak. He had introduced me to Danny when he thought I needed a listener. However, it was too soon to give him the benefit of the doubt. He seemed like a decent guy, but he was still wearing the uniform.

'No gym, Johnson?' he asked.

'Psychology appointment,' I answered.

'What time?' he asked, with a doubting look on his face.

'10:30,' I answered, my heart rate picking up.

'I didn't see it in the book,' he said. My pulse started to race and it must have shown in my face.

'Let me double check, and if it's not booked in, I'll see about you getting escorted to the gym, OK?' He must have sensed my tension. 'Come with me, we'll sort this.'

I folded my arms and he noted my reluctance.

'Ok, I'll check and get back to you.'

It may not seem like a big deal, whether she was coming or not – but in prison even the smallest of details can take on a greater significance.

I waited and listened for his footsteps on the metal stairs. At the quiet times you could make out which officers, and which inmates were on the landings, by the speed and impact of their footsteps. He had hot-footed it back up the stairs. Not many of the officers could sustain that speed for two landings. Slightly breathless, he said, 'Nothing in the wing diary, but I've spoken to psychology and they said that someone did book in for today at 10:30 and there is still an interview room available.'

'Thanks.' I turned to gather up my journal work, trying to push the thoughts of throttling Fat Bastard out of my mind. This was the last time he had fucked with me. Unable to concentrate, I turned back and was about to launch into some speech about how useless all of the officers were, but checked myself and just said, 'much appreciated' to him instead. The deliberate mix up wasn't his doing – it had Fat Bastard's fingerprints splashed all over it.

He nodded in acknowledgement, but still looking a little surprised he said, 'Make your way down when you're ready, I'll be in the wing office.'

Ten minutes and what seemed like hundreds of deep breaths later I headed down to the interview room. The only other person around was the wing cleaner. He just put his head down and squeezed the mop-head into the bucket as I walked past.

She was there, at the desk, head down, writing something. Looking up from behind her glasses when she heard the knock, she said, 'Come in'. There was no smile.

'Sit down,' she said, closing the file in which she was writing. I recognized her familiar, faint but fresh, fragrance.

'Well, it's been a while, Jed. How are things going?' A thousand racing thoughts were competing for my attention and I just didn't know what to say first.

'Fine,' I coughed.

'So you've had a break from the programme and want to come back?'

'I want to pick up where we...I left off,' I said.

'But it's been over three months, and as you know the programme criteria states that after such a long break we have to reassess.' This was starting to sound much too formal for my liking.

'But I've been right here – nothing's changed – no positive MDT's, no reports, nothing.'

'Yes but you haven't been engaging with the programme, speaking to any other psychologists...in my absence,' she finished her sentence quietly.

'I've been writing journals, waiting for you to come back so I can show you,' I blurted out. 'I've been figuring out a lot of stuff,' I said as I took out all the journal entries I'd written, except for one. I'd left the one about hitting Denise back in my cell. I laid the dossier out in front of her and beckoned her to take a look at it.

'Okay,' she said, slowly flicking through the pages. 'There's a lot of work here – are you happy for me to take it away and read it before we next meet? The programme manager can make a decision on whether or not you can continue on the programme and I can let you know, say this time next week?'

What else could I do? I had no power to demand anything else. And I had nothing to lose. The journals were already written – any insight from her would be useful. I needed to know where to go next with it all. I nodded.

'So,' she started, 'you were motivated to produce this work by yourself, for yourself? Did you have it in mind to show it to anyone else on the programme, or in the department?'

'Yes I wrote it for myself, to help me make sense of...of everything. Once I had started writing about the past I had to finish it, had to come right up to date, up to where I am now. But once I had written it I realized that wasn't enough, I needed some more help with it,' I explained.

'So why didn't you ask?' She seemed so much more serious than before, more formal, more like a member of prison staff.

'I trusted you and you weren't around any longer.' There was an awkward silence.

'Jed you will have to trust other people if you want to make any more progress with this programme'. I couldn't remember her talking so much about "the programme" before her absence. This was about me, not any fucking "programme".

Things had changed, and she had changed, perhaps this wasn't going to work out. Perhaps she had changed towards inmates, after all she had been attacked by one of us. Well, I suppose that would make sense. Why should she trust any prisoner ever again? She sensed my despondency. 'No-one said this was going to be a comfortable process for you, Jed. I explained that change is a constant, a continual process. You will be facing new situations and developing new ways to deal with things.'

I was stuck – I couldn't just ignore everything I had realized and learned about myself and yet I didn't know where to go, how to move forwards with it.

'You still have to address your violent behaviour if you want to progress through the system. You need to stick with this, Jed.'

This had become more than just me working the system. This had become real, about me, about my life. 'I want to do this for me, not just to progress through the system'. I said, frowning in frustration, and she smiled at me, for the first time in months. I felt a familiar stirring, as if life had been injected into me once again, and a satisfied smile spread over my face.

She continued, 'From here on Jed you will still have individual sessions, but it seems as if you are ready to move into the class, to work as part of the group.'

'I'll have to talk about the stuff I've written in journals?'

'Not all of it. Not the private things, but you will have to talk about incidents of violence if you are going to complete your sentence plan.' She could see I was not pleased at the thought. 'It's not about the content Jed, it's about the process, the thinking process. All the participants on the programme have convictions for violence. Some are lifers like you, others are doing lesser sentences, but everyone will be talking about their violent acts. This is where the trust comes to play. The group decides on the rules, and not talking about things that happen or get discussed in the group, outside of the group, is usually the first rule.'

My mind was buzzing with all sorts of images and ideas. This couldn't be real. There couldn't be people like me, talking openly to others the same, about their feelings and about wanting to change their lives.

'Can I come and watch?' I asked, thinking she must be bullshitting me.

'Afraid not, no spectators allowed. Everyone in the group is committed to change and has to participate in full from the outset, that way it's an equal playing field, so to speak. It's all about trust.' She continued, 'It's a long programme, can take anywhere between twelve and eighteen months to complete, so it's a big commitment. People put a lot of effort into this, and some say that they have got a lot out of it. The probation service is piloting a scheme where participants can sign up for sessions when they are released back into the community, to continue the work they have started in prison and to offer them some support when they have been released.' My mind was racing laps, my thoughts spinning around yet repeatedly ending back at the starting point. 'Think about it,' she said gathering up her things.

I wasn't ready for it to end like this. There had been so many things I had wanted to say to her. I wanted to know how she was, to tell her I had been concerned about her getting hurt. That she was on my mind, playing an important part in my life.

'I'm fine' she said in a distracted manner, answering the question I had not yet asked. Then it was real, this unspoken communication between us did really exist. I wasn't going mad, imagining there was more between us that just staff and prisoner, it was just that she didn't seem to be aware of it!

'Thanks for this,' she said, sliding my stack of journal entries in her file. 'See you same time next week? Meantime, if there are any questions you think of, about the programme or the group, ask the wing office to send me a message.' In her mind she had crossed the finish line and the race had ended. She wasn't looking back to see who else was still on the track.

I was miserable. This was not at all the reunion that I had been expecting.

But what else could I do or say? I couldn't bring myself to say anything to her, so in the solace of my cell I wrote:

## Trust

*When you're a kid you have no choice but to trust your parents or whoever brings you up, then your teachers and any other authority figures that play a part in your life, and the rest of your family and friends and people you have relationships with. So in my experience, you spend your life learning you can't trust anyone. But it's really all that you want. To trust is to feel safe and secure. And it's the same for all of us. We want to be able to trust so that we can feel safe. And so we all keep on looking, hoping that other people's trust will be handed to us on a plate, but not willing to give our trust to anyone else. But what is trust? How can you give it? And what do you do with it once you think you've got it? Fuck it up, in my experience. Then you get all paranoid because you think the people you've betrayed will do the dirty on you. It's a never-ending cycle – so the question must be how to end it?*

I re-read it a couple of times and then laughed at myself. I was becoming a right fucking philosopher! Well, I wouldn't have to make a final decision on the group thing for a week or so. The one thing I did have on my side was the time to mull things over.

Later that afternoon, when most people were on education or at work, Principal Officer King poked his head around my door and asked, 'How did it go with psychology?'

A bit taken aback, and only used to ridicule from the officers for taking part in programmes, I could only manage a stiff and suspicious, 'OK.' As he backed off, I added, 'I'm thinking of joining the group, to complete the programme.'

'Ah! Yes I've heard about that programme, some of the officers here have trained as tutors for it.' He was genuinely interested.

'Yeah?'

'I hear it gets good results.'

'Yeah?'

I was starting to sound like a parrot, repeating the same sounds, so I added, 'I have to let them know next Thursday. I'm going to think it over',

'Well I'm off shift now for a few days, back in on Monday, so if you want to talk about it, I'll be around.' No screw had ever spoken to me like that. I probably wouldn't seek him out, but if he was around, then I might find out what's what with him, I thought, knowing that Danny would have an opinion on him.

'That new screw, King, what's he like?' I asked later that evening.

'He's occupying his own space,' was Danny's considered but frustratingly enigmatic response.

# Chapter 8

# BOA ME NA ME MMOA WO:
# Co-operation and interdependence

She smiled as I walked in the room, and placed a folder on the
desk in front of me as I took a seat opposite her. 'I've read your
journal work Jed, and have some feedback for you.' It was
straight down to business. 'Alisha,' she started, 'she's the mother
of your son, JJ?'

'Yeah.'

'And she handed you into the police, which led to your arrest,
conviction and this life sentence?'

'Ye-es," I wasn't sure where she was going with all of this.

'Are you in touch? Do you have any contact with her and your
son now?'

'No, not since she visited a few weeks back.'

'So you have been in touch?'

'Yes, she hung around long enough to tell me that she's
moving away and I probably won't see her or my son again'.

I desperately tried to change the subject, 'I thought we were going to talk about the account of my index-offence arrest and trial?'

'Have you tried making contact, telephoning or writing to anyone else?' she continued.

'No I don't write to anyone, and Jon's the only approved number I can call.'

We had a special pin-number system at the prison, which meant that you could only use the phone if you put in your pin number first and then you could only dial certain numbers on the wing phones. Those numbers had to be approved by the prison authorities, so you couldn't speak to co-defendants or threaten witnesses or victims. Hence the premium value of smuggled-in mobile phones and SIM cards as prison currency. I wasn't expecting this line of enquiry.

'I thought we would be going over my account of how I ended up here,' I protested.

'I don't think I have any more to add to that, Jed. It is a very clear account. Are there any questions you want to ask me about it?' She turned it back round on me, but she was right. It had all been said, after all that had been the reason for writing it. 'You will get to examine the violent episodes in the group, looking for patterns in your thinking which led to your violent behaviour. Anything else, which has a bearing on your life, can be dealt with in individual sessions. What struck me from reading your journals, Jed, is that you've quit blaming others for your predicament, you seem to see things from a different angle now.'

Yes, that was it – exactly, we were on the same page. There was what seemed like a long silence, as we just looked at each other, again neither of us needing to say anything. Eventually she broke the silence asking, 'And on the subject of the group – have you made a decision?' I took a deep breath and said that I was going to sign up. 'Good, I'll make arrangements for you attend an induction in a couple of weeks, early January. Sessions run every week, Monday to Thursday afternoons. Fridays are usually reserved for individual sessions. You'll leave the wing on afternoon main-movement. There are a couple of group members from this wing on the programme, it might be an idea to get to know them.' I wasn't so sure about that, but I'd deal with it when I had to. 'Ok, so let's get on to the main purpose of this session.' She was still being very businesslike but seemed to have relaxed a little.

I pulled out my journal piece on trust and handed it to her, 'It's only short. I thought you might want to read it anyway.'

'Thanks.' She took the piece, filed it away and continued, ' Jed, we recommend that participants on the programme develop good relations with those people closest to them, people who are going to support their change. Is there anyone on the out who would be prepared to support you in this?'

An image of Ma flashed into my head and then quickly faded and my mood took a nosedive into depression. 'No,' I said in the hope of shutting the discussion down.

'How about your brother Jon? He's not in prison?'

'Tommy's inside. I haven't spoken to him for a few years now. Not sure what Jon would think of it. I could phone him and ask.'

'And your sister?'

'Yeah, well, I haven't seen or spoke to her since the trial.'

'Do you have her number?'

'No, but I think I've got her address somewhere'.

'And Alisha?'

'That's definitely a no-go.'

'Is it worth perhaps sending a letter asking after her and your son, and explaining what you are doing now?'

That got me thinking, but it felt like picking at scab that should really be left alone. I just wouldn't know where to start with her. As much as I would like to see my son, I was resigned to the fact that he would now probably grow up knowing someone else as his father. 'I'll make a start with Jon, and see how that goes.'

'It is an important part of the programme, Jed. The research shows that people who are supported in their change, whatever it is, stand a greater chance of succeeding. Without any support it's easier to just slip back into old ways, especially if you are around people who are comfortable with you being that way. Does that make any sense to you?' I suppose it did. 'We also ask that you find someone in here, one of the wing staff maybe, to support you whilst you are on the programme. They are given a list of things to discuss with you and they report to us on your progress as they see it, from time to time.'

'What, a screw?' I asked in obvious disbelief.

'Or maybe someone you work with – a workshop instructor?'

I didn't have a job. I had managed to avoid it so far. 'I can't do the programme and have a job!'

"Yes you can,' she replied. 'In fact it would be better for you if you did, you would still get your full pay, even though you would be spending half your time on the programme.'

'All of ten pounds a week! What a joke!'

'It would be better for you if you were to get a job, or go back into education'.

'But they only offer the basic literacy stuff here.'

'It's your choice, Jed'

This was more than I had been expecting. It seemed like a change was happening – it was like a whole new world was opening up around me and I was shying away from it all. Well, I had been going it alone for most of my life, or so it had seemed. Apprehension was oozing from every pore of my skin and she was fully aware of it.

'There is a lot to think about, many changes for you, perhaps, and all seeming to come at once. What you'll find is that it seems like a cycle of all or nothing. Believe it or not there might be times when you'll feel frustrated that the changes are not happening quickly enough. The key is, perhaps, to know that change is always happening – even when you can't see it and you have absolutely no control over it. When you can grasp the idea that the only thing you can control in this world is yourself...' I'm sure she stopped short of saying something like "miracles can happen". She was one of life's optimists, but real enough to know that my life was never going to be a bed of roses – too much shit had already happened for that.

'Well, wishing you the best of luck with it. You'll have a couple of weeks to get something sorted, and Christmas is traditionally a good time to get in touch with people.' The fact it was nearly Christmas hadn't registered in my mind. 'I'll see you the first Monday afternoon of January, in the group,' she said, gathering her papers and standing up to leave, suddenly looking very pale and tired. I guess she had been badly affected by the attack, although she was looking normal on the outside, but deep down perhaps it had taken its toll. 'I'll just have a word with the wing-office staff to tell them that you are to be included in the escort duty to the course room on afternoon movement from there on in.'

I hung back in the interview room. Sitting with my back to the door I could hear, but not see what was going on. I wanted to hear what was being said, but I didn't want to see the mocking expression on Fat Bastard's face.

When I was certain that his attention was absorbed with her, and the coast was clear for me, I headed up the landing and straight into Danny's cell to tell him about the course I had enrolled on. In his inimitable way, Danny showed absolutely no interest in what I had to say. He offered no opinion, and looked as if his mind was totally absorbed in another reality. Usually, past events appeared to hold no interest for Danny, so I was confused when he started to talk to me again about Ghana. He asked if I had any other artefacts, in addition to the Kente cloth and drum I had inherited from my old man. I thought of the golden stool trinket I had pocketed when my brothers weren't around. No-one had ever shown any interest in it anyway, except for our father, who always kept it by his bed. I described it to Danny and he asked to see it. 'Ah! The golden stool!' he exclaimed when he saw it.

Then he told me the traditional tale of a great priest, Okomfo Anokye, conjuring the famous Golden Stool from the sky and landing it on the lap of Osei Tutu, the first Ashanti King, one famous Friday at a gathering of Ashanti chiefs. The Priest declared that the soul of the new nation resided in the Stool and the people must preserve and respect it. 'The famous Golden Stool is the spiritual symbol of the Ashanti people,' he explained, 'it is never allowed to touch the ground. When a new Ashanti King is inaugurated, he is merely lowered and raised over it three times, without actually touching it. The Ashanti people have never lost the Golden Stool and it serves as a significant symbol of their culture. And it's believed to be where the soul of the Ashanti people lives. Legend has it that the Ashanti people would disappear from history if ever the Stool were taken away from them. It was King Osei Tutu I who established the great annual festival called the Odwera, where all the Ashanti kings assemble at Kumasi and renew their allegiance to the Golden Stool and their loyalty to the Ashanti people. The Odwera was usually held in September and lasted for a week or two. It was regarded as a ritual for the cleansing of society's sin and for the purification of the shrines of the ancestors and the gods. A black hen would be sacrificed and eaten by the dead spirits sitting alongside the living; and then a new year of cleanliness, good health and renewed strength would begin'.

Danny sounded as if he was reading from a guide book. How did he keep all of this stuff in his head? 'Why are you into all this bullshit?' I had to ask. 'It's all history, man, it happened to a bunch of dead people, a long time ago on a different continent!'

'Spirits never die, Jed. From the spirit form we come into the world in human form, and when we die, we re-enter the spirit world. Therefore we are essentially spirits in various states of evolution, and it is possible to pass from our state of human consciousness into spirit states and back again. The Ashanti people believed that the spirit world is as real as the world of the living, where the actions of the living can affect the spirits of the dead ancestors and in return the support of the dead ancestors ensures prosperity for the living family. The ancestors are believed to be always near, observing every action and thought of the living. It is also believed that some of the good and great ancestors, the "nananom nsamampon" might even be reincarnated to restore a family or tribe to greatness.'

'And you think my old man was into all of this?' A clear image of our father sitting in his chair raising glass after glass in toast to the ancestors flashed into my mind, closely followed by the vision of my mother's angry face. 'All of his drunken rambling to the ancestors was to show his respect and ask them for help, as his ancestors had done?'

'Could be.' Danny shrugged his shoulders and flattened his mouth in a non-committal manner. 'The Adae was a more frequent celebration, where the Ashanti summoned the spirits of dead ancestors, offering food and drink and asking for their favours. The day before the Adae, the talking drums were used to announce the impending celebrations, and the keeper of the Stool was responsible for gathering food and drink to offer to the spirits.'

He sounded like a fucking encyclopaedia. 'How do you know all this stuff?' I couldn't help but ask.

In a rare moment Danny actually mentioned his parents and gave me an insight into his secretive past. 'My parents, adoptive ones, were missionaries. That's how I got to spend time in Ghana when I was a kid. They were talking about this shit all the time, saying it was all evil, the work of the devil, and they were trying to "educate" the locals into the Christian way, the wankers, what did they know?'

So the parents he had killed had been religious missionaries. What about his real parents? I wondered. But the moment to ask that question had passed. Danny was onto the next stage of his explanation. 'The Ashanti didn't have all this pomp and ceremonial shit that the Catholic Church has, they believed that if you wanted to speak to the supreme being you should tell it to the wind, as the supreme being, "Nyame", communicates directly to us as individuals. It is Nyame who determines our individual "nkrabea", or destiny. We're all just playing our part in the grand scheme of things.'

'So you're saying that we haven't got any control over our lives, that it's already mapped out for us and we are like puppets just doing a dance? I don't get all this spiritual stuff,' I said.

'Think of it like magic – but not really, yeah? It's the invisible link with the gods and the spirit world. And knowing how to effectively use this link to engage with the Supreme Being, is one of the greatest secrets of all time. It's been kept from most people because if they had the knowhow, they would misuse it, just to have their own way, if you know what I mean.'

I was still confused, so Danny launched into an example to try and get me to understand, 'Think of the internet, yeah? The internet is like modern magic, we can't see it, but we know it works, and what's more there are some people who know exactly how it works. Everything we do or say in spiritual terms is like what we type into search engines like Google and everything we record in websites and blogs has its equivalent in the spiritual world, a massive spiritual databank, if you like, and like the internet, once recorded, it all remains encoded, forever. And the spirit world is enveloped in electromagnetism Jed. Universal laws govern these realities too and so when man has the knowledge of these things he becomes capable of transcending them all. Spiritual evolution is essentially knowledge of the subtle realities and the knowhow of how to harness them. Alchemy is the system by where, in our human form, we can acquire the power of the spirits, have you heard of the Book of Thoth?'

I was way out of my league now, but still, I was intrigued by Danny's knowledge. 'So how would I connect with the spirits of my ancestors?' I asked.

'In Ashanti legend, the Supreme Being that created the earth left his six sons on earth to allow men to communicate with him. These spirits reside in water, in the rivers, lakes and the sea'.

The memory of the shamanic journey I had taken with Danny flashed into my mind. 'Is that why I went into that river in that trance?' I asked him.

'Did you?' He sounded surprised. I thought he knew, but then, how could he? We had never spoken about it.

'Did you have anything to do with that?' I asked.

'No, but perhaps the drum was talking to you,' was his slow and considered response. I was getting used to hearing such whacked-out stuff from Danny now. With a mind full of weird and wonderful ideas I made my way back through the "reality" of the jail and to the quiet of my cell. What if he was right? What if it was all just layers, nothing real, and nothing concrete? After all, life in prison was nothing like life on the out and yet they were both versions of so-called "reality". My thoughts were in a spin. Perhaps my old man had been in touch with the spirits, and not just the sort that he poured from a bottle?

I was pulled over on the stairs by Officer King, who handed me an envelope inscribed with my name and number. 'This just came in the internal mail,' he said handing it to me. 'It's from the psychology department, and I thought it might be something to do with the course you've signed up for.' It had already been opened. 'Sorry about that,' he added as I lifted the ripped flap and looked inside, 'that's how I found it'.

It was my last journal assignment the one titled, "Trust". The irony was not lost on me. I had trusted that this was confidential and now some nosy fucker in the wing office had read it. My money was on Fat Bastard. Well at least it had eventually reached me, and now I could be prepared to respond to any officer's smart-mouthing.

'Thanks,' I said. I turned to continue on the way to my cell, when a thought stopped me in my tracks. Perhaps Officer King could be my wing support. 'You know about the programme, right?' I asked him.'Could you be my support on the wing, the one who reports back to the psychologists?'

'I could give it a go,' was the reply. 'But I haven't been trained in the programme.'

'I don't think you have to be trained,' I explained, 'I think they give you a checklist, and…' I wasn't sure what else to say.

'Ok I'll make some enquiries,' he said. I told him that I would be attending the group sessions early in the New Year. Then, in the quiet of my cell I took out the piece of writing on trust and the accompanying feedback. There was a short, typed, covering letter that read,

*Apologies for not handing this to you personally but I will not have any opportunity to come up to the wing before I go on annual leave. I will be back in the office from the 4th January so please contact me with any questions in relation to the programme after that date. I have enclosed some comments and thoughts on your work, thinking you will have some time over the holiday period to reflect further on things.*

*Will be in touch early in the New Year,*

*Elisabeth*

Elisabeth? That was her name. I'd heard other people calling her, but seeing it written down seemed to have a greater impact on me. It was like a school kid learning their favourite teacher's first name. As I've said, in prison even the smallest things take on a greater degree of significance. I had never had any need to use her name. I just thought of her in terms of her job, rather than as a person, until I heard about the attack on her. That was the first time I thought of her as a person, with feelings and a life outside of these walls. Although I had always seen her as a woman, I can't deny that! I re-read my writing and then moved onto her comments. She noted that I was asking myself many more questions, seeing scenarios as more flexible, whereas I had previously viewed many situations as fixed.

She picked up on my reference to being a kid and just wanting to be able to trust and not to be let down, and she posed a question to me that jumped up off the page and smacked me right between the eyes. *Is this what your children want from you?* I re-read it, and it had the same depth of impact the second time around. *Is this what your children want from you?*

The same gut-churning realization that my past actions would have done nothing to make them feel safe and secure, it would have caused them to worry about their safety and make them fearful of what could happen next. I remembered some feelings of guilt about Shauna peering around the doorway, seeing me with my hands around her mother's throat, but at the time I had justified it by saying that it was Denise's fault for talking to me in that way, telling me that she had moved on to one of my so-called mates. She had made me lose my temper. Suddenly I recalled Shauna's scream as she ran into the room and wrapped herself around Denise's leg. At the time I had been in such a fury that I must have blocked it out. I felt sick with shame. I remembered how it felt to be a kid caught in the crossfire between adults, scared and powerless, and I had caused my own daughter to feel that way. I pushed the paper away, trying to push away the ugly memory as if it might diminish the painful realization.

What could I do about it now? At that point I would have done anything to make it feel better, for her and for me. But this thing had happened years ago and now Shauna had a new dad and younger brothers and sisters. What good could I do now, and from jail?

My mind wandered to my son, JJ. I had never hit his mother,

Alisha. I'd maybe argued with her in front of him, but he hadn't witnessed me using any violence against her. I was relieved. Then I thought about the two occasions I was arrested at Alisha's. Once in a dawn raid by armed police, and then when I was arrested and kicked off in the kitchen. I wondered how much of those incidents he had seen or heard. The feelings of guilt deepened. I could feel them permeating the skin of my soul. How could I have been so blind at the time? So wrapped up in myself that I hadn't given any thought to how he or Alisha might be affected by my actions? My head had just been so full of rights, wrongs and revenge. I could see now, why Alisha wanted to protect JJ from me – even when I had been in his life I had only brought him fear. I was stuck. I so desperately wanted to change things, right now, but I didn't know how.

# Chapter 9

# AYA: Endurance and Resourcefulness

Christmas in jail is grim. Yes, we were served a festive meal of sorts but half the wing seemed to be of a religion that didn't celebrate it; and the ones that did seemed to be feeling even sorrier for themselves than usual. Some of the racists on the wing, unless they felt they were outnumbered by the Muslims, used the other's lack of celebration to assert their own British-bulldog style of bullying. So one way or another, there was much misery being spread around and everyone was more on edge than usual. My way was to act like there was nothing different, and get through it with as little fuss and disruption as possible. That's why the arseholes who insisted on saving up their weekly canteen allowance to buy mince pies and Christmas puddings, really wound me up. For me, Christmas meant being separated from Ma, for the first time when I was locked up in the secure unit, and more recently on her last Christmas, just as I was starting this sentence. I had nothing to celebrate. At least I could count on the company of Danny, who seemed to hate the notion of Christmas as much as I did. If I kept out of the way then I should get through it without too much hassle. The availability of dope and hooch on the wing seemed to magically increase round this time. I'm not sure if it was the bent officers taking pity on inmates or cashing in on their desperation, either way it made for a tricky time. Violence was much more likely to break out amongst men wired on speed or pissed on the seasonal speciality home-brew they made by storing up weekly supplies of sugar, yeast and rotten fruit, and fermenting them in the cisterns of the cell toilets.

And there was more to-ing and fro-ing from the wing office to see if any Christmas cards and letters had made it through security and on to the wing in time for the "big day" – as if it made any difference in here! It did seem ironic that those who were watching and waiting with the most vigilance were, more often than not, the ones that were disappointed. Still, it prompted me to do what I had said I would to Elisabeth, and call my brother Jon. To get access to the wing phone when there was not a queue full of impatient men snorting, swearing and stamping about behind me, I would have to find a reason to hang back when everyone went to the gym. When Officer King unlocked me that morning, I seized the opportunity. 'Are you on the wing all morning? I was wondering if you would have time to talk about my sentence plan and starting the programme, and some other stuff...'

'Yeah, sure, no worries, I have a meeting now at nine, should last until about until ten. Come and find me, I'll be somewhere around the wing office after ten.'

That was great, it was not worth the effort of making me leave the wing just to bring me back for ten o' clock. I had a couple of hours to chill out on a quiet wing and make that "phone call".

I was grateful that there was hardly anyone around to witness me making the call, as I lifted and replaced the receiver back on the wall mounted phone box some three or four times before drumming up the courage to press the numbers. The last time I had been with Jon had been at Ma's funeral where no-one felt like talking. It was only the sound of other voices around me, and the realization that I might be about to lose my only opportunity to call, which finally forced me to pick up the receiver and dial.

A slightly breathless Jon answered the call, 'Hallo?'

'Jon? It's Jed.'

In response there was only silence, apart from a few deep breaths.

'You ok mate?' I asked.

'Yeah, just got in, I'm working nights'.

'It's just that I've been asked to call, I'm just calling to see how you are,' I corrected myself.

'Yeah, cool, you?'

I wasn't sure how long the credit for the call would last and so I knew I had to get to the point. 'Yeah I'm good, I'm doing a programme, a course, that will help me move on more quickly through the system and look good on my parole application.' Well it was true, and I didn't have time to go into all the other stuff about change. 'They want me to be in touch with someone on the out, and they will want to be in touch with you too, so you can report to them on my progress.'

'Who'll be in touch?' Jon quizzed.

'Psychology mainly, I think'.

'What, the shrinks?'

'Well sort of, but just for the programme, Jon, nothing else'.

'What will I have to do?'

'I think they will contact you from time to time to see what you think about me, if you've noticed a change in me or something like that'.

'Change?'

I knew this would be the stumbling block, now I would have to give him some explanation. 'Listen, Jon, I can't get into this now, walls have ears, you know what I mean?"

'Oh, yeah, yeah', he was getting the message.

'If you say yes, you're up for it, I'll write you a letter explaining everything after Christmas.'

'What about Tommy and Jodie? Are they involved in this?' Jon asked.

'I haven't been in touch,' I replied. 'Are you in touch with them? Is Tommy out of jail?' I didn't think he would be on release for a good while.

'Jodie and I have been keeping in touch since Ma's funeral, but I' haven't heard anything from Tommy,' Jon explained.

'Is Jodie still at the same address? Perhaps I'll write to her .'

'I think she'll be pleased to hear from you. Things are different now, without Ma, if you know what I mean.' Jon's voice trailed off. She had been gone for a year now, the realization rushed through my body and suddenly I felt weak.

'Ok I'll have to go now Jon, I'll write to you'.

'Yeah, take care Jed,' he said.

Shakily, I hung up. I was fearful of losing control in front of the wing staff and the cleaners if I stayed talking to Jon for any longer. 'It's done,' I told myself. The first step had been taken. I was into new territory. Taking a deep breath, I closed my eyes and tried to gather myself together. Then, with renewed momentum I headed for the wing office to meet with Officer King, feeling that not even the smarmy grin on Fat Bastard's face could rattle me, now. I was on to something.

'Let's go into the interview room,' the officer suggested and I was pleased when he shut the door so no-one else could hear our conversation.

'So what's this about, Jed?'

'This programme, the one I'm starting in the New Year, they need someone on the wing to act as an observer, someone to report back to them on my progress, stuff like that. I was wondering if you'd made up your mind about it.'

I also told him that I had been in touch with people on the out, at which point he seemed more interested. 'I'm not trained for that programme Jed, but I've recently returned from training for the Restorative Justice Programme. It's about linking prisoners with their victims and/or their victims' families, opening up lines of communication, if both parties so wish to take part, that is. The idea is that the perpetrator gets a chance to say sorry to the victim, so that amends can be made and wounds healed, so to speak. Some seventy per cent of victims of violent crimes are reported to be in favour of coming face to face with their—the perpetrator, and usually there is just one question on their mind, *why me?'*

Whoa! I wasn't thinking of getting in touch with any "victims" anytime soon. 'No, you got me wrong,' I started to explain. 'I've been in touch with my brother so he can help me on this programme!' I just couldn't imagine any good coming out of me sitting alongside Tony's family, shooting the breeze. I was starting to look at this guy in a different light. Was he some sort of religious nut? I started to wonder about his motivation for doing "the job". He wasn't the usual type of screw, keen to let you know what he really thought of you.

'Yes, contact with your family's a first good step,' he commented, obviously just not getting it.

'This is about them helping me, not me helping them!' I said impatiently.

'If that's the case, what's different, where's the change? Don't get me wrong, asking for help is very important, but it can also be a one-way street.'

'What do you mean?' I frowned at him.

'Restorative Justice is about giving something back. Real change is about being able to give as well as take'.

*Was it?* I hadn't thought of it like that. When you had lived your life feeling that the only way was to take what you wanted, there had been no room for giving back. That would be a huge change, I thought – perhaps he had a point? The silence that followed helped the notion to sink in deeper with me, broken only by Fat Bastard tapping the glass panel in the door, behind me. In obvious irritation, Officer King beckoned to him to enter.

'Mail for Johnson,' was the explanation for his intrusion, as he leaned over me to hand the letter to his colleague.

King frowned and handed the letter straight to me. 'I think we're finished here anyway,' he nodded to his fellow officer and stood to leave.

'Looking at the envelope in my hand,' he commented, 'someone's wishing you a merry Christmas, Jed.' He smiled and left the room.

Glancing at the card in my hand, I didn't recognize the handwriting, and the postmark offered no clue as to the sender. I couldn't think of anyone living in the county of Dorset. However, I had a feeling about this, so I slid it into the pocket of my prison-issue jogging trousers and headed to my cell, before the wing became flooded with prisoners returning from work, hungry for lunch. As I opened the card in my cell, a photograph fell to my feet, and I bent over to pick up the image of my son, beaming a cheeky smile at me. He had the twinkle of Ma's hazel-coloured eyes; and a gap where a couple of his first teeth had fallen out. I heard a great rush, and felt it coming from behind, lifting my feet from the ground beneath me. There he was, JJ, smiling, looking like any normal, happy kid, my kid. My head was full of air and if I'd smiled any harder, I'm sure that my wide grin would have become permanently etched into my face.

As Alisha had explained on her visit to the prison, they had moved on, and the new address was written on the back of the photograph. There was also a telephone number. A nervous excitement engulfed me, perhaps there was hope for us; or at least the hope I could get to see my son and he could get to know me, as his father. My fears of them both disappearing from my life had dissipated on the sight of that innocent, toothless smile. It was a sharp reminder that there was a whole lot of life still going on out there. Sometimes it feels like time stops still when you're in prison, but events and people keep moving on, with or without you. Change was on the agenda for everyone, or so it seemed, and there might still be room for me, somewhere, somehow in the lives of those who were important to me.

That lunchtime I had no appetite for prison food so I stayed in my cell, lying on my bunk, alternately looking at the photo and just smiling. It was as if a whole other world was opening up around me. It's funny how you suddenly want something a whole lot more when it's been taken away from you. At lockup I allowed my mind to wander, trying to imagine all sorts of scenarios with my son, the stuff that normal fathers do with their kids. However, my attention kept straying back to the memories of my childhood, to my relationship with my father. Then to life with my brothers, who I looked to for guidance when our father died. With my eyes closed, my mind filled with images of Jon and Tommy fighting, our father's drunken rages and Ma's anger and tears. Was that all I could offer my son – drink and drugs, dope dealing and violence? Suddenly the picture wasn't looking so appealing. I wanted something else for my son. I didn't want him to go the same way as me...to end up here.

Something Elisabeth had said came to mind – you can't change the past but you can choose your future. Well, I was starting to realize that it's the events of the past that you can't change; what you can change is the way you think and feel about the past and that in turn can influence your future. I knew all about my past, writing about it had helped me see things so clearly. I needed now to be focusing on the future. I knew what I wanted; I just didn't know how to get it.

When I was feeling stuck, Danny was always a good bet to take my mind off things and help me switch perspectives for a while. He was one person who did not seem to be bothered by other people's angst and agitation, despite sometimes seeming to be able to read your mind.

'I got these books for you out of the prison library,' he said as

I walked into his cell that evening, when everyone was unlocked for evening association. 'I thought you might be interested in reading some stuff about Ghana.'

My own life, as I knew it, seemed as far away and unreachable as Ghana, so I figured it might be the distraction I needed.

'Adinkra Symbols of West Africa,' I read out loud, with Danny correcting my pronunciation.

'These make excellent tattoos, mate' he said, 'I'm going to get a needle and do some artwork on myself. I can do some on you too if you're interested?' he offered.

I flicked through the pages at the strong black shapes and remembered my father's tattoo. At first I rejected the idea – it reminded me too much of him.

Danny searched for the image he had in mind. He showed me a symbol, shaped like a hook. 'This is Akoban, the war horn, the symbol of vigilance and wariness. I'm going to ink it, here on my right arm,' he said, flexing his bicep and running the palm of his left hand over his smooth forearm facing the bulging muscle. 'I'm calling in a few favours and should get the gear in time for the Christmas break.'

I flicked through the pages, frowning at a bunch of weird, meaningless, black shapes.

'It's all just symbols, Jed, the language we speak, the way we dress, the jewellery we wear,' Danny explained. 'Symbols show others who we are, where we've been, and what we believe in. Tattoos are just another way of dressing ourselves up, to tell people what we're about.'

I had seen many tattoos of naked girls, names, skulls and fire but nothing like this before. And I guess that if I had seen anything like it, I would have just dismissed it, as I usually did with anything I didn't understand.

'Take the books,' Danny said, 'and take a look through – see if any of the symbols appeal to you. Like I said, I'll have some ink sometime over Christmas, so let me know if you want some artwork.'

Flicking through the pages, my eyes caught an image of some sort of leaf, a fern. "Aya" it was called, the symbol of endurance and resourcefulness. I liked it. I would take a closer look at some of the others. I had never previously considered having a tattoo. Perhaps I had never been able to sit still long enough to contemplate it, let alone sit still long enough for the needle-work. Anyhow, the idea was now much more appealing to me. I picked up and looked at the second book, "Traditional African Folk Tales". It looked like a kid's book – large, typed words and colourful drawings.

'This is the sort of stuff I was talking about – the stories that were told in groups, when I was a kid back in Ghana,' Danny explained. 'They look like stories for kids, but there's a sort of "lesson" in there, bit like Aesop's fables, remember those?'

I had no idea what he was on about, but was thinking I'd take a closer look at it later, when Officer King appeared in the doorway to Danny's cell and said, 'Danny, your temporary job in the staff kitchen is sorted, your first shift starts at ten o'clock, tomorrow morning.'

'Cool' said Danny.

'Are you, working in the kitchen?' I asked in disbelief.

'Just over the Christmas period' he explained. I was about to ask why, when King commented on the books I was holding.

'Traditional African Folk Tales,' he read aloud. 'Christmas present for your kid, Jed?' The truth was I'd never thought of sending either of my kids a Christmas present, and I had no idea when they celebrated their birthdays. I felt OK about not having contact with Shauna, when Denise found her another father, but I had no excuse for not being in touch with JJ.

There was an awkward silence, broken when Officer King asked, 'Have you heard about the programme in education, Jed, the one where prisoners get to record themselves telling a bedtime story to send to their family? If your boy's too young to read the stories himself, perhaps you could read them out for him to listen to, and send them out on a tape or a disc?'

Danny also became quite animated at the idea. 'So this could be an Ashanti storytelling experience for you Jed! Time to make your debut,' he laughed.

I felt my hackles rising; feeling challenged, and sneered in response asking if he, Danny, knew so much about it, why wasn't he doing it himself? Then I quickly checked myself, remembering there probably was no-one on the out for him. 'Perhaps you could play the drum, the talking drum as an introduction to the story?' I don't know where that idea came from, but I suggested it anyway.

Danny seemed to be mulling over the idea. 'How will the recording be made?' he asked the prison officer. 'And where would we have to go to do it?'

'I think you'll have to record in one of the classrooms in the education department, as it's their equipment and they'll have to supervise,' was the reply. 'I don't know if someone from the department will have to sit in to listen to the recording, but it will have to be checked before it leaves the prison, just like ordinary mail, you understand?'

'Can you arrange it?' asked Danny, as if I had already agreed to it.

Looking at me, Officer King explained, 'If you want to get involved with this project, you will have to put in an application to Education. Fill in the form and I'll see that they get it. It is meant to be something special for Christmas, but there might still be time, depends on how many prisoners have taken up the opportunity.'

I said I liked the idea and would collect a form from the wing office. When he left I asked Danny about the kitchen job. 'It will be handy,' is all he would say in response.

The following morning, as my bad luck would have it, my old

friend, Fat Bastard had his arse glued to his favourite chair, behind the office desk. *Did he have a life outside?* It was hard to imagine anyone choosing to share their time with him. He seemed to spend all his waking hours here, watching, listening and waiting. *That was it,* he was a like a predator, like an animal waiting for his moment to make a move; to strike and justify his actions on the basis that all the prisoners here were just scum, less than human, and so deserved whatever treatment he decided to dish out. 'What do you want that for?' he asked when I requested an application form for Education. Although I was thinking *why don't you shut the fuck up and just give me the goddamn paper,* I politely asked again for the form.

'Trying to better yourself, Johnson? Always a good idea,' he said sarcastically. 'Shame that leopards never changed their spots; that people like you can manage to persuade these do-gooders to give you all these chances, just to waste my time and public money.'

I had to fight hard not to react to his provocation, instead channelling my fury into determination to go ahead with the project. I filled in the form and handed it straight back to him. 'Storytelling!' he scoffed, 'I've fucking well heard it all now! What next? A fucking Christmas Pantomime on the wings?' He spat out the words, and I could see myself with my hands around his throat, squeezing all the poisonous contempt out of his repulsive body. I found myself in a red mist with both hands down on the desk, leaning over with my face right up against his.

'I don't care what YOU are thinking; I don't care if you are fucking breathing, or not, but as long as you are still breathing, JUST DO YOUR FUCKING JOB!' I bellowed at him, before removing my shaking arms from the desk and stepping back.

He was cowering in his seat, visibly shaken by my response, that neither of us had seen coming. I had come close to losing it and I knew I had to get out of there before the situation escalated any further. It wouldn't have taken much, perhaps just a word from him, and I could be looking at an adjudication for assault and extra years on my sentence, or even prosecution for murder and another sentence. I left him, hoping there were no witnesses to my outburst, and headed for some solitary time in my cell. If he was going to take any action against me he would have to talk to his superior officer sometime soon. I would know before the day was out if any action was going to be taken against me. I wouldn't have any say, if they decided to bring me to an "adjudication", a prison court. It would simply be his word against mine, and of course as a prison officer, he would naturally be believed by the Prison Governor, who would be presiding over the proceedings. And of course he would lie and makes things sound worse than they were to ensure the worst possible outcome for me.

I was getting good at reading between the lines, prison life does that for you. It teaches you to look beyond what people are saying and doing, to question their true motivations for their actions. I had a choice, I could either just sit there, waiting and winding myself up ready to explode at the unfortunate officer who had the task of opening my door to give me the news; or I could get on with choosing a story to read to my boy.

The prison day passed me by. I refused lunch and smoked my way through the long hours, lying on my bed reading the book of African folktales. Not just flicking through, really thinking about what was being said, about the message that was coming through. What was it that I wanted to get through to my son?

At ten o'clock lock up, Officer King looked in on me, asking if I'd submitted an application to Education. He quite clearly hadn't received any complaint about me from Fat Bastard, and so wasn't now likely to. What was my nemesis up to? I was sure he'd be looking for revenge, somehow. I'd have to be extra vigilant when watching my back.

Meanwhile, behind my door in the dead of night, my mind was filled with the powerful images conjured up by the folk tales. My thoughts were racing, fuelled by the universal truths that had jumped out at me from between the pages in the book; and I was more inspired and determined than ever to make contact with my boy. I was thinking that even if I couldn't record and send the stories out for Christmas, no-one could stop me writing them down and giving them to him in the future.

## Chapter 10

# WAWA ABA: Hardiness, toughness and perseverance

### The Lion's whisker

*This is a story told to children in Africa, where your grandfather lived as a young boy, just like you. He may have told me this tale when I was young. If so, I must have forgotten it, but what is important is that I am telling it to you, now.*

*Once there was a small boy whose mother was very sad. She was so sad that she hardly ever spoke to him, and she never smiled any more. Even when the boy pulled funny faces at her and sang one of his silly songs, her sad face stayed the same.*

*The boy missed his mother's warm, sunny smile and the sound of her long-lost laughter. And these sights and sounds that he loved so much, were also fading fast from his memory. Every time he closed his eyes to concentrate on the image of her face it faded further from his view, and her voice trailed off into the distance. Now this boy was smart, so he looked around the village for someone who could help him in his mission to help his mother find her smile. He went to see the village elder and explained his predicament.*

*'As much as I would like to help you, I'm afraid that I'm not the man for this important job,' said the wise old man. 'However, I suggest*

*you speak to the medicine man; he might be able to help.'*

*So the young boy went searching for the medicine man and asked him if he could make his mother smile and laugh once more. After much frowning, sighing and a final deep and slow breath, the medicine man looked straight into the big brown eyes of the little boy and said that he might be able to help. However, as he was old and couldn't travel far or move very fast, he would need the boy's help.*

*'There is a potion I can make, but I will need you to get the secret ingredient for me,' he told the young boy.*

*'What is the secret ingredient?' asked the boy in wide-eyed innocence. The medicine man knelt down to be at the boy's side, where he could whisper closely in his ear. 'The whisker of a lion!' the boy exclaimed loudly.*

*'Sssh,' cautioned the medicine man. 'Secret! Remember?'*

*So the boy went away to think about the medicine man's request. At his favourite resting place, the riverside, he sat and thought,* How can I, such a small boy, do such a brave thing? *As he sat pondering his problem, he noticed a pride of lions appearing a little way along the riverside. So he continued to sit quietly and watch them from a safe distance.*

*'How can I get close enough to pluck a whisker from a lion and not get hurt?' he asked himself, over and over. He was about to give up when he suddenly recalled his mother's beautiful smile, and how it made him feel all warm inside, and he decided he must try. What he needed was a plan...*

*Early the next morning, just before sunrise, the boy took a piece of meat and walked to the riverbank, where he had seen the lions gathering to drink. Placing the meat on the riverbank, he hid himself safely behind a tree and waited. It wasn't long before the sun would show its face and the lions would arrive. The thirsty lions did not notice the meat. They drank from the river and then lay down to bask themselves in the mid-morning sun. The boy thought they must have eaten their breakfast on the way to the river, and did not need to search at the riverbank for food. He would have to place the meat closer to them. So the next morning he* came back to the riverbank, before the sun was up, and lay the meat at the spot where the lions had come to lie in the sun. Then he returned to his hiding place to watch.

As the lions came to the riverbank to drink, one of them noticed the meat and ate it all up. When the lion had finished he looked up straight at where the little boy was standing, as if to say, 'I know you are there!' The little boy froze. He had never been this close to a lion, but he could not run away. After a while the lion turned his attention away from the boy and went back to the other lions on the riverbank, to lie in the sun.

When the boy was able to move again he ran and ran, as fast as he could, back to the village. When he arrived, panting and out of breath, his mother asked him where he had been and scolded him for not being around to help her with the daily chores. She had not always been so cross with him. The young boy remembered a time when she had laughed and played with him and he was determined that she would laugh and smile again. He felt much braver the next morning when he placed the meat for the lion, and so he hid behind a tree that was closer to where the lions would come to lie in the sun. Sure enough, just after the sun had shown its smiley face the pride of lions arrived and the same lion went straight to the spot where the meat had been placed. This time the boy was much closer to the lion, and he watched as the lion's sharp teeth ripped and tore the meat apart. His heart was beating so fast and so loud that he was afraid the lion would hear it and attack him. However, the lion knew the boy was there. He looked up at him when he finished the meat, and then settled down to sleep in the sun. Feeling much braver, the boy stepped out from behind the tree and looked at the lion basking in the sun. He took one deep breath and one step closer to the powerful beast. The lion, sensing his presence opened one eye and the boy knew not to go any closer. Quietly he backed off until he was behind his tree. Now he knew what to do!

For the next nine days the boy continued to pay a daily visit to the lion, bringing food and inching ever closer. One time the lion opened his eyes and lifted his head as if to he was about to warn the boy to back off. However, the boy noticed a curious look in the lion's eyes and felt *safe to venture closer.*

*Over the days, the lion let the boy get closer and closer. Eventually the boy held the meat out for the lion to take from his small hands. Then he sat quietly by the lion's side as he ate. When the lion appeared to be asleep the boy stretched out his hand to touch the lion's whisker. The feel of the lion's strong body took his breath away. From the rise and the fall of the animal's sleepy breathing he could sense its power and knew that if he was going to do this and get back to the village in one piece, he would have to be quick. Gently he rose to his feet and squatted beside the lion, ready to spring and run if he disturbed the sleeping creature. It took all his courage and strength, and so, as he could clearly see his mother's smile and hear her laugh once more, he reached out and plucked a whisker from the face of the sleeping lion. The next thing he knew he was flying through the trees, his feet barely touching the dry, dusty ground, as he headed for the safety of his village. Arriving at the hut of the medicine man, he had to wait some time before he could get enough breath back to speak. However, he was able to unclench his fist to triumphantly show the lion's whisker to the medicine man. Now it was the turn of the medicine man to become speechless. After the initial shock, he smiled widely at the boy and then chuckled, 'Well now, you are a brave young soul!'*

*But the boy was only interested in the potion. 'Now I have the secret ingredient for you, when can you make the potion for me?' he asked impatiently.*

*The medicine man smiled once more, in a kindly way, and said, 'Young man — for only a man could have achieved this great feat — you have proved that you are so brave you do not need any potion to help you. You have the strength and courage to go out and face anything in this world. You are in charge of your own destiny from this moment on. Keep that whisker always, so you never forget who you are.' And with that, the medicine man returned to his hut and closed the door.*

*The boy was stunned and confused. He looked down at the lion's whisker in his hand, and thought of the strength and courage it had taken to get it. Perhaps the medicine man was right. He certainly felt much more powerful than he had ever felt before. But how was this going to help him to get back his mother's smile? The boy decided that just as he had used a plan to gain the lion's trust, so he could get close enough to pluck a whisker from its face, so he would have to work out a way to get close to his mother, once more.*

*That evening, as he sat with his mother around the fire in silence, eating the rice and beans she had prepared for them, the boy gently approached a most difficult subject.*

*Looking up at her expressionless, downcast face he said very gently, 'Mama, I miss Papa, too.'*

*With great surprise, his mother turned and looked straight into the beseeching eyes of her little boy. Without saying a word, she reached out and took him in her arms, where she held him tight until the fire flickered low and cooled into a pile of ash.*

*When their only light was from the crescent moon, the boy's mother wrapped them both in a blanket and they lay staring at the stars, neither speaking, but both knowing that they were looking for the cosmic sparkle that was the soul of Papa.*

*The next morning the young boy was woken by the sound of his mother humming as she prepared the breakfast. And today she smiled as she handed him the urn for his daily walk to the well to collect the water. The boy headed off with a spring in his step and a lion's whisker placed safely his pocket.*

*I am telling you this story in the hope that its message will inspire you to be strong and to do the right thing, even when times seem really tough for you and for your mother.*

*I sometimes wish that when I was alone with my Ma – your grandmother – who died a little while ago, I had said and done more to help her. I will never have that chance to make it good with her. You have every chance to make it good with your mother. Don't waste it.*

I know that some of the detail in that story was just copied from the traditional version of the tale. I had never been to Africa and wasn't known for my poetry, on the few occasions I was in school. But I could remember how it felt to hear my mother shout when she was angry and see her cry when she was sad. Writing that tale for my son had a strong effect on me. I slept soundly for the remaining hours of the night and when I awoke the next morning it was not with a sense dread dragging me down, but a calm sense of everything will be okay, whatever happens. If there was to be an adjudication and I was back-staged off the wing, so be it. *Fuck the system, no-one could take away from me what I had learned over the past six months. I would work my way through, regardless.*

On morning unlock, it was the increasingly familiar face of Officer King who greeted me; and for the first time I looked straight into his eyes and saw a person, not just a uniform. He had pale skin, deep expression-wrinkles on his forehead and close-cropped hair. He always appeared as if he was fresh out of the shower. I think he must have worked out at the gym before he started his shifts as his face always looked flushed and he was much quicker on his feet around the wing than any of the other screws. He looked straight into my eyes, as he said, 'Morning Jed', and then asked, 'is everything good here?' as he cast his eyes around my cell.

There was no mention of any complaint by Fat Bastard. I was in the clear, for now. You could never rest easy for long in jail.

'Yeah, all cool here,' I answered.

With Danny starting his temporary job in the kitchen, I was thinking about spending the rest of the day alone, with my head in books. What with all the planned changes afoot, me starting the programme in the New Year for one, I wanted to get my head around all of this African stuff. It was starting to get a grip on my mind. When I was thinking about the things Danny had told me and the stories I was reading, the images appeared so clearly and seemed so familiar. It was more like remembering than learning, recalling stuff I already knew, but had somehow forgotten. I was looking forward to delving deeper into these stories with Danny.

After a few hours of browsing through my new books, I folded up the letter I had written to my son, containing the tale of the lion's whisker, and went to the wing office to put it in the out-tray for mail.

Unusually, there was no sign of any officer at the desk. Cool! Perhaps the letter would be picked up without being checked by the wing staff. Although it would be screened at some point before it left the prison, hopefully whoever got to read it would just let it go without any fuss. There was no harm in it. I addressed the envelope to Alisha and hoped it would find its way, for her to read to our son.

A sense of freedom washed over me as I walked slowly back along the prison wing. The wide, windowless corridor that ran through the length of the wing seemed less tunnel-like and, for once, less threatening. I did not feel the need to look over my shoulder when I heard voices behind me. It was just the wing cleaners finishing up their work for the morning. The prison rumour was that you got the job of wing cleaner for one of two reasons. Either you were being bullied by the other cons, and so kept where the wing staff could keep their eye on you, or you were being bullied by the wing staff into informing on the other inmates. Then the wing staff would need you to be around when the others were off the wing. It really was a dead-end job. Once you were seen in that role, you were pegged as either a victim or a grass.

As the Christmas "break" drew nearer, so the atmosphere on the wing became tenser. I don't know why, because nothing really changed, except a reduction in the levels of staffing. The screws that had to work over the holiday were always in foul moods, and there were always a few cons who came close to losing it, either smashing up their cells or their cell mates.

It's funny how the terms we used to respect or insult each other became so familiar that they started to mean nothing at all Someone had scrawled "cons r us" on the wood above the doorway in one of the wing interview rooms. The staff always referred to us as "prisoners" when talking to outsiders visiting the prison; and in meetings with probation officers we called them "officers". However, when the gates were closed, we became collectively referred to as "cons" and they became "screws". It was like an unwritten rule, something that we all just did, as part of some silent agreement.

However, all the old, familiar stuff was starting to feel a bit strange to me. Things that I had previously just accepted as part of "the way", were not now feeling quite so comfortable. Circumstances were changing, at their own pace, and I couldn't stop or control them. I could only face and deal with them. Yet my sense of uncertainty was greater. Life was less black and white, and I was starting to see how everyone around me was telling themselves a story of how it was, or listening to someone else's take on life. In lots of ways it gave me a newfound sense of freedom. I was no longer responsible for controlling anything or anyone else, just myself. I had more choices, more options. I could turn away and look for something in a different place, I could walk away from people and tricky situations instead of hurting them, or getting myself hurt.

At lunchtime, I queued only to confirm that Danny really was working in the kitchen. We said nothing as our eyes met over the serving counter. I held out my plate and Danny raised his eyebrows towards the serving scoop full of chips in his hand. I nodded silently and they were shovelled onto my plastic plate. I would seek him out later.

At evening recreation, all of us enhanced life-sentence prisoners were allowed a couple of hours to mingle on the wing. We had a room with a TV, pool table, and a small kitchen where we could store and cook our own food. I only spent time there if I wanted to see or talk to someone, to find something out. Like me, Danny usually stayed away from the recreation room, but when I saw he wasn't in his cell that evening, there was only one other place he could be. Danny was standing in the prisoner's kitchen, chatting to a guy who was getting something out of the freezer. I recognized him as the other con who usually worked in the wing kitchen. I waited until Danny clocked me and then left. I was sure he would follow.

However, it wasn't him who was behind me as I climbed the two metal staircases to the second landing. Panting heavily as he reached my cell, arriving a few minutes after me, Fat Bastard walked in uninvited to my space, locking the door behind him.

'What are you doing?' I asked through clenched teeth and with rising hackles.

'Need a word, Jed,' he said through a sinister smile, appearing very pleased with himself, 'It could be in your interest.'

*What the fuck could he have to interest me?* I thought to myself.

'As your letter got bounced,' he said, fumbling under the roll of fat overhanging the waistband of his trousers to pull out my letter to JJ from his pocket, 'I thought this might come in handy for you to talk to your boy. It comes at a price, mind you.'

From the other pocket he brought out a mobile phone, held it up to my face between his middle finger and thumb, teasingly tilting it side to side. My initial rage at seeing my letter crumpled up in his grubby hand was extinguished at the thought of hearing my boy's voice. Flooded with excitement, apprehension and then fear, my hand shook as I held it out to take the mobile phone from him and then quickly withdrew again.

'What's your problem?' he asked, looking agitated. 'It hasn't been anywhere nasty. I didn't have to shove it up my arse to get it into the prison, like you idiots have to. The staff have much easier ways to bring stuff in past the cameras and the dogs,' he smirked. 'So are you interested or what? If not stop wasting my time, there are others I can do business with.'

I was so tempted. All I could think of was talking to my boy, and hearing Alisha's voice, knowing they were safe and well. I wanted to hear about their new home, find out what was happening with them. Yet there was a slow scraping sensation, from low in my gut. I was learning not to ignore these feelings, to trust them more and not let my immediate thoughts rule my decisions. *Could it be this easy? Would I use it to make just one call and then pass it on, just one conversation? What if I lost it in the system so it would never be traced back to me?* I knew enough people and could call in a few favours to get it passed far enough away not to be traced back to me. My thoughts were flowing like a swollen river, about to break its banks yet still racing on towards its inevitable outlet. It was feeling as if something was finally going in my favour. Or was it?

I looked at Fat Bastard, unsure of what exactly it was about him that unnerved me. Then it dawned on me. It was his smile. It was always the same, false smile, whether he was sucking up to his superiors or abusing his authority to bully an inmate. For the first time I sensed the dangerous depths of this manipulative man. Although through his exterior he presented himself as a helpful, harmless soul, his dark, interior intentions insidiously leaked out through that smug smirk and his sharp, stabbing comments. I was caught between the dream of contact with Alisha and JJ and the reality of doing business with Fat Bastard. How could that ever be a good thing? Who could say that once he had his cash or his favour, that he wouldn't shop me to cover his own back? What if he got caught? I had no doubt he would rat on me. I had much more to lose, and he knew it. The balance of favour was firmly on his side. No-one would believe my word against his, and once he had me implicated in one thing, who's to say where it would end? I felt a cold wash of realization at just how close I had come to becoming enmeshed in his twisted world.

Looking him in the eye, I shook my head and said, 'I can't afford it.'

'I haven't said my price,' he snapped.

'You've got me wrong, I'm not interested,' I said defiantly.

I knew I was on dangerous ground. There was no telling which way things would go now. I couldn't guarantee what he would do or say, but I could control my own actions and there was no room for any confusion. For a minute or so the tension heightened as he just stared, cold-eyed at me. I only knew he had got the message when he slipped both the letter and phone into his pockets and turned to go, without another word. The temperature dropped in my cell as he locked my cell door, and I stood shivering, as if I had just survived an encounter with a deadly reptile. I had lost my temper with him in the heat of the moment; and he had sought to set me up, in cold-blooded revenge. The stakes had been raised. We had both shown our hands and it was anyone's guess as to what could happen next.

Danny's voice was the next sound I heard, calling from the landing outside my door. 'How are you locked up man? It's not bang-up for another half an hour.'

'A misunderstanding,' is all it felt safe to say. Danny didn't ask any more, he knew the score. It was often better not to know stuff in this place, especially if it didn't concern you.

The following day it was as if nothing had happened. That was how Danny wanted it to be, and I thought that the less people that knew about my encounter with Fat Bastard, the better.

There was more downtime on the wing now that the normal regime was being suspended for the Christmas break. There were no educational, gym or workshop classes running, although those working in the kitchen and laundry and cleaners for the segregation unit were still moving around the prison as usual. This meant that the energy from those who were being locked up for longer than usual backed up and spilled out more into evening wing-association time. People were generally louder and more argumentative and it made finding a quiet space on the wing even more difficult than usual. It made me realize why Danny had opted for the staff-kitchen job: there was extra work to do to prepare the seasonal meals for the staff and so time spent working in the kitchen meant more time away from the wing .

'So where did you learn to bake mince pies and Christmas cake?' I asked Danny.

Always the elusive bastard, he would tell me only that he had, '...done a few catering courses, in a few different places. Comes in handy, at times like these,' he explained, as I remembered that he had been in the system for many years.

As an inmate with the trusted position of listener, he also had the high-level security clearance for the kitchen. This was a place where inmates worked alongside officers, preparing food for the prison staff; and they sometimes waited on outsiders visiting the officers' mess to eat. Danny described to me how all of the kitchen knives were numbered and checked at the start and end of every session and how all deliveries and orders were closely watched and accounted for. There was no smoking allowed anywhere in the building and certain articles, such as tin foil were just not allowed into or out of the mess. At one end of the building was the gate through which prisoners were moved into and out of the kitchen; and in between the kitchen and the mess hall was a short corridor with a gate through which the staff could enter and leave. The building was so dated that there was even a bar in the mess hall, which Danny said was now only licensed for special occasions. Although Danny said he had been in some nicks, in the early years, where some of the officers returned to the wings after lunch with the smell of beer on their breath.

'If I put in a word for you, you might be able to swing a job as a catering assistant for the season.' Danny was thinking out loud. 'There'll be time when we will be left alone to clear up the mess and keep an eye on the ovens when the officers have their break.'

I was beginning to wonder why he would want us to be left alone together, when as if he was reading my thoughts, Danny announced, 'I'll be getting my Christmas present soon so I can do that art work I was telling you about.' Stroking his left bicep as he smiled at me. 'Do you want to get a tattoo, Jed?'

I was going to leave it, not sure I'd get security clearance for the kitchen. The wing staff would have some input and I was sure that some officers did not have enough trust in me. However, once again the magic of Danny prevailed and he got us some time and space in the kitchen of the officers' mess over the Christmas break. I kept my head down when the officer in charge was around – just taking basic orders and watching what was going on around me. I soon got a feel for the place and an idea of what Danny was up to. The officers have a word for it when they believe that a prisoner has hoodwinked you into unwittingly helping him do something. They call it being "conditioned". I watched how Danny gradually gained the trust of the officers and negotiated more space and time in the kitchen for him and me, alone. By doing the same monotonous task over and over without incident, some officers soon got lulled into a false sense of security and turned their attention away at a crucial moment, or allowed themselves to become momentarily distracted, so allowing the inmate the opportunity to do whatever he had been planning. Danny chose his moment carefully, believing we had been safely left alone for an hour to prepare all the extra vegetables for the officers' Christmas Lunch, before unveiling his Jack Hammer tattoo gun.

'It's a beauty,' he remarked, lifting a shiny new red piece of metal from beneath a cloth, lodged behind some industrial-size pots and pans. 'How did you get it there?' I was amazed. I hadn't seen him with it and I had been with him every time we had been moved over to the kitchen from the wing.

'Ways and means!' was all he would say, and I knew that someone must have helped him out. Perhaps one of the cons who had been working in the kitchen for a while had an outside contact, perhaps it physically found its way into the prison through one of the delivery vans that came in from outside? I didn't ask any more questions. It was better not to know.

'I've made this stencil,' he said pulling out a small piece of carbon paper with the symbol of a fern cut out from it. 'It's only going to be a black outline, so it won't take up much time or much ink. There is only one needle and if it snaps we're fucked...so no sudden movements.'

Danny held the stencil up to my left deltoid muscle. 'Sweet,' he said, 'are you ready?'

For the next hour Danny dragged the hot needle through my skin as I clenched my jaw and took deep breaths. After the initial shock of the pain, the adrenaline kicked in and the hypnotic effect of the noise of the hum from the needle helped me focus my energy into dealing with the alternating burn of the needle and sting of the antiseptic spray.

'Are you doing ok, Jed?' Danny asked. 'I'll stop if you need a break, but we haven't got much time left.' I just wanted it over as quickly as possible and so I told Danny to finish it.

When I closed my eyes I imagined it as the feeling of hot water on burning skin, and a picture of my brother Tommy flashed into my mind. This is what it must have felt like to him, when he got burned as a kid. No wonder he was so fucked up. I felt a pang of guilt as I recalled how many times I had taken the piss out of him about his ugly burns.

Eventually, Danny sat back and admired his handiwork. 'Nice one!' he said. 'Keep it moisturized. It's going to scab over but don't let it dry out or you could lose some of the design.'

He removed the needle from the machine and wrapped it in the antiseptic wipe he had been using on my skin. Then he wrapped the machine in the camouflage cloth and replaced it on the same spot on the shelf. I heard the clank of officer's keys in the gate and looked over to see Fat Bastard coming into the kitchen. Danny coolly replaced the last pot back on the shelf and turned around to face him.

'Hope you lot have cleaned up thoroughly after yourselves,' the slimeball smirked. 'We don't want any health and safety breaches in the officer's mess now, do we?'

*Fuck!* I panicked. *He knew.* He finally had something on me. No wonder he was looking so pleased with himself. Confused, I shot a glance at Danny, who showed no reaction to either me or him.

'Ok let's get going,' he said and stood ready for the routine pat down to check for any smuggled kitchen-equipment concealed on our persons. Fat Bastard just turned and walked away from Danny, failing to carry out his duty. He simply unlocked the gate to the kitchen and we all walked over the prison compound to the wing in silence.

What was Danny playing at? I knew there was no use in asking him. He never answered any direct questions. I felt a deep sense of unease. I was trying to get my head out of that twisted way of thinking but it looked as if Danny and Fat Bastard had some arrangement going on here. My head was spinning. I was torn between carrying on with the "new me" and sliding back into the old ways. If Fat Bastard and Danny were in it together then I was also implicated. Every which way I turned I felt trapped. I did want to change, but it felt like the forces were trying to keep me embroiled in the past.

## Chapter 11

# NKYINKYIM: Initiative, dynamism and versatility

I had a choice.

I could crawl back into the shell of my former self and live in constant fear of the consequences, or I could face up to the new challenges and opportunities, and live in constant fear of the consequences.

Fear is a powerful motivator. The fear we feel is real, and I had used other people's fear to get what I wanted out of life.

Fear is also paralyzing, and it was my fear of the unknown, of not being able to see clearly that I would succeed, that was holding me back from even trying to do things differently.

However, the thing we fear rarely hurts us as much as we think it will, if at all, and there is only way to discover this: to take the risk and find out.

I guess death is the ultimate fear. I had lost my mother and my liberty and yet I was still breathing. And there were other people willing to offer me support, to give me a chance. There was no way I could escape the fear, or the events of my past, but I could venture into the unknown territory of the future with the intention to do things differently.

If I got in trouble for the tattoo then I would just have to accept it and move on. I wasn't responsible for bringing it into the prison, but I could get adjudicated for knowing it was contraband and being involved with it. I reasoned that the worst thing that could happen would be that I would lose my enhanced status and get back-staged to the basic regime on another wing. If that happened I would have to bide my time and keep my nose clean until I was judged trustworthy again. My only real fear was that it might affect my entry into the programme. Well, I could only wait to see what would happen. I decided to give both Danny and Fat Bastard a wide berth for a few days, in the hope I could distance myself from any trouble if it did arise.

I spent Christmas day in my cell, mulling things over. No-one bothered me. It was an unwritten rule that lots of inmates just wanted to be alone at this time, so unless you were flagged up as a suicide risk, and subject to hourly checks, the short-staffed officers just left you alone. I was unlocked at meal times but I had no appetite and so I saw and spoke to no-one. My mind was filled with thoughts of Alisha and my boy, and wondering how they were spending Christmas. I couldn't remember any great Christmas celebrations at home. We must have had some; perhaps when I was still too young to remember. My strongest memory of Christmas was the time I had to stay in a secure unit for the holiday. Suddenly, home with Ma felt like the only place I wanted to be.

To escape the painful memories, I buried my head in books of West African tales. My imagination was firing up with the humorous stories of outwit and justice. If this was the education the kids in Ghana were getting, I couldn't help but feel how my brothers and sister had missed out by growing up in this country, where we felt that we weren't wanted and never experienced any sense of belonging.

I was imagining myself telling these tales to my boy; picturing his big hazel eyes widening, and his jaw dropping as he heard about the turtle that cheated death by learning how to swim, and the spider who was sent to earth by God to tell his stories. That's what it should be like when you're a kid, I thought. Life should be full of mystery and excitement. I had just never given it any thought before, or given myself any time to try it out that way, as a father. That's where I wanted to be, with my son, showing him the way. I didn't want him taking the same route as my brothers and me. He needed to feel wanted, to know that he belonged. I wanted him to know and experience the magic.

It was focusing on that goal and gathering cultural tales for the telling, that got me through Christmas and into the New Year, when early on, I got called into a wing adjudication, not, for once, as the accused, but as a witness. These proceedings were a sort of kangaroo court where the inmate often had no rights or legal representation. The word of the officer bringing the complaint was often enough in the way of evidence to support the charge, and it could result in loss of pay, privileges – and in some cases extra days' detention added to your sentence. For a lifer, none of this seemed very important, unless you had made some progress through the system and didn't want to fuck it all up. I would have to be very careful with my words.

The deputy governor had been called in to officiate. He was a cocky young guy, who always seemed look down his nose at prisoners, as if he was expecting a very bad smell. He had been called in at short notice and was obviously feeling very pissed off at having to cut short his holiday. I knew then it must be a serious allegation.

Adjudications were carried out in a damp, stale and smoky room in a corner of the segregation unit. I think it was meant to be a store room, as there was only one very small, barred, frosted-glass window, set high in the painted brick wall. I wasn't surprised to see Danny sitting opposite the governor and noticed that he was side on, facing the wall to his right. It was hard for

Danny to look anyone in the face for any length of time. I was ushered towards a chair at the back of the room, by officer King, but I knew the drill, only to speak when I was addressed; and not to speak to the accused directly. No-one explained to me what was happening and I was expected to sit in silence until I was asked a question. I had obviously missed part of the proceedings, but I quickly gathered that Danny was up on charges of possession of a banned item: the tattoo machine, I guessed. However as I listened in it became apparent that there was much more to this.

'So, Danny you're not denying that you have had possession of a tattoo machine, but you are refusing to tell us how you got hold of it?' Danny's response consisted of a large drag of a roll-up and an even bigger exhalation of the smoke. I had not known Danny to be involved in any trouble before, I had never seen him clash with authority. It struck me how cool and confident he seemed, despite being caught out.

'Danny, we know you have a contact who is helping you traffic contraband through the prison. If you insist on protecting him or her, then you will pay the price for both of you. Is that what you want?'

'I ain't no grass,' is all Danny would say as he still refused to look the deputy governor in the face, and talked to the wall.

'Why now, Danny?' asked Officer King. 'After all this time? Things have been going smoothly for you lately, you have been making good progress. Are you really going to mess it up for some misguided criminal code? We all know that when your back's against the wall there is no honour amongst thieves. Give it up Danny.'

With a smug smile, Danny replied rather enigmatically, 'If honour is the issue then perhaps you should be looking somewhere other than amongst us thieves.'

'What do you mean, Danny?' asked the deputy governor, shifting in his seat. 'It's clear you had help on this one. We want to know who else was involved.'

Danny remained steadfast in his refusal to give away any information and I was beginning to get twitchy. *What were they going to ask me? What did I know?* Nothing really, I couldn't confirm anything although I had suspicions. *Had Danny been caught with the tattoo gun and was simply refusing to say where he got it from?*

'OK, let's see what Johnson has to say.' It sounded like a threat. I wondered why they had called me in. *Did they know about the tattoo on my arm? What were they going to ask me?*

'Johnson, you were also working in the officers' kitchen over the Christmas period?'

'Yes, sir,' *Keep it short,* I was reminding myself. *Say as little as you can.*

'Do you know anything about a needle found in the officer's kitchen?'

'A needle?' an image of the used needle wrapped in the antiseptic wipe rolling off the pots-and-pans shelf shot through my mind. 'What sort of needle?' I asked falteringly.

'A tattoo needle was found on the ground, just outside the kitchen door. Do you know anything about it?'

I had seen Danny put the machine and the needle right at the back of the shelf. Even if it had rolled off the shelf and out of the wrap, how could it have got outside the kitchen door? 'I don't know anything about any needle outside the door,' I replied, it was true. But I was shaking, fearing what might happen next. *Were they going to ask me what I knew about the tattoo gun?* I could hardly deny all knowledge; the evidence was inked on my left arm.

'I told you Jed doesn't know anything about this,' Danny said irritably and with a sigh of impatience. 'And I haven't got any tattoo gun.'

*So they hadn't found the Jack Hammer?* I was confused. Was that going to be the end of this?

'Well we have no choice but to find against you Danny. There have been reports that you had a tattoo machine and were using it over the Christmas break. And a needle was found on the ground outside the kitchen, where you were working. You may well have disposed of the gun, but we know that you have used one recently, you have a new tattoo on your own arm, don't you?' Danny had made no effort to keep his latest piece of art under-cover. 'You know full well that needles and machines using needles are banned on the wings.' I thought I saw a hint of a wry smile on Danny's face, as the deputy governor continued, 'We are very disappointed at your refusal to co-operate.' Then looking to officer King for approval, he stated, 'We have to strip you of your enhanced status and back-stage you to the basic regime. Get your stuff packed up, we'll be moving you out of your cell on the wing today. Of course this means you can't work in the kitchen or as a listener, as you have clearly breached your position of trust in the prison.'

I was shocked at Danny's reaction. He said nothing and showed not the slightest hint of emotion as he stubbed out his roll-up between his finger and thumb, and stood up to place the remainder in his trouser pocket. As he walked past my chair I stared at him in disbelief, but he just looked straight past me, shrugged his shoulders and said, 'Shit happens.'

When I was escorted back to the wing I waited until the officers returned to the office to write up the report from the proceedings and headed for Danny's cell. 'What was that all about?' I asked him.

Danny looked outside the door to see if anyone was listening before he replied, 'It was a set-up. I was told there was only one needle, the one left on the floor was clean; and put there to be found, if you know what I mean.'

'They didn't find the gun, or the used needle?'

'Nope'

'So who…?'

*Double dealing Fat Bastard – that was who.* I thought it and Danny knew it too, but he just looked at me and said, 'What's done is done'.

'So you're not going to do anything about it?'

'Karma, Jed. He'll get his,' Danny said as he placed his Bodhran on top of the laundry bag he had been given to pack up his belongings. 'There ain't no use in making allegations against prison staff. They are always in the right, and we are always in the wrong. Just leave it up to the universe to sort it out.'

Danny confused me when he spoke like this. Sometimes he seemed to have it all under control, and on other occasions he seemed to just relinquish all responsibility for what happened to him. Right now he seemed happy just to sit back and become swallowed up by the system again. I just didn't get it.

As I watched him make his way from his cell along the landing and clank down the metal staircase, I realized that I wouldn't be seeing Danny on a daily basis any longer, unless our paths crossed at exercise in the compound. However I was learning that this was how it was in prison, people came and people went. Sometimes the wing-staff were only given a few hours' notice that someone was to be shipped out, and they did not always seem to know the reasons behind the move. Perhaps this is where Danny was coming from. After all, he had been behind bars for all of his adult life.

Things were moving on fast and I had to concentrate on the changes that I wanted to make. It looked as if there was not going to be any fallout from my part in the Christmas tattoo or my confrontations with Fat Bastard, but I was reminded that constant vigilance against everything going on around me in prison was just how it had to be. These recent incidents could have so easily resulted in me back-pedalling through all of my progress, but it seemed that for once fate was on my side and I had to take this chance to focus on my future. Danny's nonchalant attitude to the whole thing made me think that taking a step back wasn't too big a deal for him. However, I had plans for my future and they didn't include looking back.

It was with this single-mindedness that I decided to immerse "New Me" in the New Year, eager and apprehensive to see what it would bring.

As Elisabeth, the psychologist, had said, the first group session of the programme was to be held on the first Monday in January and I sat alone in my cell all morning waiting for afternoon movement. I had no idea what to expect as I had not mixed with anyone on the wing since Danny had left. I heard that he had not been back-staged to a wing on basic regime, but had actually been relocated to another prison.

However, thoughts of seeing Elisabeth again filled me with a sense of excitement and apprehension. I had no idea of what to expect. After lunch I was unlocked by a new officer who checked my name and number before telling me I was on main movement to the education block for "group therapy". I found his manner very irritating. This was my cell and I'd been there for over six months now. Who the hell did he think I was? And what's more, didn't he realize that this therapy programme was a choice, not an order? I saw no point in arguing the toss with him. He'd learn what it was all about, soon enough. I reasoned with myself that he was just trying to do the job properly.

I didn't know any of the other men moving with me, so I just kept my head down as we were escorted across the compound and towards the education block, which was contained within a large fenced area between the main part of the prison and the perimeter wall.

This was some temporary building, something like a porta-cabin office on a building site, which had been squeezed in between the old stone library and the red-brick workshops, which were a much older feature of the prison. In the mornings the two rooms in the portacabin were used for basic literacy and numeracy classes and in the afternoon for psychology programmes, or 'therapy' sessions as they were sometimes called.

Elisabeth was already in one of the rooms, arranging chairs in a semi-circle and chatting to a uniformed officer. As I walked into the room I clocked the video camera placed at the back and headed for a chair that I thought would be out of its range. As I took my seat, three others came in behind me, but only two of them sat down. The room fell silent and all eyes were on me. I was obviously in someone else's seat.

The atmosphere in the room tightened tangibly, until Elisabeth broke the silence by introducing me to the group. 'This is Jed, the new group member I told you all about before Christmas. He will need to know how things are done around here and so we will be recapping on a few things like the group rules, before we get on with today's session.'

Elisabeth waited until the standing inmate reluctantly sat in the last available seat before continuing, 'Jed has been through the same assessment procedure as all of you, but of course you are all at different stages of the programme and so I would appreciated it if you will all help to answer any questions he may have as we go along.'

I quickly cast a glance at the other men in the room, before concentrating my gaze on the flip-chart Elisabeth was bringing into the centre. I recognized a few faces but couldn't say I knew any of the guys.

'This is Steven Black, my co-tutor for the session,' said Elisabeth turning to the expressionless prison officer sitting next to her. Then she turned over a page on the flip-chart explaining, 'These are the group rules, I'll leave them on display for the duration of today's session for you to familiarize yourself with,' as she nodded at me, 'and as a reminder for everyone, generally' as she cast her gaze around the room.

I quickly read, *Listen actively – at all times. Ask useful questions and offer helpful suggestions. Show respect for each other's efforts. Offer no judgments or justifications. Keep group business within the group only.*

This was something new. I had never before been in a class where the rules were spelled out for you and actually posted on the wall. Looking around, I didn't see any sign of resistance from any of the other group members.

'We will, as always, start with a check-in. Who's got a recent incident to report? Dave? OK, when you're ready!' Elisabeth was sitting upright, looking straight at him, whilst the officer sat next to her started scribbling something down. The rest of the group shuffled around uncomfortably in their seats.

'A check-in is a verbal self-report, a sort of rewind of a recent incident in which we nearly or actually did resort to using hurtful behaviour, to deal with the situation, Jed' explained Elisabeth. 'It might be easier for you to watch at first, as a way of learning how the process works. But you will be expected to contribute check-ins from the next session'.

I nodded and watched.

Dave was a thin, blonde, baby-faced kid who looked as if he was about to shit his pants. I could see him taking deep breaths, but as soon as he started to talk, his voice broke down into a stutter. After what felt like hours of trying to speak, his face reddened all over. He stopped and looked at the floor. It was at this point that Elisabeth stepped in, 'Take your time, Dave,' she said, seeming to have an instantly calming effect on the boy. 'What was the situation? Can you describe it objectively for us?' It felt as if the whole group took a deep breath at that point and Dave started again. This time I could hardly believe my own ears at the shaky words coming out of his mouth.

'Someone disrespected me and I was forced to defend myself, with a scissors.'

I shot a look at Elisabeth to gauge her reaction. No-one seemed in the slightest bit bothered by what this kid had said. Surely he would go on report and get a warning for this?

'Someone disrespected you?' Elisabeth asked in a curious

manner.

'That's not an objective statement of fact,' piped up someone else in the group. 'That's just how you saw it. Stick to the facts.' I shot a look around the room, thinking something was about to kick off. All I saw were five serious faces.

'What did this person do or say to make you feel disrespected?' Asked Elisabeth, whilst the others looked on.

'He called me a fucking faggot,' was Dave's shaky reply.

'And what exactly did you do as a result of being called that?' Elisabeth seemed to be steering the guy, as she had done with me, many times in our sessions together.

'I threatened him with a scissors,' came the reply, with what seemed a sigh of relief.

'Define threatened,' demanded another group member.

'Yes,' added Elisabeth, 'can you please describe to us exactly what you did with the scissors?'

Reddening up again and looking very uncomfortable, Dave began to stutter, 'I...I... st...stuck it...at his th...throat.'

'OK,' I think we have it then, the scenario was *'someone called me a fucking faggot and I stuck a scissors at his throat?'* Elisabeth waited for the general consensus before nodding to the officer sitting beside to make notes.

'What were you thinking Dave?'

Again I was amazed at the words that poured out of his mouth.

*'Cheeky fucker. Who does he think he is? I ain't no faggot. I'm not having that! He's having this...Now who's smiling, arse-hole?'*

No-one challenged him on his thoughts.

'OK, and your feelings?' asked Elisabeth as if he had just described a walk in the park to her.

Dave paused before volunteering that he felt, *'Angry, challenged, disrespected, furious, crazy.'*

I watched in silence as his every word was being noted down and recorded by the video camera. What was this all about? I knew my individual sessions with Elisabeth were taped but I seemed to have gotten used to it. I had a sharp reminder to think before I spoke again and got caught on camera.

'That feeling of "crazy", seems to crop up quite often for you in check-ins Dave,' Elisabeth noted. 'Can you explain to us how the feeling of "crazy" is any different to "angry" or "furious"?'

Dave was silent for a few minutes and then explained, 'Crazy is when my head is gone, when there's no turning back.'

'So, when you get to that point then there is no doubt in your mind that you are going to use violence to sort out the situation?' Elisabeth suggested.

'Yeah,' was Dave's reply, delivered deadpan.

'What about your underlying attitude or belief in this situation, Dave?'

'It's about disrespect?' suggested another group member, rather impatiently.

'Yeah!' said Dave seeming quite pleased that someone else had answered for him.

Not letting him off the hook, Elisabeth asked, 'So what happens when you tell yourself that someone else's behaviour is disrespectful to you? Phrase it like this Dave...' and she wrote on the flip-chart the half-finished sentence, 'When I feel that someone has disrespected me, I...'

'Go crazy?' offered Dave.

'Nah, that's how you feel, man,' explained one of the others, 'This is about what you believe you have to do in such a situation, to stop the disrespect.'

Dave went quiet at this point, putting his head down and Elisabeth stepped in,

'We know getting to the underlying attitudes and belief system is not always easy, but we will keep working on it. The point of check-ins is to keep focused on our thoughts and feelings and to notice how they lead us towards hurtful behaviour in the here and now,' Elisabeth explained for my benefit. 'When we are able to intervene in these types of situations before the incidents get out of hand, then it is useful to work out how we managed to achieve it. It sounds as if Dave let this go too far in this situation and might have to face the consequences of his actions.'

'No-one saw us,' Dave volunteered. 'It was in the workshop, when the instructor was busy with another group.'

'What about the others in the room?' asked Elisabeth, and Dave shrugged his shoulders. 'What might have been the consequences, if someone else reported the incident?' she continued.

Dave shuffled in his seat and mumbled the word 'adjudication'.

'We use this process to monitor our thinking and evaluate our progress in the programme, Jed,' Elisabeth explained. 'And as we use journal assignments to explore past thinking and behaviour in individual sessions, in the group we use a tool called the "self-report" to work out how our past thoughts and feelings have led us to carry out the violent acts for which we have been convicted.'

It wasn't with the theory of this stuff I had issues; it was the public declaration of my inner thoughts and feelings that was unnerving me. Although I found the idea of learning more about myself very appealing, I was just not sure about sharing it with others. I decided that I would just sit quietly for the rest of the session and drop out of the programme before the next.

Elisabeth took a seat and the uniformed officer stood up and started to speak to the group. He was talking the same language as Elisabeth, not the usual stuff I was used to hearing from the screws, but somehow the uniform was blocking the way between us. He took control of the session whilst Elisabeth made notes and I sat back and watched the work of the programme in action.

Offering up a self-report was a prisoner in his late thirties, or early forties, who had shaved his head to disguise his balding hair. I noticed his deep-set frown and picked up on a manner which said he was tired of all the shit that came with the lifestyle of a thug.

I witnessed him exposing his inner world to the group and the tutors. What struck me was the similarity between the thoughts in his head and those in mine. I could sense that he was much closer to me than his age and ethnicity would suggest. We were both here in this time and place, not through where we were born or how we were brought up, but through the choices we had made in our lives.

'Give me a brief, objective, description of this scenario, Patrick,' requested the Officer, Steve. Then he wrote Patrick's reply verbatim on the chart as he repeated it out loud,

*I saw my daughter's boyfriend out with another bird in a pub and I glassed him.'*

'And what were the consequences of that action, Pat?' Steve asked.

'A conviction for GBH and seven years,' was Patrick's reply. Then he added, 'It was the last job I had on the doors, and neither my daughter, nor her mother, has spoken to me since.' This was followed by a respectful silence as everyone sat still in their seats and focused on Patrick's words.

Steve headed up the next section by writing and underlining "THOUGHTS" on the chart. Without any verbal prompting, Patrick started to reveal what he believed were his thoughts at the time of the event, and Steve wrote quickly, trying to make sure every thought went up on the board.

*'Just who the fuck do you think you are?'*
*'Wanker'*
*'Doing that right in front of me'*
*'Cheeky twat'*
*'She's my daughter'*
*'You've got no right'*
*'Don't grin at me like that'*
*'I'll wipe that fucking smile off your face'*

*'You're having it mate'*

I took a deep breath as the memories of the attack on Ma's man came flooding over and sank into the pit of my stomach. This could have been me, I had done something very similar, and I recognized myself in those thoughts.

I must have visibly sunk into my chair, as Elisabeth cast a glance in my direction.

'Any other thoughts, Pat?' asked Steve, before moving on to underline the heading "FEELINGS" on the chart.

*'Furious, protective, insulted, aggravated, vengeful,'* were poured out by Pat and recorded by Steve's marker pen.

'What about underlying attitudes or belief system driving all of these thoughts and feelings?' Steve looked up and placed the pen in the groove at the bottom of the chart, as if he was expecting to be listening and not writing for a while.

'Well it's about respect, I think,' said Patrick. 'Can I get some suggestions from the group before I decide on that?'

'Of course,' said Steve. 'Let's throw it open to the group and see what the others have to say.'

I looked at the remaining three guys in the room. All seemed to be concentrating intently on the chart. After a few minutes, Stan the eldest member of the group, asked in a blunt Northern accent, 'Were there any more thoughts about your daughter?'

*'I'm not having it, you treating my daughter like that.'* 'No-one *treats my daughter like that,'* Patrick suggested, faltering over his second sentence.

The group looked on as Steve wrote up the thoughts. Then Elisabeth spoke, 'Are you sure you were thinking that at the time Pat, or were they afterthoughts to justify what you had done?'

Again there was silence. She was good at this! I remember her having made me think twice about things and come clean about my real thoughts and feelings on more than one occasion.

Patrick stopped biting his bottom lip and took a deep breath. 'I remember saying *"I'm not having it"* but perhaps the bit about my daughter did come after I'd cut his face with the broken glass. She's only a kid, seventeen at the time, I think.'

'No justification, Pat' said Stan. 'What was the last thought you had before you cut him?'

I shot a look at Stan and then back to Pat.

Patrick thought before answering, '"You're having it mate". That was the last thought I remember having.'

'Let's move on to the feelings,' suggested Steve. 'What feeling or feelings go with the thought of "who the fuck do you think you are", Pat?'

He didn't have to think long about this, 'Furious,' he answered confidently, 'and that goes for when I was thinking "Wanker", too. When I approached him with that girl and he just grinned at me I felt insulted and aggravated. I was feeling rage and vengeful when I thought "I'll wipe that fucking smile off your face" and "You're having it mate".'

'Good work, Pat,' said Elisabeth, 'Steve, can we add the feeling of rage onto the chart please? Thanks. Ok has anyone got any questions or suggestions for Pat on his self-report, so far?'

The rest of the group shook their heads and Dave looked at the floor. They were all taking this very seriously. I was trying not to stare, open-mouthed at Pat's honesty about the situation. I had never explained my feelings to anyone, except perhaps in writing in some of the journal assignments for Elisabeth. And I wasn't sure I could do this in this group. I was shocked at how Pat's thoughts and feelings were similar to my own, and I began to wonder about the other men in the group. Would I become aware of more similarities with them, too?

Steve announced that it was time to take a closer look at Pat's underlying attitudes and the belief system that was driving his thoughts, feelings and actions in this situation.

Pat was concentrating, but he appeared to be struggling with this.

'Pat, I noticed the feeling of protectiveness listed under

"feelings", but you didn't link that to any thoughts,' said Steve. 'I'm wondering if this feeling has any place in the report?'

'It's my job to protect my daughter,' stated Patrick, appearing defensive for the first time. 'Was she there at the time and about to get hurt?' asked Elisabeth in a gentle but firm tone, 'There don't seem to be many thoughts about her either.'

'No,' replied Patrick, 'but I was there, working on the door and he knew I could see what he was up to. He wasn't treating her like that right in front of my eyes and getting away with it, I just wasn't having it.'

'I have a suggestion,' said Elisabeth. 'Correct me if I'm wrong, as it's only an idea, but was this particular situation perhaps more about your pride being hurt, or your reputation being challenged, than protecting your daughter?'

The look on Pat's face told me she had managed to see right through him and speak straight to his soul. I knew how that felt, and to be truly honest I felt a pang of jealousy. I had thought that level of connection was exclusive between her and me. Now I could see it being played out with another, right in front of me. I felt another surge of defensiveness rise in my chest.

Elisabeth's suggestion was then picked up by Stan who said, 'Yeah, come to think of it, those feelings of insulted and vengeful have cropped up in other reports where you have said that you have felt disrespected. What's your belief in those situations?'

Both Patrick and Elisabeth started looking through their folders, looking for copies of past self-reports. Patrick flicked through a few pages before volunteering, 'There's this one *"disrespect me and you'll deserve all that you get"*. But this situation is totally different. It's the one and only time I used a glass.'

'Did you feel disrespected in this situation Pat?'

'Yes. He had this great big grin on his face as if to say *"and what are you going to do about it?"'*

'So you felt he was challenging you?'

'Yeah that's it, the cheeky twat was in the wrong and rubbing my nose in it.' Steve added the feeling "challenged" to the report on the chart.

'So what do you do, how do you behave when you are feeling challenged? What's your rule?' asked Elisabeth.

*'Challenge me and I'll have to put you right?'* suggested Pat.

'Put you *"right"* or put you *"out"*?' asked Stan.

The atmosphere became tense and I sensed that Pat was feeling under pressure.

Elisabeth intervened with, 'That's a good suggestion, Stan, but we all own our work and so we have the final say on our own attitudes and beliefs.' I could see that she had validated Stan's comment whilst still leaving the final decision up to Pat.

I shot a look at Stan. He didn't seem at all bothered by Elisabeth's comments.

'Pat, the final word on this is yours. Was this about you feeling challenged? And if so, how do you deal with situations in which you feel challenged? Does it always result in you using violence to solve the problem?' Elisabeth summed it all up firmly.

Pat was clearly in some discomfort over this idea.

'Perhaps it's just a one-off?' suggested Stan.

'Or have you identified another thinking pattern?' suggested Steve. 'How many reports have you completed so far, five or six?'

Pat was deep in thought.

'Yes, it will be interesting to see what comes up next,' added Elisabeth. 'Pat, I think it might be worthwhile looking again at this report and deciding if it might fit another pattern, what do you think?'

'I'll take another look at it,' Pat replied. I could sense his discomfort and shifted uneasily in my own seat. I had a good idea how he was feeling. I had just never imagined that I could have something in common with a middle-aged white guy. The thought that we could actually feel the same way had never crossed my mind. Pat nodded in agreement but looked thoroughly pissed off as he shovelled his papers back into his folder.

'I think this has been a very valuable session. I'm just looking at the time now and thinking we need to wrap it up for today. Good work everybody,' said Elisabeth as she looked around, acknowledging every face in the room.

'Thanks everyone. Good session today,' said Steve, as he reached for his radio and requested collection for us, over the prison network.

'Same time, same place tomorrow,' Elisabeth reminded us, 'and as always, please respect the rule that whatever goes on in this group is not discussed anywhere else in the prison.'

As we left the room with the new officer escorting us back to the wing, I felt a rush of excitement. This was for real. Everything I had learned from my work with Elisabeth in the individual sessions had come to life in the last couple of hours. I heard that there were other people who thought just like me; and those that had clearly made the same choices in life. More importantly there were men there who had reached the stage where they wanted to change, to learn to do things differently. This programme was opening up a whole new world to me and it felt both threatening and empowering. I decided that I would come back for the next session, and see how it went from there.

Over the eighteen months that followed, I developed a greater insight into who I was, why I acted the way I did, and more importantly how to change my thinking or my "internal behaviour", which would in turn affect my external actions. It became easier to divulge my personal thoughts and feelings when I was amongst others who were doing the same. The group was where I learned the meaning of trust. If you are willing to reveal to others your intimate thoughts and feelings, then you are essentially investing in trust. It was an incredible feeling just knowing that others were trusting in me. The group also taught me a sense of acceptance, of who they were and what they had done. In turn their acceptance of me helped me to accept myself.

I learned, with the help of the others, that I had often acted out of fear of losing my reputation, which I had mistaken for the real "me". In my darkest moments, the fear had driven me to thoughts and acts of revenge. This realization had brought back up with it all the old feelings of guilt and shame, which I decided to face for the last time. If I was to ever move on I had to accept all of me and make the conscious choice to change my ways. Then, as I was a life-sentence prisoner, I had to prove to others – the prison authority and the parole-board members – that I would not behave in any of the old ways ever again.

Rumour had it that Fat Bastard had been transferred out of the prison, amidst allegations of misconduct, and I felt that a negative interference had been cleared from my path. I heard nothing from Danny, but as he was always more into pictures and stories than written words, I guess I should not have been surprised. I concentrated on getting to know the men in the group, and had no contact with anyone else on the wing. Instead of trying to avoid the trouble that was always brewing during the recreational hours on the wing, I decided to spend my time alone in my cell with the books I was borrowing from the prison library. Although there was a weekly scheduled library session for each wing, I was allowed to pick up and drop off books more frequently, as I was attending regular group therapy, which was conveniently situated in the building next to the library. It had started one day when Officer King was escorting us back to the wing and now had also become an accepted practice amongst the other regular officers.

In the group I had worked out who were the longest-serving members, and who seemed to have the longest way to go. I couldn't comment on the progress each one had made before I joined the group, but I was able to keep a close eye on where we all went from here. Stan was the oldest and most outspoken of the group. Always in control, he seemed able to present the greatest challenges to others in respect of their work, but always had the last word on his own. A lifer in his forties, it seemed that this was Stan's last chance to progress through the system and get out of jail whilst he still had time for something of a life on the outside. He rarely brought a check-in to the group, seeming to have it all sorted now, but he had presented the most self-reports to the group, which documented a long history of organized violence, using guns and "runners" as he liked to call them. He was a respected member of the group, the type of guy you would much rather have on your side. Everyone acknowledged his point of view but always kept their distance. Whilst I respected him, I was fearful of becoming like him. After all, the reason I was serving this life sentence was because I had been convicted of using a gun. The way forward for me if I continued down that road had become alarmingly clear.

The one who seemed to suffer the most on the group was Dave. He, like me, had been in care and young-offender prisons and had become enmeshed in the drug and knife culture. His paranoia popped out of him in the form of his darting eyes, sudden shifts of attention and visible jolting in his seat when someone talked to him. His mind always seemed to be racing and yet when he opened his mouth, the words just couldn't come out. He seemed to lose control of his actions very quickly, and I was very wary of him. He was jagged, unpredictable and dangerous, in my eyes. After a few sessions I got the feeling that he was trapped in a loop, some crazy fucking loop that was becoming increasingly frustrating for him. I knew I wouldn't want to be anywhere close to him when he hit the final spin.

The more I got to hear from Pat, the closer I felt to him. He too spoke of troubles with the women in his life, and the anger and sadness of not getting to see his kids. I found myself getting heavily involved in his scenarios, wondering what I would be thinking, how I would be feeling if I was in his shoes, and often volunteering assistance when he appeared to be struggling with the unearthing of his underlying attitudes and beliefs. In this way, listening to his experiences gave me some perspective on my own, and I was anticipating him giving me more insights when I presented my work to the group.

Once we had all identified our dangerous thinking, we had to replace it with stuff that we believed would lead us to behave differently. Then came the challenging part of road-testing the new, watching how it performed in comparison with the old, ingrained thought patterns. Life became something of an experiment in a safe setting. We all invested equally in the process and so each of us valued the others' viewpoints. Those members who had not been able to develop the trust had usually left the programme of their own accord. However, there was no chance to become complacent, as each man's progress was closely monitored by the programme leaders and fiercely guarded by the group members.

I soon found that identifying the old me, which wasn't really me at all, was easy in comparison with working out who was the "new me". There were days when I felt there was no "me" at all. When I was brave enough to bring this up with Elisabeth in a private session, she reassured me it was a natural part of the process for many people and that it was a sign that real change was possible. The important bit to focus on was the creation of the "new" me, not as in a completely different person but as in the "me" who no longer needed to resort to violence to get what I wanted out of life or to make myself feel better. A more streamlined version of myself, is how I liked to think of it, removing the parts that I no longer had any use for and would only serve to slow me down. I found that as I discarded the old parts of me, so there seemed more room for other changes to take place. I went further inside, concentrating on the aspects of my life that I wanted to learn about and could change, if I so chose.

## Chapter 12

# HYE WON HYE: Imperishability and endurance

My new outlook was affording me new horizons, albeit small and close to home. Participation of the therapy group required that I have a wing monitor, and Officer King showed willing and started to observe my behaviour outside of the group. Although some of the group members saw this as being "spied" upon, I chose to see him as another mirror reflecting back my progress on the programme. Our previously friendly chats took on a more formal tone, but I still felt that I could trust him – Kieran – as I'd got to know him at this point. So far, he had always played it straight with me and I respected him. In one meeting he informed me that he was recommending me for "Red Band" prisoner status, which meant I could apply for jobs in the prison where a high degree of trust was required.

'There's a job vacancy coming up in the library, Jed,' he told me, 'If you're interested I can put in a word of recommendation for you.'

'What would I have to do?' It did seem appealing, and convenient if I could get morning or evening shifts.

'Probably cataloguing new books, sorting returned books

back to their shelves and helping out when the wings have their scheduled library sessions. I think they're going to be installing a new computerized database, so I guess there might be some inputting to start with. Leave it with me and I'll have a word with the librarian.'

It sounded quite appealing, so I decided to give it a go if I was offered the chance.

Luck was on my side, or at least the librarian liked the look of me, and I was given the job and Red Band status. The shifts were split morning and evening, allowing me to continue with the programme. The evenings were busy, with regular users browsing, requesting and returning books. I was surprised to learn which inmates were quietly studying for academic qualifications, using the library resources. I found myself looking into how to go about studying from prison and found myself drawn to courses covering philosophical and spiritual subjects. I also used my position to request many more books on West African culture and read each from cover to cover, absorbing every image, symbol and word. In a strange sort of way, it was as if I already knew this stuff, and was undertaking a refresher course.

The morning shifts were quieter, as there were less inmates allowed access to the library, most being at work or in education. On these occasions I had to wait for the librarian to check every book before I could replace it on the shelf. As with the prison post, inmates often tried to pass around prohibited items in between the pages of library books. Also we had to report any coded messages found scribbled in books to the security department so they could be checked out before we removed the graffiti.

Additionally there were a few occasions when I accompanied the librarian on to the wings with the book trolley, trying to interest more people in reading, and to recover the late books that prisoners couldn't be bothered to return to the library. The first time I felt apprehensive as to the reactions of some of the other prisoners when they saw me with the librarian. However, no-one at this point had given me any grief.

I also tried to get in touch with Jon around this time. However, he never seemed to be at home when I called, usually about mid-morning, when it was quiet on the wing. I thought perhaps he had changed to day-shifts and thought to call one evening, but the phones were always busy during evening recreation on the wing and there was always some tension in the queues. For a second, the image of that mobile phone offered to me by Fat Bastard flashed into my mind, but I knew that was not the way.

During an individual session, Elisabeth brought up the subject of my contact with Jon. She told me that she had written to him, giving him some information about the programme and enclosing a form for him to fill in and return. She showed me a copy of the form, which asked such questions as whether I had been in touch with him and if he had noticed any changes in my attitude and topics of conversation. Elisabeth told me that Jon had not responded and that perhaps I should think about getting in touch with my sister, Jodie.

'Having support on the outside is crucial to your success, Jed,' she reminded me. 'You need to have someone on the out knowing how you have changed so they can help you.' This rang true with me. It was much easier to maintain changes when the people around you knew what was going on. The group experience had taught me well. I suspected that the formality had scared Jon off. *Was he still shying away from any form of authority?* I wondered.

'How about writing to Jodie and sending her the information and the form?' Elisabeth suggested.

'I'm not sure. I haven't had any contact with her since before the trial. I don't know how she would respond, if she even wants anything to do with me anymore.'

'Well there's only one way to find out, unless you can think of someone else?'

Elisabeth was being awkward with me, not as warm and accommodating as she had seemed when we first started our individual sessions together. I watched how well she worked with the other group members and felt that she must still be wary from the assault to which she had been subjected, a while back. I knew she was just doing her job, but I had realized that deep down, I wanted something more from her. I wanted to see if she was interested in me, in any way, outside of the programme.

'Well I have written to someone else, but not in relation to the programme,' I hinted.

It worked, she lifted her chin, tilted her head slightly to the left and asked, 'Who?'

I felt the warmth spread across my chest, the same comforting feeling I had as a kid, when Ma used to wrap me up in her arms and I could bury my face in her soft, sweet-smelling sweater. 'My son, JJ,' I responded with a smile. 'Just before last Christmas I sent him an African tale, a story written in my own words. I have a copy here. I made a few mistakes and so I wrote another version to send without any alterations.'

Elisabeth started to read the story and I saw a small smile steal across her lips. 'This is lovely,' she said in an absentminded way, before pushing the paper back to me across the desk. Then regaining her composure, she asked if I intended to write any more. Encouraged by her response, I told her that I had not received a reply and was unsure if I should write again. 'I think you should,' she said. 'What gave you the idea for the story?' I told her that I had borrowed books from the prison library to read about my Ghanaian heritage and that I liked what I had read.

'Now I'm working in the library, I have easy access lots of books,' I told her.

'So you've got a job also? That's good news, Jed. It's another sign of progress.' This time I got a wide smile from her, and it was hard not to smile back.

'Are you ready to present your new thinking to the group in Monday's session?' she asked. We were back to business once more, however I didn't mind as I still had that warm feeling in the centre of my chest.

'Yes, I've been working on it,' I answered her.

'How do you feel about the group process, that some members might want to challenge your ideas?'

I thought she was referring to Stan. 'That shouldn't be a problem,' I replied, hoping that Pat might help out with the developing of my new thinking, given that our patterns were so alike in many ways.

'There will be a new addition to the group, a young guy called Chris, and he should be starting on Monday. I just thought I would let you know,' she said.

Just as things started to get cosy in the group, they go and drop in a new face, and on my time, I thought to myself. I was not impressed.

'You know this is a rolling group, with people starting and leaving at different times, Jed,' Elisabeth explained, having noted my reaction. Once again I was being rudely reminded that there was no getting comfortable anywhere, anytime in jail.

'Yeah, I'm cool with it,' I told her, wishing it was the truth. I had been prepared in my mind for this important piece of work, and now I had no idea how the session was going to go. This new person was an unknown quantity. I liked having the time to sit back and work out any new people who came into my life. Instead, I was going to be on show, spilling my guts, on this guy's first day in the group. Well hopefully he would just shut the fuck up and listen on his first day, and if he didn't show respect, then he would learn very quickly if he was going to survive in the group.

I had been working on a couple of self-reports. All followed the same pattern. For me, believing that someone was deliberately disrespecting me was the green light to use whatever means I had at my disposal to get the upper hand. This usually resulted in violence. Now I had come to the end of the road using that method, I had to learn a new way of dealing with these situations. However, just because I had changed, didn't mean the rest of the world had. There would always be people wanting to take advantage, get the upper hand, call it what you want. What had changed for me was the realization that I didn't have to use violence to stop them. In fact, I didn't have to do anything. But, old habits die hard and to avoid reverting to the tried and trusted methods of dealing with situations, I had to be sure my new ways would work for me.

I had now reached the section of the programme that involved developing new thinking, or "interventions" as they were called. Reaching this stage in the programme afforded you more kudos with the group members and the tutors, as it was regarded as something of a milestone that not everyone reached, and even fewer mastered. It was these sorts of thoughts that I played over and over in my head that weekend to ensure I didn't bottle it when Monday's session arrived.

As I was on shift in the library that Monday morning, I was able to finish early and get my work over to the therapy room before the rest of the group arrived. I pinned my chart, which had a circular thought pattern written with linking arrows to show the cyclical nature of my thoughts and behaviour, on to the board. This helped me to relax a little, to make me feel as if I had some control over what was going to happen. I sat back in my seat, closed my eyes and focused my mind on getting to the end of my presentation without getting irritated or distracted by the others. Then, I sat quietly, waiting for the group to arrive.

Roused by the loud clank of keys, and the muffled sound of remote voices on the officer's radio, I realized the rest of the group had arrived. Dave came in first and slunk across the room, trying to make himself invisible in his seat. He had been much more moody and withdrawn lately, but that wasn't my concern today. Pat and Stan followed closely behind. Steve, the officer, had the new guy by his side, 'Take a seat, Chris,' he said, motioning towards a spare stack of plastic seats at the back of the room.

All eyes were on Chris as he picked up a seat and looked around to choose a space. Our eyes met and he rolled over towards me, placing his seat alongside mine. *Fuck!* I thought to myself. I really didn't want to be bothered with him today.

'This is Chris,' Steve announced, and the group all acknowledged the young black guy.

'Also known to my friends as 'Dreads'' he announced confidently, in a heavy West Indies accent, shaking his waist-length, braided hair back over his shoulders.

I picked up on a strong energy coming from him, but I had to somehow shut it out. I needed to concentrate on my own shit. Now was not the time for putting him right; that would come later. He was too cocky and would have to learn his place in this group. We were now waiting on Elisabeth. I was on the verge of a small panic at her absence, when Steve picked up a message from his radio and told us that she was on her way. Any sense of calm I had managed to find was evaporating rapidly and I was becoming more aware of rising frustrations as we all waited in the awkward silence.

I did feel a momentary sense of strength when she finally entered the room, and then we were into the session. 'Would someone please start video recorder?' asked Steve, whilst Elisabeth was sorting out a pen and some paper. 'Okay, for the benefit of our newest member, I will draw your attention to the group rules before we start. Chris is all of this clear to you?' Steve was pointing to the rules which were now in the form of a sign, sellotaped to the wall of the portacabin. Chris didn't seem to give the rules much thought. There were lots of prisoners who suffered from dyslexia, or who had never learned to read properly due to the fact they had no education. However, participants for this programme were screened at the start, so I knew he could read the rules. 'We always start with a "check-in", Chris. You will become familiar with this process, but for today we only expect you to listen,' explained Steve. 'Who's bringing a check-in?'

Stan coughed and sat up in his seat. Then he volunteered a situation, 'Something happened over the weekend that made me grit my teeth and go back into my cell.'

'Can you be a bit more specific, Stan?' asked Steve. 'What was the trigger event?'

'An officer told me I was too late to start cooking my supper in the recreation-room kitchen,' Stan said, very deliberately and with an irritated glare.

'What did you do in response Stan?' asked Steve.

'I gritted my teeth, picked up my stuff, put it back in the fridge and went up the landing to my cell.'

'What were you thinking, Stan?'

In a somewhat robotic style, Stan rattled off the thoughts we had heard him repeat so many times before, 'OK have it your way. It makes no sense. You are wrong but there's no chance of putting you right.'

'Any other thoughts, Stan?' asked Steve in a very tired way. He knew he would get nothing more out of him. Stan shook his head and continued, 'And I was feeling irritated and frustrated *but* calm...'

Part of me so wanted to challenge him on this. How can you feel frustrated and calm at the same time? The two just did not go naturally together. He always made out that he was cool with everything and always in control. I just couldn't see it. As usual, neither me, nor any other members of the group said anything to him. I was beginning to think that perhaps the world was that black and white to Stan. Perhaps he could just switch off his emotions in that way. I could see from Elisabeth's frown and bite of her bottom lip that she was uncomfortable with Stan's answers.

'Finally, what attitude or belief was driving this situation, Stan?' I sensed that Steve was trying to bring the check-in to a close.

Stan replied with the same attitudes he seemed to apply to every situation, *'I'm not doing this for you, I'm doing it for me. Just because you think you are right, that doesn't make me wrong. Maybe this is your time, but I can wait for mine.'*

Steve sighed and Elisabeth shivered. I thought that Stan was sanitizing or censoring his real thoughts to make himself seem in control of the situation. Whenever Stan was questioned about this "time" issue, he always claimed it was about him waiting to be released from prison. The thing is, Stan was serving a mandatory life sentence and had already been inside for over twenty years. With his imminent release not seeming very likely, I too was wondering how long it was before he got sick of waiting; and feeling fearful of what might happen if he was released? The man refused to consider any alternative courses of action other than to bide his time. Until recently, the only other way he had of dealing with conflict was by shooting people. If he wasn't able to do it himself, Stan had talked about a wide network of people he could contact to do the job for him on the outside. None of us really knew how true any of this was, nor were any of us very keen to openly tackle Stan on this issue.

Anyway, now it was my time to present my work. I had completed all the stages which included the identification of my thought patterns in situations where I had used violence, and in particular the most dangerous or "hot" thoughts which were always present just before I committed a violent act. In the group we had devised a cycle of typical escalating thoughts and feelings that had always resulted in me committing acts of violence. I had also given this much thought when alone in my cell, reliving the incidents where I put Ma's boyfriend in intensive care, and took a gun to shoot at Tony's house, amongst others. I was now hoping for some group support to help me finish the task, by helping me to devise alternative thinking to tackle the old and dangerous patterns. Elisabeth was going to facilitate my piece of work, and so she stood up to address the group.

'Here we have Jed's main pattern of violent thinking which he has identified as leading him to commit many of his violent offences, culminating in his index offence, of which most of you will be aware.' Looking at the new group member she added, 'Chris, this might not make much sense to you at this stage, but it also might be useful for you to see where you could be in a year or so, if you stick with the programme. Feel free to ask any questions along the way.' Suddenly the reason for bringing in a new participant for an advanced session became clear to me. Elisabeth seemed to dovetail the programme and the needs of the participants very effectively. I felt a sudden surge of jealousy at the attention she was giving Chris, and I was wondering if she was thinking about my needs when she decided to bring him into the group.

Elisabeth continued, 'So here we can see Jed's most dangerous thoughts,' and she read out, *'That bastard; who the fuck does he think he is? He's a piece of shit. He's not getting one over on me. I'll show him. I'll have him.'* Pausing for everyone to take in the cycle, she continued, 'And as a group, we have identified the types of thinking that have lead Jed to hurtful behaviour in the past.'

'Dehumanizing thoughts,' volunteered Pat, using *'he's a piece of shit'* as an example.

'Thoughts of revenge, *I'll show him, I'll have him,'* suggested Stan, 'and justification: *he's not getting one over on me,'* he added.

It baffled me how he seemed to be able to so accurately pick apart someone else's thinking, whilst not being able to assess the failings of his own.

'Let's focus on how the different thoughts affect Jed's feelings and contribute to the escalation of his violent behaviour.' Elisabeth was in command now and I felt more comfortable. 'At the start Jed reports that he was feeling *"furious"*, and by the time he gets to the last two thoughts of *"I'll show him"* and *"I'll have him"*, his feelings are intensified as *"rage"* and *"vengeful"*, can you all see the correlation?'

The group looked on thoughtfully. Chris's eyes were popping out of his head, which reminded me of my first day in the group.

'The next task is to develop thinking which is not going to escalate or intensify Jed's emotional state, but to help him keep control over his feelings so he doesn't fall into the trap of his old, hurtful behaviour,' explained Elisabeth. Then, methodically, she asked for suggestions of alternative thoughts which would help to calm me down, rather than wind me up, in these sorts of situations, where I felt I that my reputation was at stake and I was seeking revenge. Pat was hot-wired into my feelings, perhaps because his own were so similar; and he came up with some suggestions that really helped this process come alive for me. Elisabeth's words were echoing around my mind, 'The key to this process is meaning, Jed. The new thinking has to have significant meaning for you. It has to come from within you, or it just won't work.'

However the stakes were seriously raised when we came to consider my underlying attitude and beliefs in these situations.

As stated on the chart, my beliefs read, *Make a fool of me and you'll pay. Fuck with me and I'll fuck you up. No-one fucks with me and gets away with it.*

I wasn't proud of these attitudes, but I was being honest and not censoring my thoughts.

As usual, the group struggled with this part of the process. It was no surprise, really, as by nature, our core attitudes and beliefs are deeply entrenched in our minds. For a moment, my mind wandered outside the prison walls and I wondered how many people just lived their lives without ever questioning their basic beliefs about life. I suspected that many, if not most, people just wandered around, oblivious to the reasons for some if not all of their decisions in life. The thing is, once you become aware of how your thinking operates, it becomes impossible to ignore.

'Do you see any reason to change these attitudes, Jed?' asked Elisabeth. It would have been so much easier to say no, but I had to say yes. 'Firstly we need to work out the meaning of these basic beliefs; how and why they came to be part of your thinking. Then we can decide whether or not they serve any practical or helpful purpose in your new thinking, Jed.'

A stony silence fell over the group. This was the tough part, and we all knew it.

Elisabeth was waiting for any contributions from the group before making her own suggestions, when Chris spoke up, 'So this is all about your reputation, yeah?'

I nodded in response, feeling irritated that he had seen fit to invite himself into the conversation. 'How important was your reputation to you?' he continued.

'My reputation was everything to me,' I answered, a bit taken aback with his forthright manner.

'So what's important to you now?' he asked. 'Is it still about what other people think of you?'

'Yes.' I couldn't lie.

'Which people, the same people?'

I saw Elisabeth and Steve exchange expressions of surprise, and I looked straight at Chris. He got me. He had seen quite clearly to the core of me. My irritation with him had vanished. He had thrown me a curveball from the side of the pitch and I had caught it, squarely on.

'No, it's others...different people, I mean,' I faltered. 'I'm more concerned with what my son will think of me, when he's old enough to realize what's going on.'

'Then your attitude has changed?'

'Yeah...yes, it must have'.

'So what do you think your underlying attitude is now?'

Elisabeth and Steve sat back in their seats and let Chris lead the way.

He continued, 'How do you want your kid to see you?'

I felt tears welling up in my eyes and was fearful of losing control of my emotions in front of the group. So far, I had managed to keep control by refusing to mention anything about Ma, or my kids in my reports, although I had written about my feelings for them, in detail, in journal assignments. However, this was it, the point of no return for me. I was starring my inner self right in the face; and I had no choice but to turn around and show my new face to the world. Much to the discomfort of just about everyone else in the room, I cried.

I cried silent tears for the love and loss of Ma, for the father I had only ever feared, for the women I had hurt, and for my children who had no father. The group sat around me in a shocked silence. There was no scripted way of dealing with this situation. No-one had experienced anything like this in the group. There was an overwhelming feeling of confusion, yet no-one wanted to disregard or disrespect my feelings.

It was Steve who finally decided to end the session. 'I think that's it for today. How about you?' he asked Elisabeth. 'Shall we leave Jed to work on his new beliefs as a journal assignment?'

Elisabeth nodded, although looking very unsure about the choice. 'If it's ok with you, Jed?' she checked. It was. I wiped my eyes and gathered up my work. I just wanted out of that room as soon as possible.

Later that evening, Elisabeth turned up when I was on shift at the library, 'I had to collect something from the group-therapy room, and thought I'd see how you were doing,' she said to me, after whispering something with the librarian who then busied himself behind the desk. 'I think that was a very important session for you today, and I just wanted you to know that we appreciate it might also have been very difficult for you. If you want to discuss it in your next individual session, that's fine, we can reschedule the other work we were planning to cover. I think it is important to finish what you've started.'

'Yes, thanks,' I said, feeling grateful for the momentary respite, and the time to mull things over, and for the extra attention from her. We chatted a while, as I tried to convince her that I had everything under control. Then I felt a deep stirring, when she absentmindedly dropped her guard and touched my arm, as she said goodbye. It was these moments that I lived for, the rare, snatched instances of intimacy with another human being.

That night, my sleep was restless and I found myself wide awake in my cell in the early hours. Thoughts of Ma and our father were jostling for attention in my mind. I was replaying old scenes from my childhood, and I felt that there was still something I could not work out. There was something I needed to make sense of, before I could see my way clear to becoming a real father to Jed Junior.

I was on the basic-regime wing with the book trolley from the library, later that morning, when a new inmate came up to me. The prisoners on this wing were here if they hadn't yet proved themselves to be trusted for enhanced status, or if they had been back-staged here from enhanced due to bad behaviour or rule breaking. It was getting close to lunchtime, with inmates arriving back from work or education for lunch, and the mood on the wing was becoming dark. The stranger asked about a book he said he had reserved. It wasn't on the trolley, so I took his name and said I would track the status of the book for him when I got back to the library. There was something about his manner that really got my back up. There were some cheeky bastards around who thought you owed them something and expected you to do "favours" for them. I always knew that when a guy was desperate to pick up a pre-ordered book currently out on loan to another inmate, that he was usually expecting to pick up more than just the book. I wouldn't go out of my way to scrutinize the book when it came in, but if there was something suspicious, I couldn't ignore it. It was a thin line between grassing people up for stupid things, and knowing when something was a serious security risk.

Feeling pissed off at having to deal with that idiot, I looked around to ask the librarian if it was time to leave the wing. I was getting anxious to get off this wing and to prepare for the afternoon's therapy session with Elisabeth. When I turned back to the cart, the inmate had gone, and so I headed along the wing to the office, where I guessed the librarian must have disappeared. It was then that I noticed a book that had been hastily shoved onto a lower shelf, had worked its way loose and was about to fall off the cart. As I bent down to catch the book, "The Krays", a well-thumbed, old favourite amongst the prisoners, the back cover fell open to reveal a loosely-taped list inside. When I read closer, I could see this was a current, official print-out of the Schedule One offenders in the prison. *What the fuck was I going to do with that?* I think I know who put it there, that last inmate I had spoken to, just before I turned my back to look for the librarian? But who else knew about it? How many others had already seen it? What if it was meant for me to find? Was I being watched? How do I explain having that? How do I prove how it got there? This was a fucking dangerous position for me to be in. What would happen if I handed it in to the staff? Would they believe me? Would I get called to prove my innocence at adjudication? Would I lose my job and my red band? Was this a test? Was this a set up? Paranoia and confusion set in and I started to sweat. How was I going to handle this? I could feel my chest tightening and reached for my inhaler. The easiest thing would have been for me to just replace the list and temporarily "lose" the book on a wrong shelf somewhere, for the next unfortunate fucker to find. Then it would be his problem, not mine.

I stopped in my tracks by a very strong image of my mother appearing in my mind. Suddenly it felt as if I was being sucked back in time to the funeral hall again, telling her I was going to change, to make her proud of me. Closing my eyes, I started to slow down my breathing, to calm down and give myself chance to think this through. I had nothing to do with this, I had literally just discovered this list and if I was to let it lose into the hands of the other prisoners I knew what would happen. Schedule One offenders were those who had committed sex acts or violence against kids. There would many more "accidents" on the wings and maybe even some deaths, if this list fell into the wrong hands, and some inmates decided to dish out their own punishments. I couldn't say that I would blame them, no-one wants the nonces around, but I couldn't be responsible for that chaos and carnage. Besides, there was a good chance my name was on that list. I would have to trust my luck, and my new reputation amongst the staff, and tell them how and I where I had just found it. The uncomfortable thing would be grassing up the last prisoner I had spoken to. I was sure that once I gave them his name, he would be questioned about the list and he would probably realize that they had got to him through me. Well, that was a risk I had to take. The alternative scenario would be one of havoc and upheaval throughout the prison.

Shaking as I entered the wing office, I handed over the list to the officer behind the desk. The colour drained from his face as he realized what he was reading. I quickly explained that it had fallen out of a book and that as far as I was aware, apart from the person who placed it there, no-one except me had seen it. I was sweating and had to reach again for my inhaler.

The librarian spoke up for me. 'That book wasn't on the trolley when we left the library', he confirmed, 'it must have been returned from someone on this wing. I'll check the records to see who last borrowed this book and we can take matters from there.'

'Do you know who handed you that book?' asked the officer.

'I'm not sure,' I answered truthfully. I couldn't remember anyone handing the book to me, the first time I noticed it was when it was about to fall out of the cart.

The officer eyed me suspiciously until the librarian repeated that we would have to return to the library and check the records to find out the name of the last person who had borrowed the book. 'However, I won't be surprised if it's been outstanding for some time and passed around the wings,' he added.

'Well, at least it's out of circulation now,' said the officer, adding a stiff, 'Thanks' before we left the wing.

After lockdown that evening I heard the telltale clanking of keys and slamming of doors, as a dozen or so men were shipped off the wing, on the grounds of their own safety. In the morning I would probably be able to work out which of my fellow inmates had been Schedule One offenders, by their absence from the wing. That information would stay only with me.

Chapter 13

# AKOMA: Patience and tolerance

'I've changed Ma, I really have.' The twinkle in her hazel eyes and smile of approval cocooned me in warmth and safety. I nestled into her faded pink sweater, comforted by her sweet, familiar smell and the softness of her breast against my cheek. This was home, where everything always felt right.

I wanted this moment, this feeling, to last forever. Yet as soon as that thought came into my mind, I realized that I was dreaming and the magic would soon pass.

On waking I tried desperately to hold onto the comfort, keeping my eyes closed in the hope of seeing her image for a little while longer in my mind's eye. As always, she faded all too soon and I was faced with the bare, grey solitude of my cell. I could hear no sign of movement on the wing, no clanking of keys or doors banging, and so I rolled over and closed my eyes once more. Drifting in and out of sleep, I tried to conjure up more images of Ma to recreate the feeling of comfort, however, it was Elisabeth's face I could see most clearly, through each level of consciousness.

As we lay face to face, I looked deeply into her green eyes and we spoke without words. My heart was furiously pounding in my chest. Elisabeth sensed my fear and reached out to take my hand. She placed it on her chest and soon all I could feel was the rhythm of her heart. It's calm beat echoing around us until it eclipsed my own heart, absorbing the two of us, beat by beat, heart to heart, into one.

When I woke again it was to the voice of Officer King, 'Jed, you awake? There's someone here to see you.'

'What, at this time?' I was confused. 'What's the time?'

'It's early Jed, but there's someone from psychology to see you, said it's important.'

I wasn't expecting to see Elisabeth until later that afternoon for our individual therapy session.

'Ok, I'll be down as soon as I can,' I said and then thought to ask if it was her, but Kieran had already left the landing. Why did he say 'someone from psychology' and not 'Elisabeth'? What if something had happened to her, again? I felt my chest constrict and reached for the inhaler, taking two long, slow breaths before leaving the cell.

As I looked through the narrow glass pane in the interview-room door, I was relieved to see her sitting at the desk. Her mouth was slightly open and she was absentmindedly tapping a pencil on her front teeth. I knocked and she looked up, beckoning me to enter the room.

However, my heart sank as I took a seat. There was a heaviness hanging around in the air and a lurking sense of dread crept over my shoulders.

'Jed, sorry it's so early, I just wanted you to know as soon as possible.'

'Know what?' I took another deep breath as my heart started to race, what was this about? Then the fear started to well up inside me. I wanted to know, but was frightened of what she was going to say.

'It's about your brother, Jon,' she continued. 'Jed, we didn't get a reply when we wrote to Jon as he had, died. Jon died one day last week.'

Dead! Jon? She must have got it wrong. I was confused.

'What? How? Are you sure? Was it an accident or something?' I couldn't believe anything had happened to Jon. 'Was he ill?' Why didn't he tell me?'

'The cause of death isn't yet clear, Jed. We are waiting on the post mortem results,' explained Elisabeth. 'I really don't know any more than that. As next of kin, you will be informed of the results and as you and Tommy are prisoners, the authorities will probably speak with your sister Jodie in relation to funeral arrangements.'

'Next of kin...' the words rang around loudly in my head and then reverberated around my body. My big brother was dead. I felt vulnerable and exposed. It was Jon who had taken charge when our father died, and now he was gone too. I was expecting him to be there when I got out of jail. Now, I would be on my own. I gasped for breath as I saw myself tombstone through the depths of a murky ocean.

'Are you in contact with Tommy and Jodie?' Elisabeth gently asked.

'I'll write to Jodie but I've no idea where Tommy is.' I barely managed to reply.

'Where is Jodie living these days?'

I was wondering why Elisabeth was so keen to know about Jodie.

'I'll speak to Kieran King and see if we can apply for a transfer for you, somewhere closer to your family. I can't promise anything, as you know, but I can make a recommendation.'

Jodie was now my only family, on the outside, but Elisabeth was my life here and now. I didn't ever want to leave her. I was overwhelmed with the desire to be close to her, to lose myself in her softness and warmth. Closing my eyes, I wanted only to be aware only of her sweet smell; to forget the harsh realities of the hurtful world around us. I wanted to be with her in a time and place where no-one else could reach us and we only had each other to think of and care about. In her I could recognize and be myself, the real me. She knew of every aspect of me, from the cowering, scared child, to the cocky street-dealing kid who had graduated into world of vengeful, violent offending. She also knew me how I was now, as the anxious prisoner who realized that changing my behaviour was the only real option, if there was any hope of salvaging something of a life. Being with her seemed like the only place I could ever find any peace, just being me, breathing freely.

'I want to stay here, with you. You mean more to me than anyone. I can't do this without you. You're all that I have.' At just the slightest gesture of sympathy or affection from her, my overwhelming desire to be with her would have crushed any professional boundary between us.

Elisabeth was watching me intently. I could see a million thoughts floating around behind her magical green eyes. All I wished for at that point in time was for one of those thoughts to crystallize into words expressing her desire for me, and for those words to slip from her lips.

With the gentlest of restraint she replied, 'There's nothing I can say, Jed, to make things feel better for you at this very moment, but you know I will always do what I can to help you. This isn't the place for you, now. You have a chance to move on to the next stage, I think a transfer nearer home would be the best thing for you right now.'

We sat in a restrained and respectful silence for a little while, the air around us loaded with emotion. There was so much I wanted to say to her. However, she rose to leave, saying that she thought it best if I tried to get in touch with Jodie and that she would also speak to the Prisons Location Officer about a possible transfer for me. She had thrown me a line at the start of the life sentence; and just as I thought I was about to finally climb out of the trench, she had cut the cord. I plunged to the depths of despair. I thought I would never see her face again, although I would always carry a memory in my heart of how she had made me feel.

I lived through the next few weeks with my head in a haze. Everyone seemed distant and everything happening around me was doing so in a slow and painful motion. The masked daylight hours dragged and the nights became filled with dreams of my drowning.

When Kieran King informed me that I was being moved to a Category C prison near to where Jodie was living, the bubble of my existence became punctured with facts and formalities. I had written to her to ask what was happening about Jon's funeral. She told me Jon had died of multiple organ failure, with an overdose of steroids suspected to be the cause. He hadn't made a will and so she had been forced to decide on the funeral arrangements. Thankfully, she had opted for a burial over a cremation. Something told me that Jon would be happier with that choice. Meanwhile I packed up my cell and waited for the knock on my door. Prisoners are usually notified about a move, just hours before they are shipped out. I had lost any sense of rhythm or routine I had ever developed in this joint and could only focus on the practicalities of the funeral arrangements and the impending transfer.

On the day of the funeral I was finally unlocked and told to dress in my best clothes. I wore the same suit that I had been allowed to buy for Ma's cremation and journeyed in the prison van. This time I didn't care who was watching as I walked into the service handcuffed to a uniformed officer; and I refused to acknowledge anyone standing by the graveside, except for Jodie.

The communication between us over the last couple of weeks, namely a few letters and one brief phone call, had consisted of a factual exchange of dates, days and times. Amongst the itinerary items listed in my head was the fleeting opportunity to escape. I replayed the likely formalities of the transfer and thought of a few occasions when I might be able to take flight. What did I have to lose?

However, there's nothing like the sight of your dead brother in a wooden box, being lowered into a hole in the ground on a damp, autumn day to bring you down to earth.

Seeing Jodie again brought back stark memories of Ma. They looked much alike. Both had the same, small frame and twinkling hazel eyes, but Jodie seemed much stronger. She had an air about her that let you know she would help you out, but take advantage of her at your peril. I guess she learned that lesson growing up in a troubled household with three violent brothers. However, as a girl I think she was sheltered from lots of the stuff that went on. I never saw our father show her anything but kindness.

Now she was a young woman without the support of her family. Things had moved on since I had come into prison on this life sentence, she was now married and had twin girls of her own. Jon had played the role of our father in giving her away at the ceremony, whilst Tommy and I had been locked up in jail. Although she carried herself with the demeanour of a responsible woman, at the graveside that day I saw the face of a frightened girl.

There we were, just the two of us, connected by our family heritage, sharing the same genes but living very different lives. This would be the only chance I would have to speak face-to- face with my sister, as I would not be allowed to attend to funeral wake. I had accommodation booked at an overnight holding cell at the local police station, before being transported to the prison the following day.

'Jodie, I need to talk to you,' I said, as the last of the earth was scattered over the top of the coffin. As she turned to leave, I grabbed her arm, 'Jodie, things have changed now, I've changed, please!' I was desperate. She stopped and stared at me. 'Can I write to you from the prison and send a visiting order, so we can talk?' I pleaded. She nodded in agreement and I knew not to push any further. There was a glimmer of hope that we could get back onto speaking terms again. If I had any chance to build a new life, I needed someone like Jodie around, to help me keep it real.

That night in the silence of the holding cell, I stared into the void.

Closing my eyes against the blackness, my soul was still permeated by the chill of isolation. If ever there was a time and place in my life most conducive to committing suicide, this must have been it. It was a cruel awakening, to finally appreciate the people in my life, to learn how to love, trust and show respect, just to have it all turned on its head by another untimely death. It all felt out of control. I had no control over my life. I was powerless, just a pawn on the chess board of the criminal justice system, being played mercilessly by the fingers of Home Office strategy; and it seemed as if the fuckers were intent on pushing me closer to the edge. Just as I was becoming someone, taking control of my life, this was a sharp reminder that there were always greater forces at work.

My mind was a mash-up of everything that was bad about my life. I replayed all of the memories of our father's violence with my brothers; and his rows with Ma, old film footage now restored in high definition. I winced at every blow of my father's fist, my energy ebbing away with every tear falling from Ma's eyes.

What was the point of therapy to stir up all of your darkest moments, if there was no way to make it good? Perhaps Danny was right after all, we have no real control. We are all part of a bigger plan and we just have to play the part we've been assigned. Perhaps it was the way my life was supposed to be, painful and chaotic. If our lives are all pre-destined and controlled by spirits, then perhaps I was fighting, and losing, some pointless, invisible battle?

However, I could no longer just accept this, my part in the apparent "grand scheme" of things. I was excruciatingly uncomfortable with some of the hurtful things I had done in the past; and I desperately wanted my future to be different. I had glimpsed the alternative; I had spent time with people who could show me better ways of dealing with matters, and I liked what I had seen. I wanted to direct my own action, create my own scenarios from hereon in. I had learned some new skills and I wanted the chance to put them into practice. My parents, teachers, girlfriends, cops, and the courts had all played their parts in the previous scenes of my life; now I wanted to change the genre and have full artistic control over sequel, the rest of my life.

It was with these thoughts that I willed myself through the night, and was wide awake and ready to leave when unlocked from the holding cell the following morning. With a quick glance back into the cell, just as the door was closing behind me, I knew that I had left every discarded element of my past back in the void. Just as I would never return to that cell, so neither would I look back on the people and events of my past, and allow them any influence over my future.

The old film footage had been replaced with empty frames. I was moving only in a forwards direction, and I had already decided on the next step.

The transition in to the next prison went as smoothly as I could manage. I was familiar with the drill and I wasn't looking to make any statements or assert my reputation and so I just moved in quickly and quietly. A Category C prison is filled with inmates serving shorter sentences and there are some local prisoners on remand, whilst their cases are being heard in court. Lifers, like me, tend to move on to these types of prison when they are coming to the end of their sentences. Being in a place with a fast turnover of people and where no-one (apart from the staff) know anything about you it can either be a blessing or a curse. Men threatened by your arrival will act up to warn you off and to reinstate the prison hierarchy. This I knew from personal experience on previous sentences. Things had changed for me now, I didn't want to be seen as a threat, but neither did I want to be the target of any bullies desperate to make a name for themselves. I knew that to progress further, I had to speak to the wing staff, get a job and keep my head down, whilst not being seen as a grass or a pushover. I knew I was being watched closely but that was fine with me, I had nothing to hide. I had a future to plan for and it was coming closer every day.

I wrote to Jodie. I needed to know whether or not she was going to be willing or able to help me. I knew that I only had one shot at this and so I took some time to write to her explaining about the work I had been doing and how much I wanted to turn my life around, while I still had the chance. I gave her the name of the programme I had been working on and the contact details for Kieran King and Elisabeth, for her to check out the truth for herself.

I remembered something Jon had said about them becoming closer after Ma's death. I wanted to fill in those years, to find out what had been happening in her life whilst I had been inside.

I didn't have to wait long for a reply. Jodie said that talking with me further had been on her mind since the day of Jon's funeral. There was some family business she thought I needed to know about. With her agreeing to see me, I sent her an order as soon as I was eligible for visits.

The only two visits I had ever received on this prison sentence were from Jon telling me that Ma was dying; and Alisha informing me that she was moving away and taking my son with her. Waiting anxiously for her arrival, I was feeling apprehensive as to what news Jodie might bring.

On her first visit, both Jodie and I realized that neither of us were in touch with Tommy. Jodie explained that she had a stack of returned post from the last prison and wasn't sure if he had moved on or was refusing to accept her letters. I confessed that I had made no effort to keep in touch with him even before I, myself, had become a prisoner. The last time I had seen him was at Ma's funeral. Our only hope was for someone to write to the Home Office, quoting his prisoner number; in the hope that someone could be bothered to check a central database to locate him. We both felt that he should know about the death of our brother and Jodie agreed she would be the best person to try and get in touch.

I asked Jodie to help me fill in the gaps, to share with me the things that had happened in her life since I had been inside, serving this life sentence. I learned how she had trained as a nurse and worked in the local hospital, where she met her husband who worked as a paramedic. They had twin girls and Jodie had been working nights to make sure she was at home in the day with her kids. I wondered if she would want me to have any contact with my nieces, to play any part in their lives.

Jodie told me that Ma had confided in her when she became sick, telling her things she wanted to get off her chest. She wanted to explain what had happened with our father, and to explain that things had not always been bad with him.

Jodie asked if I could remember anything about our father's younger brother, Cliff.

I had seen a photograph of him and remembered talk about him coming over from Ghana to stay with Ma and our father, for a while. He couldn't get a job and went back home, or so I thought. It was before my time. Jodie explained to me that when Cliff came over, Ma had just lost a baby, the fourth child.

'We would have had another sister, but it had been a difficult pregnancy and the baby had some genetic metabolic disorder. She was never going to live for long. Ma was suffering, but our father's way of dealing with it was to drink himself stupid. He wouldn't talk about it and left Ma to deal with all of it, the funeral, the loss, the effect of it on all of us. As kids, we didn't really know what was going on anyway. Jon and Tommy were about six and seven and I was only four, so I can't remember anything.'

Jodie continued, 'Ma told me that she and Cliff had become close when he was staying with us and our father was out on his weekend drinking binges. When our father found out he kicked off big time. He threatened to kill Cliff if he didn't leave and so Cliff had nowhere to go except back to Ghana.'

I was wondering what any of this had to do with me, when a sudden fear gripped my gut.

'Ma told me that although our father suspected that you might be Cliff's kid he would never admit it. He said that you were the fifth child, and that you would bring bad luck to the family. However, Ma said that at first you were different from Jon and Tommy, that's how she knew she knew that Cliff was your real dad. She sent him letters and photos of you when you were small.'

'I was the unlucky fifth child? Is that why he would have nothing to do with me?' I asked.

'If you were his fifth child, you were going to bring bad luck; if not then you were Cliff's child. Our father couldn't accept either possibility.' Instantly I felt transported back to the scene where Denise had told me she was pregnant, by someone else, and felt a painful awareness unfolding in my gut.

'Ma said that Cliff had asked her to go back to Ghana with him, but when it came down to it our father said that she couldn't take us all with her, and she just couldn't leave us.'

Suddenly I found myself at the centre of the conversation, rather than hovering on the outside like an observer. This changed everything! This man was my real father, not the dead drunk. Was this guy still alive? Where was he, in Ghana?

'Ma thought that he got married and had some more kids, but as they hadn't spoken for about thirty years she wasn't sure what was happening with him. She says she did think of trying to get back in touch with him when our father died but she heard he was spoken for and she didn't think he would be interested in picking up with her again. Then she met Watson and you went your own way and she began to think that she was wrong all along, that you couldn't be Cliff's son after all as you were turning out just like Jon and Tommy.'

'She had given up on me hadn't she?'

'Well, to be honest, yes, when you went in on the life sentence she didn't expect to ever see you again. I think she would have come round after a while and come to visit you, or at least written to you, but then she got ill and her health went downhill so quickly after she was diagnosed with cancer.'

'I'm sorry, I never meant...'

'I know, Jed. You didn't know and there was nothing you could do anyway.'

'I never had the chance to show her I'd changed, to show here that I wasn't the thug I had grown into, that I was still the little boy she loved, underneath it all.'

Jodie just looked at me, not knowing what else she could say to make things better, then, tentatively, she asked if I thought it might be worthwhile trying to get in touch with my father in Ghana.

'I could go through Ma's box of letters and things and see if there's an address we could try. He's probably moved, but you never know, it could be worth a shot. All we need is a contact, someone who recognizes his name and could tell us where we could start looking for him.

A whole new horizon had opened up in front of me, and the landscape looked fresh and exciting.

On the next visit, Jodie brought with her a battered old shoebox, full of old letters and faded photographs. I remember feeling excited about the secret words and pictures I was about to find, and yet fearful at the same time of being disappointed. I was expecting the contents of the box to fill in many more "gaps" in my life. However, I was forced to wait whilst the security officers and sniffer dogs rifled through the box, checking for smuggled items. Watching their smirks and attempts at covert comments had little effect on me now, I was far more interested in the contents of that box.

When Jodie finally placed the box on the plastic table between us, I found a mixture of old, Polaroid photos of me, Jon Tommy and Jodie as kids, messing about in the parse lounge of the flat. We both laughed at the photo of Ma caught unexpectedly with curlers in her hair, trying to hide from the camera. Then there were earlier, photo-booth snaps of Ma and us from that one holiday in Brighton I can remember. Jodie reminded me that we went to visit a cousin of Ma's who had a B&B business by the sea. Ma helped out with serving breakfasts for the guests and took us to play on the beach in the afternoons.

I suddenly saw an image in my mind's eye, Ma crying on the train journey back home and I shuddered.

Jodie handed me a letter. It was postmarked *Greater Accra, Ghana, January 24th 1976* and addressed to Mrs Sylvie Johnson. It read,

*Dear Sylvie,*
*How lovely to finally hear from you and to see a photo of Jed. He's a handsome boy, must take after his father! I'm not much of a letter writer but am happy to keep in touch like this until you can come over. When do you think you will have enough money saved to make the journey? I am working in the city now, there's more building work here and I have enough money to rent this place. There is only one bedroom and I have to share the bathroom with the family in the next flat but there is room for you and the baby. How old is he now? Will he be walking and talking by the time you get here? Take care until then.*
*All my love,*
*Cliff*

So she was planning to leave our father and move to Ghana with Cliff.

I rifled through the photos until I found an old black and white picture of Cliff. He was standing next to our father, with one arm around his brother's shoulder. Both were in dusty working clothes and boots and looked as if they had just come in from a day's work on a building site. Where was this taken, in Ghana? So how old was our father when he came over to work in Britain? It must have been sometime in the 60s. I flicked over the photo and read *"Volta 1961"*.

What was Ghana like in the 60s and 70s?

I had so many questions floating around in my head.

I tried hard to imagine growing up in Ghana, in Africa in the '70s and '80s. It was something I knew nothing about. I heard our father rambling on about the Cape Coast when we were small and he was pissed. It usually started with him trying to tell us about his childhood when he went off fishing with his father to earn some money for the family. As my brothers and I had only ever seen the sea once, on that holiday in Brighton, we had no idea what he was talking about and soon got bored and restless. That was when he used to lose his temper and lash out at one of us, usually Tommy.

'Here's the next one.' Jodie was trying to put the letters in date order so they would make more sense.

*Accra, Ghana, June 22nd 1976*

*Dear Sylvie*
*It is glorious summer here now and you and Jed would love it. I have saved some more money for a bigger place for you, Jodie and the boys. If it will make you happy to have all of them here with us then that's ok with me.*

*I miss our moments together and can't wait until I can see and touch you again.*

*Perhaps when things have settled down and I have earned enough money we can move back to the Cape Coast and the boys can go fishing just as me and my brothers did when we were kids.*

*Is Jed talking yet? Have you told him about me? Have you told him you are coming to Ghana?*

*I will let you know when I get somewhere bigger and we can make some plans.*

*All my love,*

*Cliff*

The next letter was dated December 20<sup>th</sup> 1976 and read:

*Dear Sylvie*

*I was hoping you, Jodie and the boys would be here for Christmas. What's happening? Are you ok, is he giving you trouble? The best thing you can do is leave as soon as you can. He will never change and we could make a good life here. I have been thinking more about moving back to the Cape Coast. With the money I have saved we can rent a house not far from the beach and I can teach the boys how to fish. Between us all we can make it work. I haven't heard from the rest of the family or a while, and they won't think to look for us there, so perhaps we can make it work.*

*Please send me some photos of you and Jed. I miss you like crazy.*

*All my love,*

*Cliff*

'Are there any more letters?' I impatiently asked. I was becoming enthralled by the "other" life my mother was living in her head. Why didn't she leave our father and take us to Ghana? How different would my life have been if I'd been brought up in a different country with Ma and Cliff – my real father?

'There don't seem to be any more letters from Cliff,' said Jodie, 'but there is a letter here from Ma to Cliff which never got posted.'

There was no stamp on the envelope, and it was sealed.

'Shall we open it?' I was fearful of what it might say. Why didn't she post it?

I had to know, even if it was bad news.

The letter read:

*January 10^th 1977*

*Dear Cliff*

*I really don't know what to say, how to say this, but I won't be coming to Ghana to be with you. I can't take the boys away from him. We are trying to make things work here.*

*I hope you understand and that you will be happy.*

*I think it is best if we do not have any further contact.*

*Sylvie x*

So why didn't she send the letter? And if she wanted nothing more to do with Cliff why did she keep the letters? Perhaps it wasn't really over...maybe she wanted our father to find the letters and make her choice easier?

Part of me agonized over the fact she never went. Life could, would have been so different. I felt myself starting to blame her for staying in that shithole flat on that dog-eat-dog dump of an estate where we learned to lie and steal and just take what we wanted, regardless.

'What else did Ma tell you about Cliff and Ghana?'

Jodie frowned and said, 'She said that she and Cliff would have to face the rest of the family, in Ghana, who would not look kindly on what they had done; and she was afraid of what would happen to me, Jon and Tommy if she left us behind with our father. She knew that she couldn't take us with her, and perhaps she was afraid of what would happen to our father if she did.'

We could only wonder at her reasons for staying with our father.

'So why didn't she get in touch with Cliff when our father died?'

'I don't know. Perhaps she thought it was too late?' Jodie suggested.

'I was only six when he died. It was years before she took up with that Watson. Why didn't she go to Ghana when our father died?' I was finding it hard to accept.

'She was a single mother with four young kids, remember?' Jodie reasoned with me. 'Perhaps it just wasn't that easy?'

Jodie passed me a very old black and white photograph. 'Look at this.' I saw two young men standing in front of a sign that read "The Akosombo Dam". Jodie explained that the brothers worked on that hydroelectric dam back in 1961. 'They were both active in the building of the infrastructure of their homeland, Ghana, after they were granted independence in 1957.'

I wondered why our father never told us about it. Then again, perhaps he did in his drunken rambling way, it's just that we didn't listen to him. I was curious to know why he and Cliff came to England when Ghana had just obtained its independence. Were they both intending to go back?

Now I could see of our father as a man with a life of his own before me, Jon, Tommy and Jodie...and before Ma.

Did he stay over here for Ma?

A whole new perspective suddenly lurched before my eyes.

What if our father stayed here for Ma? That would make sense. Perhaps she felt guilty about keeping him here and couldn't bring herself to go to Ghana with Cliff. Maybe he was unhappy here but stayed for her – after all she was born and brought up in England. Perhaps she refused to go and he felt he had to stay and that's why he drank so much – to forget his misery and the life that he could be living?

My heart started pounding and I became light headed at the realization.

I was seeing my father, both of my fathers and my mother through a 360 degree lens for the very first time. I think as kids we tend to only think of our parents in that role, we fail to consider them as people with a past, or a future.

'I think our father couldn't see a future for himself in this country, and perhaps that's why he drank so much,' I said to Jodie, starting to feel uncomfortable with all the years of condemnation and blame I had laid at our father's feet; all of the excuses of an abusive father and unhappy childhood I had given to lawyers, judges, juries, probation officers and prison psychologists.

'Perhaps,' she replied, thoughtfully. We could only theorize, as neither he nor Ma were around to answer all of these questions.

I was also seeing myself differently now. I had a rich, cultural heritage. Although half British and half Ghanaian, I had only ever acknowledged the English aspect of myself; the part of me that was born into a poor family. I had never questioned my place in the world, just worked hard to carve myself a niche in the underworld, so to speak. A place where the rules were made to be broken and everyone I knew thought they were playing the winning hand.

Now, I had become aware of the other "half" of myself, I had woken up to a whole new continent of possibilities.

# Chapter 14

# FAWOHODIE: Independence, freedom, emancipation

Ghana became my obsession for a while. I became a regular user of the prison library service, reading as much information as I could on the country, its history and its people – my people.

My imagination ran riot when I first learned that "Ghana" translated into English means "Warrior king", and that the country's motto is "Freedom and Justice". Avidly I read about the Portuguese building Elmina Castle as a permanent trading base on the Atlantic Coast in 1482, with a Thomas Windham making the first recorded trading voyage from England to the Coast in 1553. During the next three centuries, the English, Danes, Dutch, Germans and Portuguese nations all exercised control over the various parts of the Cape Coast, building forts to allow them to develop and manage their various trading businesses. I learned that it was the English who named Ghana "The Gold Coast". As the precious metal was in natural abundance the Europeans traded items such as copper, brass and glass beads with the West Coast occupants for their gold. However, it was the slave trade which proved the most lucrative to the Europeans and Africans, alike. The Ashanti Empire was a pre-colonial state, established by the Akan people who lived deep in the rainforest area of central Ghana. In 1821, the British Government took control of the British trading forts on the Gold Coast, fighting a series of campaigns against the Ashanti, from 1826 to the early 1900s for control of their inland kingdom. In 1902, they succeeded in establishing firm control over the Ashanti region. However, as I already knew, Ghana became an independent state in 1957.

I looked at images of Kumasi, the capital city of the Ashanti region, and fantasized about travelling with my son to see the real Golden stool, the seat of the Ashanti soul, at the Manhyia Palace. I imagined us travelling out West of the city to see the Anokye Sword marking the spot where the Golden Stool first appeared out of the Heavens; and to the villages around the city where the traditional crafts of gold-smithy, cloth printing, pottery and weaving are practised. I saw us standing on the shore of the Bosumtwi Lake, where it is said that the souls of the dead ancestors come to say goodbye; and walking out onto the wooden veranda of my father's beach house, to go fishing off the Cape Coast. Then I remembered that I was a British prisoner on a life licence, unable to leave the country without permission from the Home Office. My reality consisted of the cold loneliness of my cell, and if I was lucky, a glimpse of the sky overhead, between the thick, grey clouds. There I could fester for days without seeing or speaking to anyone, except the officer whose duty it was to check I was still alive. It was the contact and conversations with Jodie that was helping me to reconcile the events of the past, and to keep focused on my new direction. She was still talking about getting in touch with Cliff, and she was becoming more interested in her heritage.

In one of our telephone conversations she eagerly told me about her recent discoveries, 'Did you know, Jed, that it's an old tradition in Ghana for a wife to marry her husband's brother, if she becomes a widow? The brother of the dead man is also expected to bring up his nieces and nephews, as his own. If Ma had gone to Ghana with Cliff when our father died, no-one would have batted an eyelid.' It was the family matters she seemed to have most interest in. 'The eldest surviving son inherits all the family property when the father dies, Jed. If there is no son then the daughter will inherit it, I wonder if there is anyone else…' We didn't know if Cliff had ever married and had more children. 'The traditional attitude to children, is interesting too,' Jodie informed me. 'Ashanti parents consider childhood to be a happy time, and that kids are harmless and cannot be held responsible for their actions. They don't see any need to be worried for the soul of a child. That's why they don't bother with the usual funeral rites for children who die young. And that could explain why our father didn't want to make any fuss when our baby sister died, he just didn't see any need. However, Ma took it all the wrong way, thinking that he didn't care.'

It was as if we were working on a jigsaw puzzle, using our newfound knowledge to fit the pieces of our childhood together, so that they formed a recognizable picture. I had begun to understand some of the more obvious elements of my culture through Danny; Jodie was providing me with insight from another angle.

'The Ashanti believe that we are made up of two elements, blood and spirit, both of which they obtain from their parents,' she explained. 'The blood which comes from the mother determines the clan or Abususa, and the spirit which comes from the father determines the Nton. Therefore it is the mother's birthright that determines the clan of the children, not the fathers.'

'So a person can only be Ashanti if their mother was?' I was confused.

'It is possible for an Ashanti not to have Nton, which is the father's spirit, but impossible not to belong to an Abususa.'

'So as our father was a member of an Ashanti clan, and Ma was not, we can't be Ashanti?'

'Our spirit is!' Jodie laughed into the telephone. 'We have

Ashanti spirit from our father – I mean fathers. Don't take it all so seriously, I'm sure our relatives in Ghana would welcome us as family.'

This was no joke to me. 'What about our kids? Where do they belong?' I was starting to feel uncomfortably isolated again. Just when I thought I had found some heritage, it felt as if it had been cruelly taken away, again.

'Well isn't this all just history, as far as we are concerned, Jed? We were all born and brought up in this country, we are British, like it or not.'

I couldn't agree with Jodie, the more I came to know about the African aspect of my ancestry, the further removed I felt from anything that was "British".

'What about Alisha?' A thought flew into my mind and perched expectantly. 'Jed Junior's mother, I'm sure she had family in Ghana.' I felt a flutter of excitement. *What was her heritage? I needed to know.* If her mother was Ashanti, then my son would have both the spirit and the bloodline.

'Alisha?' asked Jodie in a surprised tone. 'Are you in touch with her?'

'She wrote to me a while back with her new address,' I answered. 'And I wrote back, with a story for JJ, but haven't heard anything further.'

That night as I lay calm and motionless on the top bunk of my cell, I became aware of a flash of purple feathers, as a large, red-crested bird landed on the branch of a tree, just above my head. Jolting in surprise, I felt a strange swinging sensation beneath my feet and looked down to see that I was standing on a narrow, wooden walkway, suspended by rope from the surrounding trees. Looking up, above the tops of the trees, I was forced to close my eyes as the burst of golden sunlight landed on my face. To balance I grasped at the waist-high, mesh netting to each side of me and took a deep breath. *This must be a dream.* Opening my eyes again, I marvelled at the bold, black markings on an orange-winged butterfly, now perched on my right hand. Then I looked below. The forest floor lay one hundred feet, or so, beneath me, its native red antelope, with their white stripes and wavy antlers, appearing as miniatures playing hide and seek in the under-growth. The shock turned my in-breath to ice and I gripped on tighter, telling myself that I would wake up at any moment from this dream.

However, the swinging motion of the rope bridge beneath my feet continued and I felt the urge to move forwards. I could see that the rope bridge curved towards some tall, verdant trees, where I imagined I would be able to climb down to safety. With each step, my confidence grew and the swinging slowed to a gentle sway. I started to look around me and marvel at the brightly-coloured birds and butterflies darting in between the ebony trunks of the tall trees. Navigating the curve, I could see that the rope bridge led to a platform wrapped around the trunk of a majestic, Mahogany tree. The sturdiness of the stage encouraged me to stop and marvel at the scene unfolding around me, and I found myself under the curious scrutiny of a group of small, black monkeys, with white brow and cheek markings. Tilting their heads from side to side as they looked at me, they appeared to chatter amongst themselves, before turning to reveal their red-furred rumps, and disappearing back amongst the branches. I smiled in amusement. Time seemed to have taken on a quality of stillness, everything around me was happening in slow motion, and there seemed no sense of danger.

However, I soon realized that there was no way down from the forest canopy to its floor, from this point. My only option appeared to be to take another rope-bridge, reaching across a wide clearing to reach a network of shorter bridges and lower platforms at the other side, which would lead me lower into the forest. Relaxing, I became more aware of the vibrant colours and strong scents of my surroundings. The air was warm and moist and I wiped a light covering of sweat from my forehead, as I descended through the verdant foliage to the forest floor.

On reaching the bottom, I felt relieved to rest in the shade for a few moments, smiling in the expectation that I was about to wake up at any moment from this bizarre dream. Closing my eyes, I concentrated on the sounds of the forest surrounding me. I could hear the call of the birds from high in the tree tops and tried to imagine how it might feel to rest weightless, on a wing, and soar high in the clear, blue sky. I stirred only on hearing a faint rustle of leaves beside me, and when I opened my eyes every nerve-ending in my body screamed out in full alert. My eyes met with the paralysing stare of a snake, poised upright, directly in front of me. Every muscle of my body contracted, in an attempt to get me out of there, yet I remained motionless, mesmerized by the hovering, hooded eyes of the cobra. My heart was pounding furiously and yet my blood was running cold through my veins. Without any warning, the head of the snake flew towards me, and as if in slow motion, I raised my hands in defence of my face. Firstly there was an excruciating pain in the back of my left hand, where the creature had sunk its razor-tipped fangs. Then a deadly, dull ache spread into my wrist and forearm. As the feeling of turning to stone spread to my upper arm and shoulder, I believed that death itself had just been brutally injected into my body. The last thing I remembered was the feeling of floating above myself, watching as the creature slunk away into the undergrowth. When I opened my eyes once more, the fearful pounding of my heart had ceased, and I was greeted by the familiar staleness of my cell, in the chill of the early hours. I looked at the back of my left hand, expecting to see an open wound. It was sore to the touch, but there was no puncture wound, just a faint bruise. However, as I rose from the bunk to take a piss, my whole body shook in weakness, and I slumped on the floor next to the toilet pan, too weak to stand.

I was awoken with a rude reminder of the confines of my reality. The officer unlocking me that following morning shot a questioning look at the puddle next to the toilet, told me to get my arse up off the floor, and then informed me that I had an interview with the Sentence Planning Officer. I knew the drill. They would have my "Lifer's file", with all of the wing-officers' reports on me and would be looking to see what courses they could get me to do next. These officers weren't the same breed as those working on the wings, and I was keen to see what they would suggest, and so I pulled myself together as best I could.

I was escorted to an interview room on the wing and introduced to a young officer, who looked hardly old enough to be wearing the uniform.

'So, Mr Johnson, you have completed the "Cognitive Strengths and Emotional Management" programme, and you have specifically addressed your violent offending. Is that correct?'

'Yep,' I replied.

'It says here that you were an enhanced prisoner, with red-band status, in your last location.'

'Yep, that's correct too.'

'Ok then, as you've been here over a month now with no positive drug test results and no adverse wing reports, we can see about arranging a job for you. We have a small library here.'

'Yeah, I'm familiar with the library,' I replied, 'but I would like to try something else.'

'How about working as a gym orderly?' the officer asked. 'Those jobs are reserved for red-band prisoners; it's a position of trust.'

That seemed like a good idea. I said that I would like to give it a try and the officer looked very pleased. 'I'll have a word with the gym officers and see if there are any openings,' he said, scribbling down a reminder for himself.

'The other thing here is a remark about the Restorative Justice programme. I can't quite make out the name of the officer who wrote it,' the officer said, straining to read Kieran King's signature on an entry in the file.

'I talked about that with Principal Officer King,' I explained, 'but it didn't go any further than that.'

'We are running a pilot for the programme here,' said the young officer, quite excitedly. 'I'll put you forwards for an assessment.'

*Yeah, what the hell,* I thought. It was all progress.

One week later, I was having an induction into the gym. I found myself cleaning the changing rooms and doing safety checks on the weightlifting equipment with the staff. Here there were all sorts of heavy-duty metal objects ripe for adaptation into effective skull crushers. Initially, I remember feeling vulnerable in this new environment, watching the other orderlies in the mirrors. In prison, you learn never to drop your guard, however well you think you know a person, and these inmates in this environment were all new to me. However, it felt good to be learning something new and the gym was a positive environment. The instructors assigned the work and we just got on with it. As the main hall and the weights room were all on constant CCTV coverage, our every move was monitored, and I soon adjusted to the regular rhythm of daily life in the gym. It was another world within a world, somewhere for me to feel safe and yet challenged at the same time. I wasn't interested in destroying places or people any longer. I had invested heavily in the construction of my future and the gym officers soon came to realize this.

After a few weeks of proving my worth, the senior officer approached me and asked if I was interested in gaining any gym-based qualifications. He explained that the prison offered some inmates the opportunity to work towards nationally recognized certificates which could be used to gain employment on the outside. He told me that although there was some written work involved, the qualifications offered by the department were more practical in nature. This appealed to me as a welcome break from all of the "headwork" I had been doing over the past couple of years. I started by enrolling on the popular BAWLA course, and learned about weightlifting, first aid, and health and safety aspects of working in a gym. I could see how this might be useful to me when I was released from prison and would have to start looking for a job. This sort of certification would be recognized on the outside and demonstrate that I was qualified to work in a gym or a health club. I enjoyed the new focus of working out, the awakening of muscles and discipline of movements. After a couple of serious aches and minor injuries, I soon learned to respect the sanctity of rest days, and fell into a new rhythm. My routine of alternating targeted muscle-development with cardio-vascular workouts ensured an effective, whole-body workout, which I always ended with satisfying stretch.

After a few months of my daily workouts in the gym, I noticed that my general mood was elevated; my new feeling of mastery over my body had brought with it a satisfied sense of calm. I also noticed that others around me seemed more relaxed, as relaxed as a prison setting would allow. As I was stretching out one afternoon, one of the instructors called me into the office. 'Jed, I've just spoken to a Kieran King, Principal Officer at your previous place, who has requested that you are assessed for the Restorative Justice Programme. This prison will be piloting the scheme over the next couple of months. They are looking for volunteers. Are you interested?'

'Yeah, I think it was part of sentence plan,' I replied. 'I'm up for it, who do I need to talk to?'

'I'll speak to Officer King, and ask him to mention your name to whoever's running the programme here. He seems to be in charge of rolling out the programme in this area, Jed, and he's got you on his radar! You must have made an impression on him at your last place.'

I felt like the first kid picked for the team. This was good. Things were moving on, new opportunities opening up around me, and the feeling was one of excitement at the prospect of freedom. Participating in the Restorative Justice Programme could be my ticket to a "D" category prison, the last stop before home. There I could live in open conditions, where unsupervized weekend town visits are a privilege, and lots of prisoners can actually work outside the jail during the weekdays. When you are serving a life sentence, the only goal you can set your sights on is your day of release. Every action you take can impact on this. Positive achievements make it appear closer; whereas one false move can completely obliterate the image. Willing to do all I could to keep the image sharp in my mind's eye, I requested an appointment with the Sentence Planning Officer; I did not want to miss this opportunity.

I was soon summoned for an assessment of suitability for the programme.

'There is more to this than just saying sorry, Mr Johnson.'

I felt offended by this girl's attitude towards me. She knew nothing about me. Then, I asked myself, *why should she?* This was the first time we had met. I knew nothing about her. She came to the interview with a backpack full of assumptions, and I had a life sentence hanging around my neck. She had the power to loosen the grip of the sentence, and it was up to me to help her unpack her assumptions, to show her my suitability. This wasn't about her; the focus was on me to prove myself.

So I listened patiently to her speech and waited for my chance to let her know who she was dealing with. When she started to ask questions, they were all related to the events and actions that comprised my index offence.

'What happened?'

'I took a gun and shot at the windows and doors of the house of someone I believed had wrongly grassed me up to the police,' I stated, factually.

'What happened then?' she asked, and I thought that I had

better get to the crux of the matter.

'I injured the young lad inside the house. When I shot through the letterbox, the bullet hit him in the leg'.

'What were you thinking at the time?'

'At the time I accidentally shot the kid, or the whole time?'

'Tell me all of your thoughts,' she instructed me, her pen poised to jot down a few quotes.

'OK,' I said slowly, 'there were quite a few, tell me if I'm going too fast and I'll slow down, in case you miss any.' She shot me a warning look as if she thought I was messing with her, but said nothing, and so I continued, 'I was thinking, *you cheeky fucking bastard, who do you think you are? You're not getting away with this! I'll show you not to mess with me.*'

I paused and watched her scribbling furiously. 'Shall I continue?' She looked up and nodded and so I continued, 'When I got to the house and Tony refused to come out and face me, I felt even angrier, and took my frustration on his car. Then, when I saw someone moving behind the curtains, I just saw red and tried to get in through the back door of the house. Everything was locked up, and in a rage I shot at the doors and windows. I can't really remember what I was thinking at that point, I just felt as if I was on fire.' I stopped and took a deep breath.

'What have your thoughts been since?' She asked.

'My thoughts have been mainly for my situation and the effect of my actions on my family,' I replied, and she frowned in response.

'Who has been affected or harmed by what you did?' She asked.

'As I said, my family, my kids...' I started and she interrupted with another question.

'In what ways?'

I tried to stifle my irritation. She wasn't giving me chance to explain myself properly, it seemed as if she was looking for short answers to neatly package up and box off. Well it just wasn't like that, and I needed to let her know. 'Look, I admit, for ages I was only concerned with my own situation. It was only when I started in therapy that I started to realize how my actions were affecting those around me. I realized I wanted to change things. I don't mean the past, I know I can't change the past, but I want things to be different in the future. I want better things for my kid, I don't want him going down the same road as me and ending up like this. When I was first approached about doing this programme, my reaction was *why should I say sorry?* I thought they deserved what they got and I thought that as I didn't intend to shoot the kid, Jake, I shouldn't be serving a life sentence.'

'So what's changed?' she asked, tartly.

'I've changed,' I responded. 'I can see things from more than just my own perspective and I know that I want things to be different. I'm not going to keep making the same mistakes, I'm breaking that cycle.'

She was now looking intently at me, 'And how do you think participating in this programme is going to help you?'

I thought she was trying to catch me out and I wasn't going to let it happen. 'I'm hoping it will help me, my family and Tony's family. His kid didn't deserve to get caught in the crossfire between us and I want to do what I can to make up for that.'

'So, how do you think you can achieve that, make up for what happened?' She asked slowly and deliberately.

*There it was, the chink in her armour, this was my chance.* 'I want the kid to know that I didn't want to hurt him, and that he doesn't have to be scared of me ever doing anything to hurt him in the future.' I was thinking on my feet. This was new ground, unfamiliar territory to me, but it felt so good. 'I would never want my kid to be hurt like that, and that's all he was when it happened, just someone's kid.'

Her expression told me she was deep in thought. Had I said enough to get on the programme? 'As I said at the start of this interview, Restorative Justice is more than just saying sorry,' she said thoughtfully. 'And so the next question is what are you prepared to do to make up for the harm you have caused?'

This was my Achilles heel. *What could I do?* I had no idea. I started to flounder. I didn't want to sink now, not after coming so far. This wasn't fair. I wanted to ask her what she thought I could I do, but I knew that any suggestion, any ideas, had to come from me.

This was miserable, I was struggling. Weakly, I finally responded saying, 'I'll consider doing anything Jake suggests. I'm prepared to do whatever I can.' *Was this enough?* I had no idea. I watched helplessly as she continued to make notes, not even trying to make out what she was writing.

She looked up, nodded at me, and placed her notes in her folder. 'Thank you Mr Johnson,' she said, holding out her hand to shake mine.

'Is that it?' I asked. 'Am I...?'

'I will pass this assessment on to my supervisor, with the recommendation that we move on to the next step in the process.'

Once again, I could do nothing but wait. Waiting and trusting were the dual challenges at the core of my existence, like spiralling strands of DNA, continually rising up to face me. I could do nothing else, except to focus on the small details that gave my life meaning. I mopped the changing-room floors, checked the safety of the gym equipment, rehearsed a future conversation between Jake and myself, and dreamt of freedom.

Redemption day dawned, under a grey and featureless sky. I turned over on my bunk to face the wall, hoping that something would happen to prevent the scheduled meeting from taking place. Perhaps Jake would back out. I turned back to look out from between the bars of my cell window, imagining a weak and lonely figure limping off into the distance. Maybe some security issue might arise at the prison, resulting in a lockdown. I closed my eyes and re-created the sounds of clanking keys and the shots of bolted locks. I would have welcomed any event which would have prevented me finally coming face to face with the victim, *my* victim. However, there was nothing but a curious silence. The day for which I had waited so patiently, had finally arrived, and not in a glorious haze or with a fanfare of ceremony. I was simply unlocked by an emotionless officer, who informed me that I was to be escorted to the closed visits area. All I could do was to walk slowly and breathe deeply. I had refused the option of having a friend or family member present, as I wanted to concentrate fully on the job in hand. A thin and pale Jake was already in the room, sitting with his mother on a sofa. Across the low table there were a further two chairs, one seating Kieran King. The escorting officer knocked and opened the door, announcing, 'Jed Johnson', as Kieran beckoned me to sit in the empty chair next to him. All of the calm I had conjured up with deep-breathing exercises, was now caught up in the chaotic pounding of my heart. I stopped at the door, and sensing my hesitation, Kieran was on his feet and making his way over to me.

'Take your time, Jed, there's no rush,' he reassured me in hushed tones. 'We all know the procedure, and I'm here to make sure that no-one loses the plot or takes advantage of the situation, OK?' I took a shot of Salbutamol and then a seat in the room.

Jake was looking at the floor, whilst his mother stared at me, with a steadfast gaze and a wide-eyed expression. Thankfully it spoke to me more of disbelief, than of disgust. Gone were the fake tan and the revealing clothes she had worn at my trial. She too looked pale and tired and I felt that she wasn't just here to bawl me out, although I was expecting some recriminations. I acknowledged her and then turned to Kieran for some guidance.

'Just a few simple rules to remember,' he said, turning sideways in his chair so that he could address all three of us. 'We only want one person to speak at a time. Please try to answer the question being asked, rather than just saying whatever comes to your mind. There will be the opportunity to say everything you wish, it's our aim for everyone to benefit from this meeting. My role here is to help us keep focused on the reasons for this meeting and to make sure that everyone is treated with civility. I won't intervene unless I am asked to do so, or if someone is becoming abusive or offensive.'

We all nodded and then Kieran indicated for me to start. I had rehearsed this moment in my head a thousand times and yet it had never felt like this. There was so much I wanted to say, I had prepared many explanations and yet I could say nothing. *If only I could think of some way to start.* Yet the silence continued. The tension was building and I sensed that other people were struggling to contain their emotions.

'Jed?' Kieran looked at me and nodded for me to say something. Each time I tried to say one of the many things I had floating around my head, and summoned the will from the pit of my stomach, the words got stuck in my throat. Something or someone was strangling me, they didn't want me to make good. Each breath got tougher and a sense of panic started to rise in my chest. I looked around, there was no-one else in this room with the power to take away my breath. *Get a grip,* I told myself. 'I'm sorry', I managed a breathless, constricted apology. At least it was a start.

Jake's mother exploded in disbelief, 'You're sorry! Is that all you can say?' I barricaded myself behind closed eyes. 'My son has permanent damage to his leg, and he's too scared to go outside the house, and all you can say is *sorry!*'

She broke into tears and Kieran reached forwards, offering her a tissue. Then he intervened, 'I think we've made a start, Jed what else do you want to say to Jake?'

Jake's gaze was glued to the floor. It was up to me to make something of this situation, to help change the way he saw things. Things were becoming clearer, I could help reframe his experience, to help him see it from a different perspective. He needed to view his past in a way that would allow him to look up from the floor, and see a way back into the world.

'I'm sorry, I never meant to hurt you, I didn't even know you were there. I was angry, furious, but that wasn't your fault, and I had no right to even be there, at your house that day. You have nothing to fear from me.'

Jake continued to look at the floor, his mother was still crying. I could sense the emotional distance between them. I knew what I had to do. I had to bridge this gap between them. I remembered that Tony, Jake's father, was doing a 20-year stretch for manslaughter, over the death of Tania. It was the sordid situation for which he had tried, and failed, to frame me.

'I have a son, and because of my actions, he and his mother are struggling, without my help. It's my fault and I am truly sorry and I am doing everything I can to help make things better for the future.'

I had learned that I had the power to inflict great hurt; I now realized for the first time that I also had the ability to facilitate great healing. A sense of calm washed over me and I felt we were all safely afloat on a raft heading for the shore.

'I don't want you and your mother to struggle, when all you have is each other,' I continued. 'And I don't want my son to waste his life in the same way I have wasted mine.'

Jake's mother leaned over and rubbed her son's arm, he looked up and Kieran gently grasped the moment, 'Jake, can you tell us how this has affected you? What has been the hardest or the worst thing for you?'

'He's become…,' Jake's mother started to speak, then looked to the prison officer for permission to continue.

'Yes…?' encouraged Kieran.

'He's become too scared to leave the house,' she continued. 'He just can't face going out any more, he still walks with a limp, he thinks that everyone is looking at him, threatening him, and he just can't trust anyone.'

'Is that how it is for you, Jake?' asked the officer and I was grateful for him taking control of the situation.

We all waited for Jake to speak. I looked at this silent, shaking kid, who I had only ever previously seen in court, during my trial. If it wasn't for that episode in my life, I wouldn't have known our paths had ever crossed; let alone realized how my actions had made such a devastating impact on his young life. 'How old are you now Jake?' I asked tentatively.

'Twenty-one,' he replied. *Shit, he was just a young kid when I had shot him.* I choked on the realization.

'Are you working?' asked Kieran. He was obviously keen to keep the momentum going.

'No, I'm not working,' Jake replied. 'I was in college but I...'

'He dropped out,' Jake's mother finished the sentence of for him. 'He can't hold down a course or a job, he gets anxious about things and then it all gets too much for him. The doctors have prescribed him pills; the therapists have said that his problems and fears will seem less, the more he gets out and about in the world. But it's as if he's stuck, he just can't seem to move on. His therapist advised him to come here today, hoping it will help him move forward.'

The kid was feeling stuck, something I understood all too well, and he wasn't just on prescription medication. I recognized the signs of regular drug use. His life was going in just one direction, with a father in prison and nowhere else to turn, I could see exactly where this kid was headed, unless someone stepped in and helped him see the other options. If he didn't overdose or become another addict's victim, he was going to get himself a criminal conviction, and maybe a life sentence. I was struck by the clarity of my vision. It was as if I was looking in a mirror which reflected my inner self, me as a kid.

'Let's take a moment to consider how Jake's life has been affected by your actions, Jed.' Kieran knew my mind was ablaze with realization. He was helping me to focus, but I didn't need the time.

'I can see how my actions have harmed Jake and his mother and I want to do whatever I can to repair the damage. I can't change the past but I can help in the future.'

Kieran turned his attention towards Jake and asked, 'What would you like to see come out of this meeting?'

Jake looked at me for the first time and said, 'I don't want to be afraid of...of being hurt like that again.'

I was filled with shame. *He thinks I'm some sort of monster.* Well of course he did, I reasoned with myself. All he knew was that I had terrorized his family and fired a gun at him. Everyone else, the police, courts and press will all have contributed to this very real fear, and embellished the image of me in his mind's eye as nothing but a dangerous beast.

Suddenly I realized how much was being asked of him, just to be sitting here, facing me, and I felt small. This kid was stronger than I could imagine. If he could sit here and face me then he could get grip on his own life and make something of it. *Still, he wouldn't be sitting here in this state if it wasn't for my actions,* I reminded myself. I had long given up trying to blame Tony, the Police and everyone else for my actions, it was only my finger on the trigger of that gun. 'I never meant to hurt you, or your mother, and I will never do anything like that again, to anyone.' I stated. 'I have worked hard in prison to change and I'm not going to do anything to mess up my progress, or to cause harm to anyone else.'

'Jed made up his mind at the start of this sentence that he needed to change is ways, and he has made considerable progress in the prison system,' explained Kieran, 'and we hope that coming here today to meet with him has helped you, Jake.'

'I hope this is the start of a change for you,' I said directly to Jake. 'Living in fear is paralysing, I don't want you to be living in fear of me any longer. You have no reason to be afraid of me.' Jake nodded and his mum wrapped her arm around his shoulder.

'It won't be an overnight change,' added Kieran, thoughtfully, 'but hopefully things will start to get better for you, from hereon in. Is there anything else you want to say to Jed, or to ask him?'

Jake shook his head. Just being here today was a milestone in itself, for him. I wondered how many people, aside from his therapist realized how much it meant to him. I could feel his fear. I wondered if he could feel my shame.

'Is there anything that anyone would like to add before we draw this meeting to a close?' asked Kieran.

Jake's mother clearly had something to say. 'I came here for Jake's benefit, not yours. I thought you were a monster and I didn't want my kid to suffer any more because of you. I don't know if I can ever forgive you for what you've done to my son. All I hope is that by coming face to face with you, he can see that you can't ever hurt him again.' Her words felt like a rip in the lining of my soul. It would only heal if she allowed it to and she wasn't ready for that. I couldn't blame her. God knows what I would have done if someone had hurt my kid like that. I could only respect her, despite her contempt for me. All I could say was that I was grateful for the opportunity to make amends and that I hoped Jake would feel able to get on with his life from this point on. Kieran went through the formalities of thanking everyone for attending. He told us he would be filing a report and we would all get a copy.

Walking out of that room, through the locked gates and over the compound, I looked up at the top of the perimeter wall and was hit with the realization that there was more to freedom than just walking out through that main gate. I felt more expansive with every step I took closer towards my cell. My existence had taken on a deeper dimension. I had peeled off a few more layers of myself today, and exposed a glimpse of the real me. Other people had seen another side to me, and hopefully realized that there was much more to me than just the mindless, violent criminal they had the misfortune of meeting first. Exposing myself to the victims of my crime had been one of the greatest challenges I had ever experienced. It wasn't for the faint-hearted, and I had struggled at times. There was no way of telling how it was going to go, Kieran had kept reinforcing that notion, warning me that recriminations were likely. However, it had simply unfolded in its own time and at its own pace. Not one of us had owned it, the dynamic between us all seemed to have taken on an energy of its own. There had been no-one telling me what to say, and I had spoken straight from my heart. When Jake had talked about his fear, in a strange way it had helped me to feel closer to him, allowing me to open up about my shame. I realized that people can't challenge your feelings. Others can tell you that your actions are unacceptable, that your thoughts are twisted, but only you know the truth of your feelings. Acknowledging your core feelings, owning and taking control of them is very empowering, this was my first real taste of freedom.

# Chapter 15

# MMU SUYIDEE: Good fortune and sanctity

D-Cat day arrived.

My transfer to an open prison was confirmed. I had jumped through every hoop, completing every rehabilitation course suggested to me. I had kept my head down and my drug-test results sheet clean. I had channelled my energy into learning new skills, giving both my mind and my body a major workout. Those who were keeping a close eye on me could testify to my path. There had been many diversions and distractions along the way, although few were aware of those. I had shared some of these experiences with others, such as Fat Bastard, who, I now realized, had played a crucial role in the proceedings, teaching me valuable lessons about myself. I decided that I would thank him, if I was ever unfortunate to cross paths with him again.

However, Danny was the one person I was destined to meet up with again.

I felt nervous when I heard on the grapevine that he was already in the open prison where I was headed. At this point I hadn't seen or spoken to him in over three years. Much had changed in my life since our last encounter and I was curious to see how things had played out for him also.

Conditions in the open prison were very different from those in my previous establishments. There were no high-fenced, concrete compounds or imposing Victorian buildings. Small, pre-fabricated hut-like dormitories replaced the vast red-brick wings as accommodation, and the security was hardly visible as some inmates regularly left each morning to work in the nearby town. The idea was to put down roots on the outside, to help smooth out the transition from imprisonment to freedom.

Of course there was no entitlement to this opportunity; it was much more a case of luck or chance, along with the willing assistance of interested parties on the outside. However, those who took advantage of the regime and stayed out past their curfew, would arrive back to find themselves locked out. One such abuse of the system was enough for you to have your privilege withdrawn. It was a system based on trust; a notion that some still were unfamiliar with. For them, the open system failed and they were returned to environments with a higher level of security. That didn't look good on your parole application. I wasn't going to rise to that temptation.

On arrival I was impressed by the well-tended prison gardens and excited at the prospect of trying my hand at yet another new skill. The thought of working outside in the fresh air, and with the natural rhythm of nature appealed to me, and I decided to apply for a gardener's position. I was informed that as soon as one became available, I would be given the opportunity. Until then, it was up to me to bed in as best as I could, in my new environment.

As fate would have it, Danny was in my dormitory. I wondered how he felt about sharing his space with strangers, albeit there were only four of us, each with a single bunk and locker, placed in the four corners of the room.

'Good to see you, Jed,' Danny said when I was introduced into the dormitory, as if we had only been apart for a few weeks. The other two occupants were "out at work" and so we were left to our own devices. I soon learned that Danny had only been here for a few weeks and was still waiting on his privileges. 'Town visits, mate, you get to go out in the town, all day. At first you have to be accompanied by an officer but after a while, you can go out alone.' He appeared very animated and part of me recoiled slightly from him. There was something very different about Danny, his energy was slightly abrasive, although he looked and sounded the same. Maybe it was me. I knew how much I had changed, and so I couldn't expect things to feel the same between us. 'Yeah, it's been a while but I remember from my last stint in open prison.'

'You've been here before?' I asked in disbelief.

'Well not this gaff, but I've done open conditions before, yeah.' Danny's words were causing a painful twisting sensation in my gut.

'What happened?'

'Oh, you know, I was younger, and the temptation of it all was a bit too much for me.'

After a few weeks in the new jail, I was seeing a more sociable Danny, one who was mixing more with the other prisoners. Yet I viewed the scene with a distinct feeling of discomfort. Perhaps it was me who was out of tune with life in an open jail. However, when I watched him arsing about in front of the others, I got the feeling that he wasn't being himself. If he was, then this "class clown" was a side to Danny that I had never seen. In our previous prison together he had been very circumspect with his company, and had appeared seriously-minded. But what did I know? People change, and this was the first time I had been around him all day and night. He would never fall asleep before me at night, and was already up and about when I woke in the mornings; the guy unnerved me.

I wondered whether to talk about some of the spiritual stuff he had been interested in. Perhaps we might be able to rekindle some of our joint interests.

'Are you still doing the shamanic journeys?' I asked him one day, breaking the silence, as we both lay, smoking, on our respective bunks.

'Sure,' he responded. 'Although, not for a while now. I haven't come across anyone here who's interested in that shit, how about you?'

Hesitatingly, I told Danny about my dream experience in the rainforest, where I came face to face with the snake. His imagination captured, Danny sat up on his bunk and turned to face me.

'So did it actually bite you?'

'It felt like it, I had a bruise on the back of my hand for a few days. There was no puncture wound though,' I answered, finding myself rubbing the back of my left hand.

'Hmm...the snake can be symbolic of a message coming to you, from a higher plane,' Danny explained thoughtfully. 'My sense is that you are being challenged in your life, something to do with the circumstances of your birth and family.' He stopped and took a long, last drag of his roll-up before stubbing it out.

A cold shiver passed through me. *How did he know?* I wondered how could Danny have known about the news that Cliff, my father's brother, was my biological dad, and that I was technically the unlucky fifth child of the family? Then again, perhaps he didn't know anything. I decided to test him. 'Tell me more – about the snake, I mean'.

'Snakes on journeys are a sign of transformation, of death and rebirth. Think how they shed their dead skin to take on new. I think this is about you having new roles and responsibilities and the Cobra is an indication that you are afraid of the changes coming your way.'

*How did he know?* I had been careful not to mention the type of snake that had appeared in my dream.

'So am I making the right changes?' I asked

'Only you know that,' Danny replied tartly.

'Well, all of the work I've done in jail has resulted in me being here, a few steps closer to release.'

'Yeah, well this isn't about the world of parole boards,' Danny reminded me. 'This is about stuff happening on the inner realms. The snake can mean the opening up of a new inner dimension, which can then also manifest on the outer realms.'

Then I wondered if Danny knew about the Restorative Justice experience, if he knew the inner shift that occurred when I had met with Jake. *How could he?* I doubted he had given me a second thought since we had last parted company. He hadn't asked me a single question about where I had been or what I had been doing for the last three years.

'The ancient Greeks used the snake as a symbol of alchemy and healing, think of the rod of Asclepius,' Danny continued. 'And even modern Western medicine tried to get in on the act, with the United States medical industry adopting the Caduceus as their symbol. The snake is a very powerful totem.' Death, rebirth and healing, this was some heavy-duty stuff. Danny was, once again impressing me with his knowledge of the world.

'So you think this is all about serious life changes?' I was looking for confirmation.

A wide, uncharacteristic grin spread over Danny's face as he replied, 'Either that mate, or you're desperate for a fuck! How long has it been?' He laughed and continued, 'Some believe snake dreams are about sex, about repressed sexual energy, that sort of stuff. It could just have been your inner manhood telling you to sort something out before you implode.'

It was true, I had been taking myself very seriously. I couldn't remember the last time I had thought about women, or sex, channelling all of my energy into making positive changes in my life. However, with a parole hearing on the horizon, this wasn't the time for messing about. As soon as I secured my release, I could start thinking about women.

'I'll be getting mine just as soon as the town visits are agreed,' Danny announced, and I wondered whether he was referring to the accompanied visits. His relations with the screws in this prison were not as respectful, in comparison with the staff in our last place together. Then I remembered the incident with Fat Bastard. Perhaps I had just not been seeing clearly back then, or maybe just seeing what others wanted me to see. Things were very different now, and I had no intention of getting caught up in Danny's web, a second time around. I was playing it straight, this time. It was spring when I was told that I could start work in the gardens. This was good timing, and I took it as a good sign. My parole hearing was set for early September, I would only know the exact date much closer to the time, and so I had a good few months of working outdoors, to demonstrate that I could be trusted under the open conditions of minimal supervision. It was just basic digging, and planting of the vegetable patches, and pruning and weeding of the rose beds, with some tomatoes growing in the greenhouses. However, I enjoyed the freedom of working at my own pace, in the fresh air. We supplied some of the local shops and garden centres with our produce, the owners often visiting the gardens and the prison café that was open to the public. Danny was popular with the locals, turning on the charm when serving up prison cake and coffee. However, back in the kitchen, it was a different story. I didn't trust the others inmates working there, and the building itself felt unsafe. It was old, timber-framed, with ancient equipment, and Danny frequently complained of mechanical breakdowns. He often returned late to the dormitory at night, complaining he had to stay late to "fix things".

I wrote to Jodie, telling her of my new job and asking to meet up with her, and maybe my twin nieces, when I was granted a town visit. The thought of asking for a meeting with Alisha and JJ had flashed through my mind, but I knew there were other matters I need to sort out before I went there. I wrote telling them my change of "address" and of my recent achievements, gaining the BAWLA qualification and participating in the Restorative

Justice programme. In response, I got a copy of JJ's first school report. I glowed inside with pride when I read that he was "a polite and helpful child, with a talent for understanding the feelings of others". He must have inherited those traits from his mother. There was hope for him, despite my early, negative influence in his life. Besides, he was Cliff's grandchild and not the progeny of our father. I waited eagerly for a response, to find out if Jodie had made contact with Cliff, and what, if anything, she had told him about me, about us all.

In the warmth of the greenhouses, my mind was caught up in the notion of travelling to Ghana. It was not likely to happen any time soon, but if I complied with the terms of my parole then it could be a dream for the future. I needed ideas to place on my horizons, strong images on which to focus. I saw myself and JJ standing on a deserted beach watching the Atlantic rollers crashing to the shore. I could hear the roar of the waves and feel the spray on my face. I could feel the softness of my son's small hand gripping mine, and I squeezed it in warm reassurance that we were both safe.

When the previous occupants of the dorm had been released, leaving just Danny and me, I started enjoying the peace of the evenings and weekend. Working in the gardens was physically tiring and being alone was the only way I could truly relax. Danny had also started on his weekend visits. He had been out, accompanied, on two occasions and the on the third visit he was allowed out alone.

He arrived back late one Sunday evening, in August, after spending the sunny day "alone" in a nearby town. Danny was buzzing. He was bubbling over with excitement, like a child. He couldn't settle and was bouncing around the room, blabbering on about what an amazing time he had enjoyed. When I didn't respond with the same enthusiasm, he became provocative, accusing me of being a killjoy. He reached into his locker and brought out his Bodhran, saying that this would be a great time for a journey. He came and sat on the edge of my bunk and started to drum. It all felt wrong. Danny's chaotic energy in such close proximity was making me nauseous and an irrational fear came over me. I felt as if I was being sucked into something that I would regret. It took all my power to resist when Danny got into a rhythm. It felt as if he had some hypnotic hold over me.

'No I'm not up for this, not now,' I protested. 'I've been in the garden all day, I'm knackered. I just want some peace, and to sleep.'

'No worries,' said Danny, reaching into the pocket of his jeans. 'Here, have this, it will help you loosen up,' and he held out a tab of acid.

A slow, cold, fear wrapped around my body as I realized what was happening. Danny had been shopping for gear on the outside. He was high, and now he was tempting me to join him. If we were caught with drugs in this building, we would both be shipped back to high security. Then it would take years to work our way back through again to this point in the system, if we ever managed it.

The cold fear evaporated, as the fury rose in me like a wild bush fire

*How could he put me in this position so close to release, to fuck up my chance of freedom?*

Old thoughts of revenge loomed large in my head, violent images that I thought were long-buried were now rushing about in my mind. I scanned the room, looking for a weapon. Like an agile predator I was looking for the kill, and as was the way with potential prey, Danny froze, wide-eyed, sensing the danger from me.

Backing slowly away from my bunk he asked, 'What's the problem? It's only a bit of fun. There ain't no-one else around. What's your problem, mate? It's easy to switch piss samples for drug tests in this place, I can vouch for it.'

*You're no mate of mine* I thought, as I got up from the bunk and backed Danny against the wall. Ripping the acid tab out of his hand, I forced it into his mouth and told him to eat the shit.

'Where's the rest?' I demanded. His mouth filled with my hand, Danny could only shake his head wildly from side to side, trying desperately to say there was no more. I wasn't taking any chance. I searched his clothing and then left him standing, afraid to move, whilst I searched his locker. I was not going to lose my chance at freedom for this junkie shit. 'Where is it?' I bellowed at him.

'There's nothing else' he insisted.

'You had better not be fucking with me, or I will fuck you up,' I said, grabbing him by the throat, my own words ricocheting around my head like a warning siren. Those old words, old ways, where did they get me?

I closed my eyes and dropped my hands from around his neck. *What the fuck was I doing?*

He looked pathetic. I remember thinking that he was just not worth it, risking my parole, my release and my future freedom. I knew I had to get myself as far away from him as possible, even though another part of me wanted to rip his lying head right off his puny shoulders. I ran outside and sat alone behind the greenhouses in the dark, tensely chain-smoking roll-ups.

The anger echoed around my body for hours, as I sat alone. It was the only safe place for me at that point. As I relived the moment so my heart rate increased fourfold, and I struggled to bring myself down again. I kept telling myself that I hadn't done anything, I had stopped myself, I had kept control. But now all the rage was running riot in my body, rampaging through my veins, desperate for an outlet. Danny's face kept looming large in my consciousness, and the only way to get rid of it was to try and replace the image with Ma's face, as I sat hugging my knees in the dark.

It was whilst I was sitting in the dark, trying to summon the fading face of my dead mother in the hope it would bring me a sense of calm, that I heard shouts and stood up to see flames licking the roof of the kitchen block. Fire was filling the windows and smoke had started to pour out from the open emergency exit. There were lots of figures milling around, and I was aware of a growing sense of panic. *What the fuck?* I ran over to the kitchen block and tried to find out what exactly what was happening.

'Get back! The kitchen has caught on fire,' announced one harassed officer, trying desperately to keep the inmates away from the scene.

Something told me to watch my back. There was more to this, I was sure. It was clear that there were not enough staff on duty to attend to the fire and keep a check on all of the inmates. The blaze was out of control now, spreading to the health-care building and the officers' administration block. I could see prisoners in places where they would not normally be allowed, clearly taking advantage of the confusion, for their own ends. The contents of the dispensary were being raided; the culprits running off with their pharmaceutical loot, to indulge in and to sell on. I looked around but could not see any sign of Danny and so I headed over to the dorm, to wake him if he was managing to sleep through all of this chaos. The building was empty. There was no sign of Danny. *What if he was in the kitchen when the fire started?* As head chef, Danny was the only inmate I knew who was allowed to hold keys to the place. I ran back to the kitchen yelling that there was someone inside. I was sure he was there, perhaps unconscious, from breathing in the poisonous smoke. The flames had now destroyed the roof of the building, and its burning timbers were falling to the ground. Where was the fire engine? Had anyone called the fire service?

'No-one's going in there, it's too dangerous,' shouted the officer. 'The fire service is on its way.'

Watching, as more black smoke billowed out from the building, and another roof-rafter collapsed, I had an idea. Running around to the garden buildings, I unhooked the hose used to water the flower beds and hauled it towards the kitchen block. A few men saw what I was trying to do and came to help, whilst others just ran past me on their way out of the main gate, which had been opened in anticipation of the arrival of the fire service. They would blame the fear and chaos at the prison for their absence when they got picked up by the police in the next couple of days.

The hose was heavy, and I wasn't even sure it would reach as far as the kitchen. However, I had to try something. I didn't want to watch my parole hearing going up in smoke. Those who enjoyed seeing the place burn obviously had no vision for what might come next in their lives and so had nothing to lose by their action. Mattresses and bedding were being thrown on the pyre, along with chairs from the classrooms and books from the library. The perpetrators were whooping in glee at the spectacle.

We managed to get within ten feet of the fire and to get the water running through the hose, when the fire engine arrived. The professionals thanked us for our efforts before taking over, and the prison officers returned to take control of the rioting inmates.

I could do little except sit on the periphery and watch the drama. When the fire was finally extinguished in the early-morning hours, the few of us inmates left were rounded up by the exhausted officers and located in the gym. It was the one building left completely intact. We were provided with makeshift beds and told to use the changing-room facilities. I wondered how long it would be before we were all shipped out of the prison. However, a core of us asked to stay on and help clear away the debris and rebuild the kitchen. As the gardens and greenhouse were largely untouched, I volunteered willingly to help out with the reclamation of the dormitories. I was prepared to do anything to hang on to my chance of freedom. It was on clearing the burnt rubble from our own dorm building, that I found Danny's Bodhran, unharmed, at the bottom of his metal locker. *Charmed bastard!* I thought, wondering where he was and what he was doing now. No-one had heard anything from him; Danny was on the run. He had well and truly fucked up his second chance at freedom.

My compliance paid off and the Parole Board hearing was delayed only by a few weeks. It was a last minute, nerve-wracking experience for me. I was briefed only one hour beforehand, by my court-appointed solicitor, in the temporarily refurbished administration block of the prison. It was to be chaired by a judge and consist of two other parole-board members. They would have read all of the reports on me, about my work and progress in prison, and would be looking to question the Prison Service professionals about my rehabilitation. It would also look better for me if there was a personal statement from my victim, amongst the papers, he added, hastily flicking through to see if there was one. I asked him who the "professionals" would be, and he mentioned the possibility of a psychiatrist or psychologist. My heart missed a beat. I didn't dare ask for their names.

I was stubbing out a roll-up when I looked up to see *her,* walking into the building. Elisabeth was here for my parole hearing, accompanied by Officer King. I had never expected to see either of them again. Good Fortune, or the ancient, Ashanti ancestors, were indeed smiling on me. This was it. This was my chance, my last chance. I was taking a shot of my inhaler as the door opened and an officer informed us that the Board was ready to start.

My eyes fixed on Elisabeth as soon as I entered the room, she smiled politely in acknowledgement, and then looked back at her notes. Kieran King nodded as I took my seat at the table. *Why was he here?*

The eagle-eyed judge started the proceedings by reminding everyone of the purpose of the meeting. He clarified the board members' responsibilities in relation to the public-safety element as to the board's decision, and looked at Elisabeth to question the efficacy of my rehabilitation. The debate started with a review of the perceived level of risk I now posed to the public. The questions about me were being batted back and forth across the room. I was watching people jousting in the cause of for my freedom, or not, as the case might be.

'Has the prisoner completed all the required offending behaviour courses?' asked the male parole-board member, seated to the right of the judge, one of the complete strangers who would be determining the next step in the journey of my life. Elisabeth listed the names of the courses I had attended and provided a general summary of my achievement in each, without as much as a side glance towards me. I had no idea how this was going to work out for me.

'What about recent adjudications?'

'None,' replied my solicitor. 'My client gave evidence in relation to the adjudication of another prisoner, some three years ago, there's nothing else on record.' An image of Danny and the tattoo machine flashed up, unwelcomed in my mind's eye. I rubbed my tattooed bicep in discomfort. 'What issues do the wing reports raise? Are there any ongoing issues with Mr Johnson?'

'Mr Johnson is noted as being "a helpful individual, who appears to complying with all prison requirements, at present",' my solicitor continued, quoting from the wing reports. I thought the prison staff might have been a bit more forthcoming in support of all of my efforts since I had been here, but then what did they owe me? *Absolutely nothing!* I had heard that a prisoner could never be sure that all the encouragement from the staff would translate into favourable answers at a lifer or parole board. Luckily for me, there were others present who knew the other sides to me.

'Also, all drug tests, both mandatory and voluntary, have

returned negative results, and no further charges have been brought against client since commencing this life sentence.' My solicitor concluded his comments with, 'Also of note is the fact that during the recent troubles at this jail, Mr Johnson co-operated fully with the staff, actively helping to put out a fire and join in with the reclamation and rebuilding exercise. He has held a position of trust at this establishment for a number of months.'

'Has Mr Johnson addressed his violent offending?' It was the turn of the only woman member of the Board. This was where Elisabeth sat up and spoke at length. In response to the question she described the programme she had worked on with me, talking about my individual and group work. At first I was listening just to enjoy hearing her voice, once more. She was referring to me as 'Mr Johnson' and was using quotes of my own words from my journals to illustrate some of her points. Once again, I felt naked in her presence.

'In your opinion has the risk of Mr Johnson re-offending been significantly reduced?' The female board member addressed the question to everyone in the room. This was the bottom line.

The silence was deafening. Was anyone going to speak up for me? *Somebody say something, say YES.* The thoughts were so loud in my head I was sure someone in the room could have heard them. This was the hook that no-one wanted to pin their conscience on. After all, none of them had any real control over me or my actions once I was out of the system. Who could blame them for not wanting the responsibility of saying I wouldn't re-offend?

'Yes,' came the muted response, eventually from Elisabeth, as I felt a part of myself soaring high into the sky.

Another uncomfortable silence followed and then, amidst a little shuffling of papers and of muttering asides to his colleagues, the judge addressed the room.

'Is there a witness statement available?' he asked, flatly.

Kieran King coughed before speaking up. Addressing the

Board members he explained, 'Some months ago, Mr Johnson successfully participated in the Restorative Justice programme. He met with the victim and was able to assure the young lad that he was no longer a threat to him.' *That was the reason he was here!* I winced at the mention of "young lad" and looked at the Board members. Their expressions soured and I felt a panic rising from the pit of my stomach.

'I believe Your Honour has a copy of the report there?' Kieran continued. 'What you won't have, as I only received this yesterday, is a statement from the victim. I have copies for you here,' he offered up some papers. In irritation, the judge reached into his jacket for his spectacles case. I shot at look at Kieran who was quick to suggest that perhaps he should read out the statement for the benefit of the Board. All three nodded in agreement and so he read:

'I, *Jake Delannoy, of* (the address is omitted for confidentiality purposes) Your Honour,' Kieran explained and continued, *'have attended a meeting as part of the Restorative Justice programme with the offender, Jed Johnson. Although I was at first very unsure about doing this, my therapist suggested that it might be the best way to overcome the fear and anxieties which have affected my life ever since that day, when I got shot in the leg through the letterbox of my house. I was running up the stairs with my mother trying to get away from all of the shooting going on outside the house, when I slipped on the carpet and lost my footing. The next thing I knew I there was a loud bang and I had a burning pain in the top of my left leg. I collapsed in pain, there was all this blood, and my mother started screaming. I thought I was going to die.*

*I received emergency hospital treatment and I lost a lot of blood. They gave me a transfusion but my body rejected the blood and so I was very ill for a few weeks. They finally got a better match, I've got a rare blood-group, and I started to get better. I was looking forward to getting out of the hospital but after a few days at home I started to have panic attacks, especially when there was any noise outside the house and when anyone knocked the door. I had been unable to finish college or get a job since this happened, but since the meeting I have been feeling better and have managed to attend at the recruitment centre for a few interviews. I have also moved house, although I still live with my mother, and feel much safer in the new place. I am still attending counselling sessions, but have reduced the dose of medication prescribed by the doctor. My leg still aches but I am now sleeping better and feeling more confident about the future.*

*Coming face to face with Jed made me realize that he is not the monster that I imagined him to be. He reassured me that he never intended to hurt me although he admitted that he was in the wrong to even be there, at my house, that day. I don't really know what that was all about, I was only fourteen when it happened. Jed told me that he has a son and he understands how hard it is for kids when their fathers are in jail. If he comes out of jail at least there will be one less kid struggling in the world. Since I have met him, I realize that he is sorry for what happened and he is not out to hurt me or my mother and so we can now just get on with our lives.'*

Kieran looked up at the Board members as he placed the report on the table in front of him.

'In your opinion, has the applicant demonstrated any remorse for his crime?' asked the judge, in a most matter-of-fact manner, and as if he was oblivious to my presence in the room.

At that point, all other eyes in the room focused on me. However, their faces were blurred as I looked back through the tears, pouring silently from my eyes. I could see only hues, the colours of the room and its occupants merging into warped, vertical stripes before me. I felt removed, as if watching from behind a pane of glass, onto which the torrent of rain was falling thick and fast, so as to obliterate its transparency.

'Jed, are you OK?' I heard Kieran's concerned tone.

Then the judge, anxiously asking, 'Is he going to faint?' before the muttering voices of the others merged into a low hum. My vision was opaque and the sounds around me, so muted, so I couldn't respond to their questions. I wasn't passing out. I had a vision in my mind's eye of a blinding light. I felt the rush of great heat flow right through me, followed fast by a total whiteout. It looked to the others in the room as if I had lost consciousness for a few moments. My memory is of reaching a new state of consciousness. I had been somewhere new. It was a quiet, clean and calm place.

Two weeks later I got confirmation of a release date, subject to a life licence with specific conditions. I heard that I would have to stay initially at a hostel and report in daily to my probation officer, but the euphoria blurred all the details and all I could see was one rosy- coloured future. I would be free, what else could be better, right?

Walking out of the gate of an open prison was a very low-key event. With five pounds for public transport and directions to the local bail hostel in my pocket, I was released on a grey, cloudy morning by an officer who looked at me as if to say, "we'll be seeing you back soon, no doubt". *No you fucking will not!*. I was feeling determined to break away from this cycle and create a new life for me and my boy.

I wrote to Jodie from the hostel, telling her of my plans. She wrote back saying that if things went well in the hostel, I might be able to move in with her and the kids in a few months. She also told me that she had heard from Cliff, who seemed interested in keeping in contact with us all. The probation officer assigned to me suggested that I contact some of the local garden centres to enquire as to the possibility of any job vacancies, and so I contacted some of the owners who would know me from the prison gardens.

I had no problem with the hostel rules of no visitors, drink or drugs, or curfew times. And I had no truck with the other inhabitants of the hostel. They were on a one-way ticket back to the slammer. Nothing had changed for them. They were still involved in the same old shit, whilst I was more interested in building a new future for myself.

However, I was a mess, a bundle of anxiety and stress. You have this idea in your head that it will be such a reward, such a relief when it finally arrives, and instead it's all fear and panic. It's one of those experiences that no amount of advice can prepare you for. You're going out to what you think is familiarity, home. What you find is that the world is much bigger than you remember, and far less friendly. It seemed like everything had changed. I felt like I was in some foreign country where no-one spoke my language. Leaving the cocoon of prison, the room at the hostel felt cold and strange. In comparison, the memory of the cells I had been so keen to see the back of, now felt so warm and comforting. It was November, and being on the outside was a bleak and harsh experience. Cold-hearted, hard-faced strangers looking straight past you in the street, and refusing to accept job applications, in spite of the "Vacancies" sign hanging in the window. Everyone seemed preoccupied with their own problems, and the security of having your food bought, cooked and served up for you had vanished. Some of the jails I had done time in were far better equipped than the hostel. In short, it felt more alienating than the first few weeks in prison.

However, I knew I had to get my shit together pretty quick so, holed up in the icy hostel, I started work on a list of "stuff to do". Things were just not happening for me as quickly as I wanted. At the top was contacting my family, Jodie and maybe getting in contact with Cliff. However, I wanted to have a job sorted out first, so I could pay my own way and show everyone that I was getting on. I had written to Alisha telling her about my release, but I had not received a response. Every time I thought about it I got a sharp, stabbing pain in the pit of my stomach.

I kept looking at the list, hoping for some fresh ideas about where to look next for work, when, in one weak moment, I turned to my list of contact numbers and I picked up the hostel pay phone.

'Hi, it's me'

'Jed?'

The sound of Alisha's surprised voice rendered me a complete arse.

'Yes, I wrote to you, I'm in town, When can I see you? Can I come round…'

I knew I was going about this all the wrong way, but I just couldn't stop myself.

I hated my desperation but I couldn't stop it pouring down the dirty, public receiver.

'Not now…soon. Yeah Jed…soon. Give me a chance to explain some things to JJ.'

Spun out by the rejection, I slammed down the receiver, my mind flooding with all the nasty, twisted, old thoughts about women. I recognized them, just as you always recognize the sly, school bully, when you see him out on the street, years later.

I was battling hard with myself, but I did not want to just give into the old me. I had come too far to lose my grip now. I needed to be strong and I thought of a place where I could go to cool off and come back to my senses.

I got myself across town and into the graveyard where my mother's charred remains stood in some cheap vase, beneath a plaque bearing her name. It took a double take for me to recognize my mother by her name, her married name. It looked so cold and impersonal etched in gold-effect lettering. She was Ma to me, yet known by the rest of the world as Sylvie Watson. 'Ma, I need you', I said, out loud for the first time ever. As the dampness and misery surrounding me closed in I could feel my breathing start to labour, I reached for my inhaler. For the first time in a long while, I felt completely alone What was the point of all the help and support in jail just to be left on your own when you got out? All the programmes and therapy in the world couldn't prepare you for that isolation and self-doubt. *What had it all been for? Had it all been worth it?* Suddenly I could see why so many had said they would expect to see me back in jail before too long. It would be so easy to call up a few old friends and arrange for some gear. A rash of panic spread over me and I told myself that I needed to get off the streets and back to the hostel, to the comfort of the rules and the safety of the walls, before the temptation to do anything stupid turned into a real-life opportunity.

With no money left for bus fare, I legged it as fast as my asthma would allow, back across town towards the bail hostel. Breathlessly turning the corner into the side road of the place I now called home, I saw him, Danny. He was in a doorway, nervously smoking a roll-up, and from his reaction when he recognized my face, I knew he had been waiting for me. *Fuck,* he was the last person I needed to see right now. Danny was twitchy, I thought it best to lay it on him first, tell him how it was with me now and make it clear that there was no room for any fucking around. In between breaths I asked, 'What are you doing here, man? How did you know where to find me? Are you still on the run? Yeah? Well, you don't want be seen here, I can't afford to be seen with you.'

Danny was saying that he wouldn't be around long, he didn't want to get in my way but he needed some money. If I could lend him some money he would disappear again. I told him I didn't have any money, and that he needed to get the hell out of my face. He wasn't listening, just looking over his shoulder as if he was waiting for someone, and saying something about being cursed if he couldn't pay his dues. I turned away from him and tried to leave, hoping he would just disappear. However, the guy was desperate, he grabbed me by the shoulder and I turned back to see him flashing a blade in my face.

'Just give me all the money you've got,' he demanded. I was

confused. *What the fuck?* 'Don't fuck with me, or we're both dead', he hollered, backing me into a filthy, graffiti- stained alleyway.' I could see the whites of his eyes, the man was terrified.

In shock, everything merged together in slow motion for me, including the shouts I heard coming from the alley way behind me. The next thing I felt was a blow from behind, and as I lurched forward, the knife that Danny was holding was thrust between my ribs.

That was the last thing I felt as I sunk from a hot pit of pain into the welcoming comfort of oblivion. Danny's throat was slit for the sake of some drug debts, and we were both abandoned in that alleyway to die.

Danny never made it out of that dark alleyway. However, thanks to the brave paramedics, I woke up in intensive care, with the local police waiting for me to gain enough consciousness to question me. So, here I am under twenty-four hour supervision, but feeling immense relief just to be alive. I had luck, or the ancient Ashanti ancestors, on my side that day, and I have lived to tell this tale. I have the comfort of a hospital bed and the care of good people, and I have a future. My physical injuries will heal, and staring death in the face has only served to make my resolve stronger. My desires run more deeply and the vibrancy of my dreams overpowers any of the scenes of reality playing out around me. I have an inner sense of peace that no-one can rattle. I'm here for a purpose; I have things to do, people to see and places to be. Following the seven years of experience in prison, I know no greater fear, or joy, than of freedom. I have been given another opportunity to create a great life for me and my son and this time I'm not leaving any of the details to chance.

Soul Rocks, is a fresh list that takes the search for soul and spirit mainstream. Chick-lit, young adult, cult, fashionable fiction & non-fiction with a fierce twist.